The Slaughter Man

Tony Parsons

W F HOWES LTD

This large print edition published in 2015 by
W F Howes Ltd
Unit 4, Rearsby Business Park, Gaddesby Lane,
Rearsby, Leicester LE7 4YH

1 3 5 7 9 10 8 6 4 2

First published in the United Kingdom in 2015
by Century

A CIP catalogue record for this book is available
from the British Library

ISBN 978 1 51000 965 3

Typeset by Palimpsest Book Production Limited,
Falkirk, Stirlingshire

Printed and bound in Great Britain
by TJ International Ltd, Padstow, Cornwall

MIX
Paper from
responsible sources
FSC
www.fsc.org   FSC® C013056

For Yuriko

Crimes reverberate through years and through lives. It is a rare homicide that destroys only one person.

Joyce Carol Oates, 'After Black Rock'

Most gypsies fear the dead.

Raymond Buckland, *Buckland's Book of Gypsy Magic – Travellers' Stories, Spells & Healings*

PROLOGUE

New Year's Eve

The boy awoke to his father's scream.

Somewhere in the darkness down the hall, behind his parents' bedroom door, his father cried out as if his world was suddenly undone.

There was terror and rage and pain in that scream and, before the boy was fully awake, he was out of bed and opening his door just a crack, just enough to stare down the dark landing to the closed bedroom door where now there was only silence.

'Dad?'

He stood, staring into the darkness, the only sounds his ragged breathing and the drunken voices that drifted up from the city streets, celebrating the death of another year.

A bell tolled at the back of the house, moved by the wind, the deep resonant sound of the temple bell in his mother's garden, tolling as if to mark the end of all things.

And from behind the bedroom door at the end of the hall, his mother began to scream.

1

And when at last she stopped, his father began to sob as though his heart had been broken.

Terror and shock choked in the boy's throat.

His kind, calm father, with his slow easy smile and his air of amusement, a father who never raised his voice, let alone his hand, sobbing as if everything he loved was being taken away.

Then he heard a voice that he did not know.

Insistent.

Inhuman.

Tight with fury.

'I'll not tell you again,' the voice commanded. 'I want you to watch.'

And then sounds that made no sense.

A sound like wood being chopped. *Chunk . . . chunk . . . chunk . . .* And accompanying the low moans of misery from the bedroom down the hall came the drunken cheers of the revellers in the other world.

None of it seemed real.

The boy slumped against the door, his breath coming in shallow gasps, suddenly aware of the tears streaming down his face.

Somewhere in their home the dog began to bark, and the familiar noise, that unexpected reminder of a world he understood, made him move.

He slipped out of his bedroom, his heart hammering and his legs heavy and a slick film of terrified sweat covering his body.

He moved quickly away from the terrible sounds, down the landing to his sister's bedroom.

He went inside and found her sitting on her bed, fully dressed in her party clothes, dry-eyed, her face white with shock as she fumbled for her phone and punched 9 once.

They both looked up at the sudden eruption of violence coming from the bedroom down the hall. Unknown, unknowable sounds. A struggle of terrible ferocity, flesh and bone colliding with walls and floor. Dull thuds and muffled groans.

The sound of something fighting for its life.

He saw his sister punch another 9.

He closed his eyes, dizzy with sickness.

This would end. He would wake up and the nightmare would be over. But he opened his eyes and it was more real than anything he had ever known.

His sister's hands were shaking as she punched the third and final 9.

The dog was barking furiously.

And then there were heavy footsteps coming down the hall, no attempt at stealth.

Coming for them now.

'The door!' his sister hissed and the boy reached it and locked it in one desperate motion.

Then he stepped back, staring at the locked door.

Somebody was knocking.

A gentle, almost playful tap with the knuckle of the index finger.

He looked at his sister.

The door seemed to press against its frame as if it was being tested by a powerful shoulder.

Then the wood shattered and splintered and cracked as the kicking began.

'Emergency services – how may I direct your call?'

'Please,' the girl said. 'We need help.'

Then the boy was at the window, opening it, freezing air rushing in and with it the sound of distant music, parties, laughter drifting across the final few minutes of the year's last day.

He looked back as the door caved in and a dark figure loomed in the hallway, reaching through the shattered wood for the key he had left in the lock.

It did not look like a man.

The figure in the doorway seemed like some deeper darkness and as it came into the bedroom, the boy could smell him, the sickening scent of sweat and blood and sex and the kind of industrial stink that reeked of old cars and dead engines and puddles of grease.

There was a voice in the room coming from his sister's phone.

'Hello? How may I direct your call? Hello?'

Then he was suddenly falling, dropping through the cold air and almost immediately hitting the driveway below with a grunt of pain.

He looked up at the first-floor window.

His sister had one leg out of the window and one leg still in the room.

The dark figure must have got her by the neck, because she was clearly choking, yes, the boy saw it now, thick fingers were wrapped around the chain on her necklace, twisting it in his fist, the way you twist the collar of a dangerous dog.

The black figure was trying to strangle her.

Then the necklace must have snapped because she was falling through the air sideways for what felt like a long second and he stepped quickly back as the ground rushed up to hit her hard.

Then he was helping his sister to her feet and she was struggling to walk, something wrong with one of her knees as they went out into the street.

They lived in a gated community at the highest point of the city, six large houses behind a tall iron gate and high brick walls that were topped with discreet razor wire.

All of London fell away beneath them.

It felt like the top of the world.

He left his sister in the middle of the street, rubbing her bloody knees, and ran across the road to the nearest house, leaning on their doorbell, screaming for help, shouting about murder.

But the house was in darkness.

And he saw that most of the other houses in that exclusive community were in darkness too. There was only one house at the very end of the road that was ablaze with light and noise. The boy ran towards it and banged on the door.

But the music was too loud and they were getting ready for midnight.

And he heard happy drunken voices in a babble of languages.

Polish. Tagalog. Spanish. Italian. Punjabi. And broken English.

The owners were away and the help were having a party.

And the help didn't hear him.

Then his sister was coming towards him, hobbling badly, only putting her full weight on one foot.

They both looked up as a firework exploded in the sky. In the distance, people cheered, suddenly much drunker and much happier. They both stared back at their home.

And from somewhere deep inside that house, a small child began to cry.

The boy cursed.

'We can't leave him,' his sister said. 'Can you smell it?'

There was a smell of burning, of smoke and gunpowder and the flames to come.

'It's fireworks,' he said.

She shook her head.

'He's burning our home.'

He saw it now.

Black smoke drifted from a ground-floor window.

'You go,' she said. 'Get help. I'll get the little one.'

He wiped his face and choked down a thick knot of bile as his sister began to stumble back to the burning house. The smoke was already thicker, the voices of the party people were suddenly raised, and he found he could not move.

'*TEN!*'

His sister turned to look at him just once, her face white in the moonlight.

'*NINE!*'

He watched her hobble up the drive, limping round the side of the house. And he knew with total certainty that he would never see her again.

'*EIGHT!*'

He shivered with cold and fear. And tried to think.

'*SEVEN!*'

He could still hear the celebrations at the house with all the lights and noise and laughter, but they seemed very far away now, removed from anything he understood, from anything that made any kind of sense.

'*SIX!*'

He screamed, panic and frustration overwhelming him.

'*FIVE!*'

Nobody heard. Nobody cared. He was completely alone.

'*FOUR!*'

From the highest hill in London he saw bursts of colour and sound start to blaze and pop and explode across the city sky. It was beautiful, like a jewel box being emptied across the heavens by some careless god.

And he knew that he could do this thing. He would go beyond the iron gates that were there to keep out the wicked and the poor and he would run down the hill and find help. That is what he would do. And the nightmare would end.

'*THREE!*'

Their dog was barking again and the smoke was thicker still. He could not see his sister. His family were relying on him now.

'*TWO!*'

He began to run towards the iron gates.

'*ONE!*'

As the New Year dawned and the sky exploded high above him, the car smashed into him, hitting him low on the back of the legs.

'*HAPPY NEW YEAR!*'

The car was going very fast and knocked him backwards across the hood then immediately threw him forward, the rear wheels passing over his legs and reducing them to a bloody mush of crushed flesh and pulped bone.

Somewhere people were cheering.

Then he was lying on his back and staring up at a midnight sky that was brighter than daylight, the colours everywhere all at once, yellows and reds and whites and greens erupting among the stars and then drifting to earth, and it was very peaceful lying there watching the sky until the pain came to claim him, the kind of pain that makes you empty your stomach, and the boy felt the reality of his ruined legs, and the agony was more than he could stand.

He watched the fireworks set the night ablaze without seeing them because now he could think of nothing but the pain. He heaved up a thick wad of blood as a dark figure bent above him.

'Please,' the boy said. 'Help me.'

The dark figure lifted him up.

With strong hands. Kind hands.

The boy wasn't sure if that was the right thing to do. He wasn't sure if he should be moved. Perhaps that wasn't the best thing. But he felt weak with gratitude.

Until he smelled that same stinking cocktail of stale sweat and used grease, both mechanical and human.

Until he saw that the hands and arms that held him as if he weighed nothing were drenched in the lifeblood of his family.

The fireworks above London were a riot of colour now.

But as he was carried back to what remained of his family, the boy surrendered gladly to the blackness, and he did not see them explode with light, and he did not see them die.

JANUARY

GHOST HOMES OF LONDON

CHAPTER 1

New Year's Day was big and blue and freezing cold. The single shot from the block of flats ripped the day apart.

I threw myself down behind the nearest car, hitting the ground hard, my palms studding with gravel, my face slick with sweat that had nothing to do with the weather.

Every gunshot is fired in anger. This one was full of murder. It cracked open the cloudless sky and left no space inside me for anything but raw terror. For long moments I lay very still, trying to get my breath back. Then I got up off my knees, pressing my back hard against the bright blue and yellow of an Armed Response Vehicle. My heart was hammering but my breathing was coming back.

I looked around.

SCO19 were already on their feet, staring up at the flats in their PASGT combat helmets, black leather gloves hefting Heckler & Koch assault rifles. Among them there were uniformed officers and plain-clothes detectives like me. All of us keeping our bodies tucked behind the ARVs and

13

the green-and-yellow Rapid Response Vehicles. Glock 9mm pistols were slipped from thigh holsters.

Close by, I heard a woman curse. She was small, blonde, somewhere in her late thirties. Young but not a kid. DCI Pat Whitestone. My boss. She was wearing a sweater with a reindeer on it. A Christmas present. Nobody chooses to own a reindeer jumper. Her son, I thought. The kid's idea of a joke. She pushed her spectacles further up her nose.

'Officer down!' she shouted. 'Gut wound!'

I looked out from behind the car and I saw the uniformed officer lying on her back in the middle of the street, calling for help. Clutching her belly. Crying out to the perfect blue sky.

'Please God . . . please Jesus . . .'

How long since the shot? Thirty seconds? That's a long time with a bullet in your gut. That's a lifetime.

There is a reason why most gut-shot wounds are fatal but most gut-stab wounds are not. A blade inflicts its damage to one confined area, but a bullet rattles around, destroying everything that gets in its way. If a knife misses an artery and the bowel, and they can get you to an anaesthesiologist and a surgeon fast enough, and if you can avoid infection – even though most villains are not considerate enough to sterilise their knives before they stab you – then you have a good chance of surviving.

But a bullet to the gut is catastrophic for the

body. Bullets clatter around in that microsecond, annihilating multiple organs. The small intestine, the lower intestine, the liver, the spleen and, worst of all, the aorta, the main artery, from which all the other arteries flow. Rip the aorta and you bleed out fast.

Take a knife wound to the gut and, unless you are very unlucky, you will go home to your family. Take a bullet in the gut and you will probably never see them again, no matter what the rest of your luck is like.

A knife wound to the gut and you call for help.

A bullet in the gut and you call for God.

I heard another muttered curse and then Whitestone was up and running towards the officer in the road, a small woman in a reindeer jumper, bent almost double, the tip of an index finger pressed against the bridge of her glasses.

I took in a breath and I went after her, my head down, every muscle in my body steeled for the second shot.

We crouched beside the fallen officer, Whitestone applying direct pressure to the wound, her hands on the officer's stomach, trying to stem the blood.

My mind scrambled to remember the five critical factors for treating a bullet wound. A, B, C, D, E, they tell you in training. Check Airways, Breathing, Circulation, Disability – meaning damage to the spinal cord or neck – and Exposure – meaning look for the exit wound, and check to see if there are other wounds. But we were already

15

beyond all of that. The blood flowed and stained the officer's jacket a darker blue. I saw the stain grow black.

'Stay with us, darling,' Whitestone said, her voice soft and gentle, like a mother to a child, her hands pressing down hard, already covered with blood.

The officer was very young. One of those idealistic young kids who join the Met to make the world a better place.

Her face was drained white by shock.

Shock from the loss of blood, shock from the trauma of the gunshot. I noticed a small engagement ring on the third finger of her left hand.

She died with an audible gasp and a bubble of blood. I saw Whitestone's eyes shine with tears and her mouth set in a line of pure fury.

We looked up at the balcony.

And the man was there.

The man who had decided at some point on New Year's Day that he was going to kill his entire family. That's what the call to 999 had said. That was his plan. That's what the neighbour heard him screaming through the wall before the neighbour gathered up his own family and ran for his life.

The man on the balcony was holding his rifle. Some kind of black hunting rifle. There was a laser light on it, a sharp green light for sighting that was the same bright fuzzy colour as Luke Skywalker's light sabre. It looked like a toy. But it wasn't a toy. I saw the green light trace across the ground – the grass in front of the flats, the tarmac of the road – and stop when it reached us.

We were not moving. Everything had stopped. The light settled on me, and then on Whitestone. As if it could not decide between us.

'She's gone, Pat,' I said.

'I know,' Whitestone said.

She looked back at the vehicles with their bright markings, the blocks of blue and yellow of the ARVs and the green and yellow of the RRVs. Between them I could see the dull metallic sheen on Glocks and Heckler & Kochs, the medieval curve of the combat helmets, the faces drawn tight with adrenaline.

Whitestone was shouting something at them. The green laser sight on the black hunting rifle played across the reindeer on her sweater and settled there.

'Put him down!' she said.

Then I heard their voices.

'I have the trigger!' somebody said.

But there was no shot.

And I thought of the palaver that came with every discharged firearm. The automatic suspension and then every shot endlessly analysed, pored over, suspected. The prospect of jail and the dole queue. No wonder they were scared to shoot.

But this was not the reason for holding fire.

When I looked back at the balcony I saw that the man was no longer alone. A woman was with him. She was wearing some kind of headscarf, although from this distance I could not tell if it was faith or fashion.

He was calling her names. He was calling her all the names that kind of man always call women. Then he seemed to shove her back and pick up something from the ground. Holding it by the scruff of the neck. Shaking it.

A child. A toddler of two or less. From where we were kneeling with the dead officer I could see the chubby look that they all get at that age. The kid squirmed like a tortured animal as the man held it over the edge of the balcony.

Four floors up.

Nothing but concrete below.

The man was shouting something. The woman was weeping by his side and without looking at her he struck her in the face with the butt of the black hunting rifle. She stumbled backwards.

Then the child was suddenly falling.

The woman screamed.

'Take the shot!' someone shouted.

There was a single crack that sounded very close to the back of my head and immediately a spurt of blood came from a hole in the neck of the man on the balcony. He did not fall. He staggered backwards and smashed though the glass window behind the balcony, and as he disappeared from view I thought how fragile we all are, how very easy to break, how always so close to ruin.

And then I was running, my shoes slipping on grass slick with ice, the call for God's help coming unbidden from my lips, holding out my arms for the falling child.

But the distance between us was too great, and there was never enough time, and the child was always falling.

CHAPTER 2

The meat market of Smithfield was silent. I walked under the market's great arch, shivering in the early death of New Year's Day, past the line of old red telephone boxes and the plaque marking the spot where they killed William Wallace. Not yet four in the afternoon, and the sun was already going down behind the dome of St Paul's Cathedral.

There was a strip of shops on the far side of the square. They were all closed for the holiday but in the flat above one of them, music was playing. Fiddles and flutes and drums played at a mad pace. A song about a girl called Sally MacLennane. Irish music. Happy music. Probably The Pogues, I thought. On the front of the darkened store the painted words were worn by time.

MURPHY & SON
Domestic and Commercial Plumbing
and Heating
'Trustworthy' and 'Reliable'

I went round the back of the shop and up a flight of stairs to the flats. A few of the residents had already thrown out their Christmas tree, but they were still celebrating at the Murphys. It took them a while to hear me ringing the bell, what with Shane MacGowan singing about his Sally MacLennane and the shouts of the adults and children inside.

My daughter Scout answered the door. Five years old and breathless. Rosy cheeked. Having the time of her life. There was a little red-haired girl with her, Shavon, maybe a year younger, and the girl's kid brother, Damon, plus a ruby-coloured Cavalier King Charles Spaniel, panting with excitement. Our dog Stan, who had a bandy-legged black mongrel pup I hadn't seen before shyly sniffing behind him.

'We don't have to go yet, do we?' Scout said by way of a greeting.

'And who's this?' I said, looking at the mongrel, by way of a response.

'This is Biscuit,' said Shavon.

'You'll have a sausage roll,' Mrs Murphy predicated, appearing behind her.

Scout dashed off with her friend, trailing kid brother and dogs behind them. Mrs Murphy took me inside where I was greeted enthusiastically by her husband, Big Mikey – a thin, dapper man with silver hair and a neat moustache, not very big at all – and their son, Little Mikey – a black-haired giant of a lad around thirty, nothing little about him. Little Mikey's wife Siobhan was nursing a new baby boy in blue. Baby Mikey.

The Christmas tree twinkled and shone. Kirsty MacColl and Shane MacGowan were telling their fairytale of New York. I was given a plate of sausage rolls and a beer. I stared at the bottle of beer as if I had never seen one before.

'Too late in the day for coffee,' Mrs Murphy said. 'You'll need your sleep.'

I nodded and mumbled my thanks to the Murphys for looking after Scout and as one they raised their voices in protest, telling me that she was no trouble, she was a joy and company for the kids. They were the kindest people I had ever met.

I suppose they were a small family. Defying all the Irish Catholic stereotypes, Little Mikey was an only child. But the three generations of Mikeys seemed like a mighty tribe compared to me, Scout and Stan.

The Murphys were a family of self-employed plumbers and I saw that, even today, they weren't really on holiday. Big Mikey was consulting his iPad to see when they could fit in a woman from Barnet with a burst pipe, while Little Mikey talked to a man in Camden with a broken boiler. And when my phone began to vibrate I knew that my own working day was not yet over.

I looked at the message and it was bad. A muscle by my left eye began to pulse. I placed my hand over it to hide it from the Murphys.

Big Mikey and Little Mikey were looking at me with sympathy.

'The holidays,' Mrs Murphy said. 'Busy time.'

The big house stood in a gated community in Highgate.

The Garden, it said on the gate.

This was London's highest point, the far north of London's money belt, and up here the air was fresh and clean and sweet. I stood outside the electronic gates with my warrant card in my hand and inhaled a draught of air that was almost Alpine.

A uniformed officer signed me in on the perimeter pad. The electronic gates began to open. DC Edie Wren was walking towards me on high heels. Her red hair was up, and she looked like she had been on her way to a dinner date when she got the call.

I took another look at the gated community. 'Are these houses all lock-up-and-leave-thems?'

Now that London had more billionaires than any city in the world, we were seeing a lot of high-end property that was bought and then left empty, as its value increased by millions.

The rich always had somewhere else to go.

'Some of them are lock-up-and-leaves, but not our one,' Wren said. 'It's a family, Max.' She hesitated for a moment, as if she could not quite believe it. 'Parents. Two teenage children. It's very slick. Looks like they've been executed.'

The gates closed behind us.

There were six large houses in the complex. Our tape was up outside one of them and beyond it the SOCOs were pulling on their white protective suits and uniformed officers stamped their feet for warmth. The winter darkness was really closing in now and the blue lights of our cars pierced the gloom.

Beyond the high walls of the gated community I could see what apppeared to be a wild green forest stretching off into the distance. But among the trees and the mad tangle of undergrowth there were huge crosses and stone angels and glimpses of ancient vaults. It was a graveyard that had been claimed by nature.

Highgate Cemetery.

Uniformed officers were knocking on the doors of the other houses where Christmas lights twinkled in the windows. In the middle of a road clogged by our cars a private security guard was being interviewed by a young black detective: DI Curtis Gane. He saw me and nodded and placed a hand on the guard's shoulder. The man was slack-jawed with shock. He was wearing no shoes.

'The guard called it in,' Wren said. 'He was doing his rounds when he saw the front door was open and he went inside.'

'And walked all the way through the house,' I said.

'Nothing we can do about that,' she said. 'Forensics have got his size tens and it's easy enough to eliminate.' She indicated the electronic

24

gates. 'He reckons nobody comes in without him knowing.'

'Then they came from the back,' I said. 'On the far side of the wall is Highgate West Cemetery.'

'Where Karl Marx is, right?'

'Marx is in the Highgate East Cemetery. The other side of Swain's Lane, the part that's open to the public. The far side of this wall is the West Cemetery and it's closed to the public. They only open it up for the odd guided tour and funerals.'

Wren looked doubtfully at the graveyard in a forest. In the twilight all you could see were the stone angels bowing their heads in the darkness.

'They're still burying people in there?'

I nodded. 'That's the way I would come,' I said, snapping on a pair of protective gloves.

We showed our warrant cards at the tape and I signed in again. It was very early in our initial response and the SOCOs had not yet gone inside. They were ready to work, white-coated and blue-gloved in their bunny suits, but they had to wait for the Senior Investigating Officer to view the scene and for the Crime Scene Photographer to record it – untouched, pristine, as horribly messed up as we first found it. Because once we all went inside, it would never look that way again.

There was the blurred electronic chatter of the digital radios, and in the distance the sound of more Rapid Response Vehicles rushing to the scene, their sirens splitting the air and their spinners turning the night blue. They would all have to wait for DCI Pat Whitestone to take that crucial first look.

Just before we reached the open front door where two uniformed officers were waiting, Wren stopped.

'Look,' she said.

A wooden pole had been shoved deep into some bushes. It was maybe ten feet long, made out of bamboo with an S-shaped piece of silver metal at one end. A butcher's hook. It resembled a primitive fishing rod. And that's what we called this popular form of breaking and entering.

'Fishing,' Wren said. 'Must be how he gained access.' She turned to call to one of the SOCOs. 'Can we get this grabbed and bagged, please?'

The bamboo pole must have been slipped through the letterbox and the butcher's hook had helped itself to a set of front-door keys that had been casually tossed by the door.

'Everybody thinks they're safe,' I said, shaking my head.

Inside, the smell of petrol was overwhelming.

White spotlights lit a long white hallway leading to a massive, two-storey atrium, a great open space with a wall of glass at the back. Someone had tried to set it on fire. Two senior fire officers were inspecting a blackened patch that totally covered one high wall and half the floor of a kitchen and dining area. There was a dinner table with places for twelve people. Beyond the glass wall there was only blackness.

DCI Whitestone was standing above a half-naked body. The corpse was a teenage boy with a single entry wound in the centre of his forehead. His legs splayed at awkward angles and his eyes were still open.

'Max,' Whitestone said quietly, taking off her glasses and rubbing her eyes. It had been a hard day and I saw the strain of it in her face. But she sounded calm, professional, ready to go to work. 'What do you think did that?' she asked me. 'Nine millimetre?'

The boy looked as though he had been shot at point-blank range.

'Looks like it,' I said. The floor was polished hard wood and I was expecting to see a telltale gold cylinder of a cartridge casing.

'I don't see any casings,' I said.

'There are no casings,' Whitestone said, and she was silent as we thought about that.

Taking the time to collect the casings was impressive.

'What happened to his legs?' Gane said. 'Looks like somebody hit him with a sledgehammer.'

'Or a car,' said Edie Wren, peering closer at the boy. 'I think he could have been outside. Looks like gravel on his arms and hands.'

There was a dog basket in one corner. It was for a big dog and on the back of it was stitched, MY NAME IS BUDDY.

'What happened to the dog?' I said.

Gane erupted.

'The dog?' he said. 'You're worried about the dog?

Up to our knees in a Charles Manson bloodbath and you're worried about *the dog*?'

I couldn't explain it to Gane. The dog was part of this family too.

'Anybody check on the goldfish?' Gane said. 'How's the hamster doing? Get Hammy's pulse, will you, Wolfe? And somebody check the budgie.'

'All right,' Whitestone said, silencing him. 'Let's go upstairs and see the rest of it.'

The giant glass wall suddenly burst into light.

The SOCOs had turned on their arc lights out the back.

Outside was a stone garden, swirls of pebbles around rocks, like a lake made of gravel. A Japanese garden. There was a temple bell in the centre of it all, a green bell stained with the weather of centuries, and it tolled as it moved with the breeze.

I did not move for a moment, stilled by the presence of all that unexpected beauty. There was a dog, a Golden Retriever, in one corner of the garden. He looked as though he was sleeping. But I knew he wasn't.

When I turned away Whitestone, Gane and Wren had already gone upstairs.

As I followed them I saw that there were photographs all over the wall of the staircase. Tasteful black-and-white photos mounted inside slim black frames. They were photographs of the family that had lived in this beautiful house.

And I saw that they had been the perfect family.

I felt I could tell their story from the photographs.

The mother and father looked as though they had married young and been fit and happy and in love for all their lives.

The man was big, athletic, with a look of mild amusement. A youthful mid-forties. The woman, perhaps ten years younger, was stunning, and vaguely familiar. She looked like Grace Kelly – she had exactly the kind of beauty that looks like a freak of nature.

If they had problems, then they were beyond my imagination. They had health, money and each other. And they had two children, a boy and a girl, and I watched them grow as I ascended the staircase.

They were good-looking, sporty kids. There was a shot of the girl on a hockey field aged maybe twelve, her gumshield showing orange in her serious face. And the boy, her brother, joyously holding up a cup with his football team. It was hard to equate that smiling child with the corpse downstairs.

Near the top of the stairs the boy and the girl were in their middle teens, almost a young man and a young woman, and I saw that the boy was slightly older than the girl but not by much more than a year. There was a photograph of the family together under a Christmas tree. Another photograph at a restaurant on a beach. In the later pictures there was a Golden Retriever who looked like he was laughing at his good fortune to find himself with this perfect family. The dog who now lay in the Japanese garden. And in the final photo-graph the woman who looked like Grace Kelly was holding a child.

A boy. About four. I guessed that his arrival had been unexpected. Their lives were full. The photo-graph wall was full. You could imagine that they did not think they would have any more children. Then the boy had come along and put a seal on all their happiness. Yes, he looked about four.

A year younger than Scout, I thought.

The Crime Scene Photographer came down the stairs.

I touched his arm.

'You absolutely sure there's nobody left alive?' I said.

'The Divisional Surgeon hasn't arrived yet so death hasn't been officially pronounced. But I've been up there. And all we've got in here is bodies, sir. Sorry.'

Something rose inside me and I choked it back down.

An entire family.

Gane was right. A Charles Manson bloodbath.

There was another body on the landing. The girl, all dressed up for New Year's Eve, lying on her side. I could not see an entry wound but around her throat there was what looked like a necklace made of blood. I heard voices at the far end of the hall, coming from the master bedroom. I moved towards it, steeling myself for what was inside.

The woman who looked like Grace Kelly was in

bed, a veil of blonde hair over her face. The pillow she lay on was stained but I could not see an entry wound. Like her daughter, she appeared to have been killed with a single shot to the back of the head.

'Looks like it was the father they came for,' Whitestone said.

The man's naked body was propped up against a dresser. He had been shot twice, once in each eye, at point-blank range and he stared at us with empty sockets. I inhaled deeply, forcing myself to look at the holes of ruined pulp. A halo of blood and brains was splashed over the white dressing table.

'Looks like it,' Gane said. 'They came for the father then decided to take out the family. The woman. The girl. The boy. They've been executed. But the father – that was personal.'

The four of us stood there like mourners.

'What about the little boy?' I said.

The silence grew like something that could kill you.

'What little boy?' Whitestone said.

The Specialist Search Team were there in fifteen minutes.

They are part of SO20, the Counter Terrorism Protective Security Command. They collect evidence after a terrorist attack and they clear an area before a state visit or major ceremonial event. They also work with Homicide.

While we were waiting for them to arrive we searched in every corner of that house for a small broken body. Then the SST methodically tore it apart.

They pulled up carpets, ripped up floorboards and punched holes in walls. They looked in the attic and in the recycling bins and in the drains. They looked in the oven and in the microwave and in the washing machine. And when they had done all of that and found nothing, they went out to the Japanese garden and searched under the neat grey stones. Then they went over the wall and into Highgate Cemetery.

The sun did not rise until just before eight a.m. And when it did, the men and women of the Specialist Search Team were still on their hands and knees, crawling inch by inch across the green hills of Highgate Cemetery. Hours before then DCI Whitestone had sent out the alert that a child was missing.

But as the sun came up our people still crawled across the graveyard, their fingers reaching in ancient tangles of ivy, their torches shining inside dusty crypts, watched from the wild by the angels with empty faces.

CHAPTER 3

The missing boy smiled shyly down at us from the wall of Major Incident Room Two.

Missing children always smile in their pictures. That is what rips up your heart, those childish smiles of joy captured on some beach holiday or birthday party, with nobody ever dreaming what is waiting down the line.

'You all know how it works,' DCI Whitestone said. 'We find him quickly . . .'

She left the rest of it unsaid because we knew it by heart.

Or we never find him at all.

This cruel fact had been hammered into us since our training days. All the statistics said that a child is found quickly or it's likely that they will never be found alive. If we didn't find the boy within twenty-four hours – seven days at the outside – then if we ever found him at all his body would probably be stuffed into an abandoned suitcase or tossed on a skip or at the bottom of a river or buried in a shallow grave. When a child has been missing for over a week, happy endings are hard to find.

We had come straight into 27 Savile Row from spending the night at the house on the hill.

And the smiling little boy had a name now.

Bradley Wood.

Bradley was four years old and he had a wonky, lopsided smile. At some point in the night, the Divisional Surgeon had officially pronounced that his mother and his father and his sister and his brother were all dead. And as I looked at Bradley Wood's smiling face I wondered what kind of life we would be bringing him back to with his family gone.

I bolted another triple espresso and pushed the thought aside.

Find him first.

He held a favourite toy in his small fist. An eight-inch plastic figure of a little man with a white shirt, black waistcoat and high boots. I looked closer and recognised Han Solo, the cocky captain of the *Millennium Falcon*.

'Where are we with the victims?' DCI Whitestone said, taking off her glasses and giving them a brief polish with a crumpled Caffè Nero paper napkin. She looked exhausted. We were all exhausted. Our Murder Investigation Team had spent the night at the crime scene and then come straight into 27 Savile Row – West End Central – at dawn, working through the morning on identifying the dead. Now it was early afternoon and the pale winter sun was already sinking over the rooftops of Mayfair.

'This is the Wood family,' I said, hitting a key on my laptop. 'The victims.'

There was a huge HD TV screen on the wall of MIR-2 and it was suddenly filled with one of the family photographs that I had first seen on the staircase of the Wood family home.

They smiled at us. The good-looking woman and man. Their two teenage children. Wealthy, athletic, beautiful. In the photograph they were all huddled up and laughing at some ski resort with baby Bradley at their centre.

'The father, Brad, was a sports agent. The mother, Mary, she was a housewife. The boy is Marlon, fifteen, and the girl is Piper, fourteen. They were both at private schools in Hampstead. And then there's Bradley.'

Whitestone shook her head. 'Why do I feel like I know them?' she said.

'You recognise the mother,' I said. 'Mary Wood was once Mary Gatling and she was briefly very famous.'

Whitestone blinked with surprise behind her glasses. 'The Mary Gatling of the 1994 Winter Olympics?'

I nodded. 'At Lillehammer in Norway. The Ice Virgin, they called her.'

'Mary Wood was the Ice Virgin?' Whitestone said. 'The girl who said she wasn't going to have sex until she got married?'

'That's her. She was part of the UK's team. A downhill skier. She didn't get a medal but she got a lot of headlines. Announced that she was going to save herself until she got married. It was big news for about five minutes.'

'She met her husband at the games in Lillehammer, right?'

'Yes – Brad Wood. American. From a blue-collar family in Chicago. He was in Lillehammer for the biathlon. Cross-country skiing and shooting. Nearly won a medal. Met Mary in the Olympic Village.'

'That's the Ice Virgin,' Whitestone said, shaking her head with wonder. 'Mary Gatling. She didn't lose her looks, did she?'

'Gatling?' DC Edie Wren said. 'Like Gatling Homes? The property developers?'

'Exactly like Gatling Homes,' I said. 'Mary was the eldest of Victor Gatling's daughters. She came from serious money. The old man started out as a runner for slum landlords in the Sixties. Then he bought a one-bedroom flat in Tottenham – did it up – sold it. And took it from there. The company has been upmarket for the last twenty years. Victor Gatling has to be seventy now at least. A lot of the new developments in prime London real estate are Gatling Homes: Kensington, Chelsea, Mayfair, Hampstead, Knightsbridge. They say Victor Gatling made two fortunes. Building homes for poor immigrants in the last century and building homes for rich immigrants in this century. They call him the man who built London. His son Nils has been running the show since the old man semi-retired.'

'And Mary's husband has been a sports agent for the last twenty years?' Whitestone said.

'Not so long,' I said. 'After Brad married Mary he worked for the father-in-law for a few years. Apparently that didn't work out.'

There were shouts and screams from down in the street and we all turned to look at the window. Four floors below MIR-2, the fury of the traffic was one unbroken howl. Savile Row is a narrow, canyon-like street, a place of bespoke tailors and hard-core Beatles fans looking for the scene of the band's final gig. And from Conduit Street in the north to Burlington Gardens in the south, right now it was clogged with the world's media. Banks of paparazzi, large vans with transmitting dishes, milling hordes of reporters were all waiting under the blue lamp of 27 Savile Row.

'The MLO called again, boss,' Wren said.

The MLO was our Media Liaison Officer.

'Yes?' Whitestone said.

'She wants to know when you're going to brief the press,' Wren said. 'That photo of little Bradley is going to be on every front page tomorrow morning. It's going to be all over the evening news tonight. And it's on every social network right now. And nothing's moving down there.'

'Tell the MLO I'll brief the press when the next of kin have formally identified the bodies,' Whitestone said impatiently.

Wren hesitated. 'And I had a call from the Chief Super's office.'

'What did they want?'

'They also want to know when you're going to brief the press.'

Whitestone nodded grimly. 'You can tell DCS Swire's office exactly the same thing: I'm not talking to journalists until the family has seen the bodies.'

'That's happening now,' Wren said. 'Mary Wood's next of kin has arrived at the Iain West.'

The Iain West Forensic Suite was the Westminster mortuary, named after the country's legendary forensic pathologist.

'Who's over there?'

'Mary Wood's sister, accompanied by the FLO.'

The FLO was the Family Liaison Officer. Every police station in the world is acronym central.

Whitestone nodded, and turned to look at a map of London that reached from floor to ceiling.

'How are we doing with the search, Curtis?

'The major problem for the search teams is that our crime scene is in the greenest part of London,' DI Curtis Gane said. 'Lots of undergrowth, ditches, trees. Highgate Cemetery. Waterlow Park. Highgate Woods. Hampstead Heath. A couple of golf courses. It's like looking for a body in a forest.'

'And there's a lot of water,' Whitestone said. 'The ponds in Highgate and Hampstead. Three reservoirs within – what? – a twenty-minute drive?'

'Yes, boss,' Gane said. 'Brent Reservoir to the west. Manor House and Tottenham Hale to the east. We've called in Underwater Search and the Dive Team

38

are working their way out. It's hard-going for the search teams, but they've got the full kit. Not just sniffer dogs – EVRDs.'

Enhanced victim recovery dogs are trained to detect human remains.

We stared at the photograph of the Wood family in silence.

'It doesn't make sense, does it?' Whitestone said. 'Spree killers don't hit gated communities with a private security guard outside. And contract killers don't abduct children.' She paused, pushing her glasses up her nose, struggling to understand. 'Who kills four people and then steals a child? Why does anyone steal a child?'

'Extortion,' Gane said. 'That might fit. Demanding a ransom for the return of the child. These are seriously wealthy people.'

'Trafficking,' Wren said. 'Abduction with the intent of sexual abuse, illegal adoption or organ farming.'

'And murder,' I said.

'Get Dr Joe in here,' Whitestone said. 'Let's have a psychological profile of the kind of creep who can kill a family and then abduct their child.'

Wren reached for her phone and hit the speed dial for Dr Joe Stephen, a forensic psychologist based at King's College London.

'No weapon?' Whitestone said.

Gane shook his head. 'Not yet.'

'No prints? No partials?'

'We heard from forensics,' I said. 'The house has

been wiped down by a pro. But that fits with the lack of nine-millimetre casings. If he's going to pick up his shells, he's going to wipe the place down.'

'He?' Wren said. 'Subduing an entire family is a big job for just one man. What makes you think—'

There was a roar down in the street.

I went to the window.

'Someone's talking to the press,' I said.

Whitestone scowled, roughly pushing her glasses up her nose. '*What?*'

We leaned from the window but all we could see was the massed crush of reporters. So we turned on the TV and watched it on the rolling news.

Directly under the old blue lamp, a man and a woman were standing on the steps of 27 Savile Row. The woman was a slightly younger version of Mary Wood with the same cool blonde beauty. Like a girl from a Hitchcock film. The man was older, with thinning blond hair. Beside them I could see the FLO and the MLO, two young women in business suits, both looking pained.

'Ah – ladies and gentlemen, your attention, please,' said the MLO. 'Can we stop pushing forward? Please! Ah, I am joined by Mr Nils Gatling and Ms Charlotte Gatling, the brother and sister of the deceased, Mary Gatling-Wood.'

The pack surged forward. Uniformed officers frowned under their helmets and attempted to keep the cameras and the microphones and the bodies off the steps outside West End Central.

Whitestone cursed. 'Please don't tell me they're actually going to give a statement,' she said.

'Isn't that going to get the public to help us?' Wren said.

'We don't want their help,' Gane said.

'We rely on the public for help,' Whitestone said. 'But you can get too much help, Edie, and you can get all the wrong kind.'

'We don't want volunteers tramping through Highgate Woods,' Gane said. 'We don't want telephone calls every time someone spots a fair-haired kid of four. We don't want the cranks and nutters and fruitcakes. We don't want a gang of squirrel-brained loonies giving us a helping hand. Because none of that helps us. All it does is get in the way of us doing our job.'

'Too late now,' Whitestone said.

The man – Nils Gatling – had begun to speak, his voice ragged with shock and pain.

'My sister and I have just seen the body of our beloved sister and her beautiful family,' he said, to an explosion of cameras. A forest of microphones was shoved towards him. 'It is still difficult to comprehend that this tragedy has actually happened,' he said. 'Our sister's family has been destroyed and our hearts have been broken. My family and I will of course cooperate in any way we can to bring those who did this to justice. Our thoughts now are with my sister's youngest child . . .' He looked up. 'Bradley.'

'Please,' his sister said, her voice as soft as a

prayer, and the camera swung towards her. 'Please don't hurt my nephew.'

She did not cry. Yet her grief was so palpable that I found I could not breathe.

'Bradley is a beautiful little boy who never hurt anyone,' she said. 'Don't hurt him. Please, please. Just bring him home – bring him home to the only family he has left. *Bring Bradley back.*'

The camera held her.

The camera loved her.

'That's their headline tomorrow,' Gane said. '*Bring Bradley back.*'

'She looks like God's second attempt at – what's the name of that old actress?' said Wren. 'Oh, yeah. Michelle Pfeiffer.'

And still the camera could not pull itself away from that hypnotic combination of beauty and grief.

Her brother Nils said a few more words, and then there was some meaningless soft-spoken waffle from the MLO about respecting privacy.

But still the camera lingered on Charlotte Gatling.

The TV cameras could not get enough of her. The photographers gazed up at her, desperately capturing her face as it was on those moments under the blue lamp of 27 Savile Row on a cold day in January.

And I found that, just like all those cameras, I could not look away from her face.

I heard Whitestone sigh.

'We're going to need a bigger room,' she said.

★   ★   ★

42

I awoke with a start in the dead of the night.

4.10 a.m., warned the clock by my bed.

Too early to get up. Too late to go back to sleep. What had woken me?

I quickly went into Scout's bedroom. But she was sleeping peacefully, her school clothes for the morning waiting on an old-fashioned wooden stand, carefully placed there by Mrs Murphy.

I watched Scout's sleeping face, marvelling that I had somehow helped to produce the most beautiful little kid in the world. I know that every parent feels that way. What was different about my daughter was that she really was the most beautiful little kid in the world.

I padded to the kitchen, hearing Stan snoring in the darkness, the old-man wheeze of the short-nosed dog. I made myself coffee and looked at my phone. Edie Wren had left me a message fifteen minutes ago:

I know why they died.

As I called her number, I walked to the window of our loft and looked down at the blazing lights of Smithfield meat market.

Four in the morning and the men were in the middle of their work. It made me feel better, like less of a freak for being awake at this hour. Wren answered immediately, and I sensed that she had not slept at all.

'They had a strong digital presence,' Wren said. 'The Woods. Try Googling them, Max.' I was already turning on my MacBook Air in the kitchen.

'You get seven million results in just under half a second.'

'Because of Lillehammer,' I said. 'Because she was the Ice Virgin, half a lifetime ago. You're not just famous for fifteen minutes now. It all stays out there forever.'

'Not just that,' Wren said. 'Not just the Winter Olympics and Mary the Ice Virgin. I mean *now*. This family – they put films online. You know – happy family stuff: Here's us having fun at Val d'Isère. Here's us celebrating one of our birthdays. Here's us on a boat in Barbados. Oh, and here's us looking gorgeous.'

There were so many results for the Woods that I didn't know where to start.

'What are you talking about?' I said. 'Sharing their happiness or showing off?'

'Is there a difference?'

By now I was on YouTube looking at the Woods on their Easter holiday in Geilo, Norway. They looked like a family in an advertisement for something you realise that you desperately need. And under their beautiful smiling faces, I scrolled down the comments section, and I flinched at the spite, the malice and the abuse. Their happiness enraged the great anonymous public.

'I want to turn these comments off, Edie,' I said. 'It's like swimming in a sewer.'

'You can't turn them off, Max. You can never turn them off.'

'So what's your theory?'

44

'It's not a theory,' she said. 'I felt like saying it in MIR-2 but I didn't have the nerve. Because it sounds stupid.'

'Say it, Edie.'

'Look at those comments, Max. Look at all that filth. Look at how much the world hates the beautiful people, the rich ones, the lucky ones with all the money and love. Look how the world hates the happy ones. Can't you see it, Max? Somebody killed the Wood family because they were happy.'

CHAPTER 4

We got up early to see the Queen's horses. It was still freezing dark when Stan, Scout and I took our places on the corner of Charterhouse Street and Farringdon Road. As usual, our conversation revolved mostly around our dog.

'Stan doesn't have one of those happy dog faces, does he?' Scout said.

I knew what she meant. He was a beautiful dog but he didn't have one of those upturned, grinning, ain't-life-grand? mouths that dogs sometimes have, with tongue lolling and eyes twinkling, the kind of dog face that you see in commercials for pet food. Stan would never wear a rakish smirk. He had the mournful downturn of the spaniel's mouth. But his windscreen-wiper tail told me he was happy to be out on an early morning adventure with all of our little family, and his ruby-coloured coat was like molten silk, and he gazed up at Scout as if she was the absolute centre of the universe.

'He's laughing inside,' I said. 'Here they come.'

Two dozen horses came slowly down the road, all of them pitch black. The heat of their bodies sent up clouds of steam in the freezing air. The Household Cavalry Mounted Regiment on their watering order – exercise for the horses who would not be participating at Horse Guards later that day. In some ways, I thought this was more magnificent. No gilt and gold and swords and plumes, just mounted soldiers in khaki fleeces, but the sight of them on these city streets seemed to touch the day with magic.

Stan pulled at his lead in an attempt to go with them. When Scout restrained him he looked up at her with eyes as huge as black marbles in his little head.

Oh, come on, he seemed to say.

When the horses had passed by, clomping down to Victoria Embankment on their way back to the stables of the Queen's Life Guard, we went for breakfast in Smiths of Smithfield.

Stan greeted familiar faces. Our dog was very people-orientated. When the first wild dogs were tentatively approaching the campfires of man ten thousand years ago, the start of the greatest alliance between two species in nature, man's food and shelter fair exchange for the affection and protection of the dogs, there's no doubt that Stan's ancestors were right at the front of the queue, licking hands and wagging tails and rolling their huge eyes.

Through the massive windows we could see the meat porters of Smithfield finishing their long night shifts.

'Did they find Bradley yet?' Scout said.

'What?'

'Did they find Bradley yet? Did they bring him back?'

'How do you know about Bradley, angel?'

'I saw him on the news. The lady was talking.'

'Angel, you know you're not meant to watch the news.' It had been one of her mother's rules. And we tried our best to stick by all the old rules. 'There are things on the news that are not suitable for children your age.'

'I know. I was watching kids' TV and then the news came on. And Mrs Murphy turned it over quick to the cookery show. But Bradley was the first thing on the news. And I wondered if they got him back yet . . .'

'Not yet. But we will. We're going to find him and we are going to bring him home.'

'How can you be so sure?'

'Because it's my job.'

My phone began to vibrate. It was Whitestone.

'We need you at the Iain West,' she said. 'There's a problem with the bodies.'

'These are not gunshot wounds,' said Elsa Olsen, forensic pathologist. 'The entry wounds you saw on the victims, and that you understandably took for GSWs, are in fact circular fractures. Circular fractures of the skull in the case of three of the victims and circular fracture of both eye sockets in the other. The manner of death was murder.

48

But it wasn't a gun that killed them. It was blunt-force trauma.'

Wren had met our little family at the door of the Iain West Forensic Suite at the Westminster Public Mortuary on Horseferry Road and immediately whisked Scout and Stan off for fun and games at 27 Savile Row. Scout liked Wren. And of course Stan liked everybody.

Now DCI Whitestone, DI Gane and I were deep inside the Iain West, looking lovely in our blue scrubs and hairnets, not quite freezing but shivering in a room where the temperature was always just above zero.

The Wood family lay in a neat row on their stainless-steel slabs.

Elsa Olsen moved slowly between them as she spoke. You could see where Elsa had opened the bodies up for examination and then stitched them back up again. On each of the four bodies there was a Y-shaped incision starting at the top of the shoulder where Elsa had gone in with her rib-cutter shears – like many pathologists, she favoured ordinary gardening pruning shears – to examine the internal organs. At the top of each head there was a skullcap where Elsa had sawn open the skulls with a vibrating Stryker saw.

Whitestone nodded at the visible wounds on the boy and the man. You could not see the single entry wounds we had found in the back of the head of the mother and daughter. But you could see the single entry wounds in the centre of the boy's forehead and you could see the gaping black holes where the father's eyes had been.

'But there are abrasion collars,' Whitestone said.

Abrasion collars are the black burn marks that you find in a gunshot wound fired at close range. And it was true you could see burn marks around the wound in the boy's head and the holes where the man's eyes had once been.

'There might be abrasion collars,' Elsa said. 'But it wasn't a firearm that did it, Pat. It was a *tool*. A tool with enough brute force to punch a hole through the skull and push a section of bone into the brain. These people were not shot. They were slaughtered.'

I understood now why there were no shell casings. It wasn't because the killer was a professional. It was because he had not used a firearm.

Elsa Olsen was tall and dark, a blue-eyed Norwegian, one of those Scandinavians who speak English far better than the natives.

'Have you seen the toxicology report yet?' she asked.

Whitestone shook her head. 'It's not back from the lab.'

'It will tell you that all four family members had traces of flunitrazepam – Rohypnol, the date-rape drug – in their system at the time of death,' Elsa said. 'I found evidence of it in each family member's gastrointestinal tract. As you know, Rohypnol has no odour. You would not have been aware of it at the crime scene.'

'So that's how they were subdued,' Whitestone said. 'They were dosed with Rohypnol.'

'Manner of death was murder,' Elsa said. 'White male, forty-five years old – Brad Wood. White female, thirty-five – Mary Wood. White male, fifteen – Marlon Wood. White female, fourteen – Piper Wood. Their bodies were all in the rigid stage of rigor mortis. As you're aware, rigor mortis sets in after around two hours and then the body becomes progressively stiff. Based on the twelve-twelve-twelve rule – twelve hours to get stiff, twelve hours to remain stiff and twelve hours for the body to start relaxing as it gets accustomed to the fact that it is dead – I can state with some confidence that the Wood family died eighteen hours before they were discovered on the evening of January first.'

'New Year's Eve,' Whitestone said.

'Why weren't they out celebrating?' Gane said.

Whitestone adjusted her glasses. 'Perhaps they were celebrating with each other.'

They now lay naked in a row on four stainless-steel tables.

'The boy – Marlon Wood – has multiple abrasions and bruising all over his body,' Elsa said.

Whitestone looked up sharply. 'Those marks on Marlon – that's not lividity?'

Like many dead bodies that have lain undiscovered for a while, the bodies of the Wood family all looked as though they were bruised. With the heart not pumping, the blood settles and stagnates and lividity sets in, and it looks exactly like bruising. They all had it. But as we took half a step closer, you could see that it was clearly more extensive on the boy.

'Marlon has broken femurs,' Elsa said. 'As you know, the thigh bone is the strongest bone in the body. It takes a hell of a lot to break it. In fact, 99 per cent of broken femurs happen the same way.'

'A car,' I said. 'Somebody ran him down in a car. He was run down and then carried or dragged into the house.'

'But it wasn't the car that killed him,' Elsa said. 'Let me show you his brain. I left his skullcap loose to show you.'

Elsa gently removed the very top of Marlon's head. Then she carefully peeled the front flap of his skull over his face and peeled the back flap of his skull over the back of his head. The features of his face were now replaced with the blank, bloody mask that was the inside of his head.

I took a breath and let it go, making a small cloud of steam in the bitter cold. We gathered at the top of the table for a better look.

'I can remove his brain if I cut the connections to the spinal cord and cranial nerves,' Elsa said. 'But I think it's clear enough *in situ*.'

She pulled back a thin layer of what looked like chicken skin etched with a road map of blood and we saw the thick channel burrowed deep into the brain, blood so dark that it was black.

'Marlon here died from epidural bleeding – he was hit in the front of the head, as you can see from the extensive damage to his skull and brain. Mary and Piper died from subdural bleed – blunt-force trauma to the back of the head. In all three the cause of death was blunt-force head trauma leading to intracranial bleeding. But the father was different. He died of a heart attack. I suspect it was after his first eye was destroyed.'

'Defensive wounds?' Whitestone said.

'Piper fought for her life,' Elsa said. 'The rest of them went quietly.'

'Did she have broken nails?'

Broken nails would be good because they would mean she had clawed the killer and possibly had some of his skin still under there.

'No, a broken thumb,' Elsa said, and she looked at the body of Piper Wood. 'But she fought like hell. She was an incredibly brave girl.'

'Sexual abuse?' Whitestone said.

'Piper had non-motile sperm in her vagina, sperm with no tails, indicating she had consensual sex a few days prior to her murder,' Elsa said. 'But I also found evidence of a sexual assault. There was a rape before the murder.'

'So Piper was raped?' Whitestone said.

Elsa shook her head. 'The mother was raped,' she said. 'Mary. There was motile sperm in her mouth, vagina and rectum. As you know, sperm survive in a dead body for longer than they do in a living body. When the heart stops beating, the body stops producing the chemicals to destroy sperm. They're still there, in fact. They can last for up to two weeks in a corpse.'

'Perhaps watching that caused the father's heart attack,' I said.

'Perhaps,' Elsa conceded.

'Does the family know?' I asked.

'I informed the sister – Charlotte Gatling – that Mary had been raped when she identified the bodies,' Elsa said. 'And she asked me not to make that information public. I agreed.'

'How does that work?' Whitestone said. 'Rape would come out in court. It would come out at the point of prosecution. DNA evidence would mean it had to come out.'

'Of course,' Elsa said. 'Charlotte Gatling understands it has to come out in court. But she requests that it doesn't come out now. Her father is unwell. Her brother was devoted to her sister. She feels that her family members are already suffering enough without revelations that Mary was raped.'

'Understood,' Whitestone said. 'No problem. And the mechanism, Elsa – what was used to kill them? What are we talking about? A hammer of some kind? A metal spike?' She shook her head. 'Because I feel that I've seen this somewhere before.'

'And so do I,' Elsa said. 'But not in this country. Not in this job.'

She began to sew the top of Marlon Wood's skull back to his head with a Hagedorn needle. She used a thick twine and the stitching looked similar to what you see on a baseball. It's not as messy as it sounds. The heart is no longer pumping so the dead don't bleed.

Only the living bleed.

'When I was a child, growing up on a farm in Norway,' Elsa said, 'there was one year when we had had floods in the spring followed by a drought in the summer. That meant there wasn't enough fodder for the cattle. So all the farmers, including my father, slaughtered their herds for beef. And before my father killed his cattle, he stunned them by firing a metal bolt into their brains. That's when I saw these wounds.' She indicated the Wood family. 'This is exactly what it looks like when livestock are prepared for slaughter.'

CHAPTER 5

'Who kills with a cattle gun?' Edie Wren said quietly back at West End Central. 'Spree killers – all spree killers – every single one of them – come to the party armed like Rambo.'

We had moved our investigation down the corridor to MIR-1, the larger Major Incident Room, but the four members of our MIT were huddled in one corner and keeping our voices down because Scout was sitting in the middle of the room, Stan dozing at her feet, doing her drawing at one of the workstations until Mrs Murphy picked her up.

'This wasn't a spree killing,' Whitestone said, equally quietly. 'For a start, it wasn't multiple locations. A spree killer would have wandered through that rich little road taking out the neighbours until we cornered him and he worked up the nerve to blow his brains out. And spree killers love soft targets. Spree killers love shopping malls and cinemas.' She glanced across at Scout and made her voice even lower. 'Spree killers love schools. A spree killer doesn't select a gated community with a security guard for his target. And you're right, Edie – he doesn't choose a cattle gun for his weapon. He comes armed with more firepower than he can ever possibly use. This was a hit.'

'But a contract hit doesn't fit,' I said. 'Despite what he did to the father's eyes.' I had left the Iain West Suite more convinced than ever that he – or they – had come for Brad Wood. 'The cattle gun rules out a pro,' I said. 'Or even an aspiring amateur. And a pro would have killed Bradley or left him alone, but they wouldn't take the kid with them.'

'Hitman, gang member, psycho,' Gane said. 'Nobody kills with a cattle gun. Why would they?'

'It happens,' Whitestone said. 'Once every ten years or so some local yokel runs amok on a farm and reaches for the nearest thing that looks like it can cause serious harm. Picks up a cattle gun. But they don't steal a child . . .' She shook her head, as if the memory she was searching for was just out of reach. 'Tends to be an impulse kill rather than premeditated. It's not unknown. Except in the middle of London. It's unknown here. Where's Dr Joe?'

We were still waiting for our favourite forensic psychologist to come in and explain to us what particular flavour of psychopath could make the kind of mess we had found in Highgate.

'Dr Joe is in the States for the holidays,' Wren said. 'He's flying back early for us.'

'Edie?' a little voice said.

We all turned to look at Scout.

'Yes, sweetheart?' Wren said.

'Check this out, Edie,' my daughter said. 'My picture.'

Wren crossed the room to Scout.

'Wow, so that's you and your dad and your dog – Stan, right? – and these are the Queen's horses?'

'Right,' Scout said. 'And they're all black, see?'

Whitestone turned to us.

'I want Edie on the missing boy for now,' she said. 'Bradley. We're getting sightings all the time.'

'How many?' I said.

'The last time I looked it was over two hundred. We're going to need some extra hands to sort the fruitcakes from the genuine leads.' She nodded at me. 'Your friend in 101 might be able to get us up to speed on precedents.'

'Right.'

She meant Sergeant John Caine in Room 101 of New Scotland Yard – the Black Museum, a unique archive of the most notorious crimes of the last hundred years. It wasn't officially called the Black Museum any more – it was the Crime Museum, in case calling it the Black Museum hurt any ethnic minority's feelings. And it wasn't actually a museum at all – the days when Arthur Conan Doyle had the key to the place were long gone. Now the Black Museum was used as a training facility to impress on young coppers that every day on the job could be their last day on earth.

More than anything, the Black Museum was a memorial to evil.

'Curtis, run the MO through HOLMES,' Whitestone told Gane. HOLMES, or more accurately the new improved HOLMES2, is the Home Office Large Major Enquiry System. 'See who's been convicted for murder with a cattle gun. Living, dead, the lot. I believe there's at least two of them currently doing time. Couple of farm boys who were unlucky in love or didn't get their Christmas bonus.' She looked thoughtful for a moment as a memory stirred. 'Now I remember – it must have been thirty years ago.'

'Someone took out a family with a cattle gun?' I said.

'A father and his three grown-up sons. There was a girl – and her mother – but he didn't touch them.' She shook her head; it was all a very long time ago. 'But he's probably dead by now.'

Whitestone looked across at Scout and Edie chatting away to each other and totally oblivious to the rest of us. But still she kept her voice low.

'The Slaughter Man,' she said.

I had arranged to meet Mrs Murphy under the old blue lamp that marks the entrance to West End Central but as soon as Scout and I stepped out of the lift, I saw that was never going to work.

The press pack seemed to have grown. The TV

vans now stretched all the way down Savile Row. Uniformed officers were doing their best to keep the crowds on the pavement and the traffic moving on the narrow road, but reporters with orange tans kept sneaking into the middle of the road so they could do their pieces to camera with the blue lamp of 27 Savile Row in the background. They jabbered dramatically in a dozen different languages.

'It's very crowded, isn't it?' Scout said.

'It is, angel.'

It was also bitterly cold. I fastened the top two buttons on Scout's coat and jammed her hat over her ears and picked her up, scanning the crowds for an old lady sporting the kind of hat, coat and handbag that the Queen would favour.

'There she is,' Scout said.

Mrs Murphy was sensibly standing just beyond the crowds, a black cab with its engine running waiting beside her. She saw us and began to smile and wave. I called over a uniformed officer.

'You see that lady in the green hat and coat?'

'Yes, sir.'

'Can you get her to the door?'

The young copper nodded and stepped into the street, waving Mrs Murphy and her cab forwards. Suddenly the crowd stirred. Two police motor-bikes were turning into Savile Row from the Conduit Street end, the blue lights pulsing on the big BMW bikes and piercing the misty morning. And then two more. Photographers began to sprint towards them. And then there was the car, a black 7-Series BMW with its windows blacked out, edging past the paparazzi, now followed by another two motorbike outriders, all of them shouting at the press to get back. The first two outriders pulled up just behind Mrs Murphy's black cab. I saw her worried face at the window and I carried Scout down the steps, my arms wrapped tight around her.

My boss got out of the black car. Detective Chief Superintendent Elizabeth Swire – the Chief Super. She stared coldly at the press and then smiled at Scout.

'Hello, young lady,' DCS Swire said. 'Are you helping your father today?'

'No,' Scout said. 'I'm only five.'

'Excellent,' DCS Swire said and turned back to the car. Nils Gatling got out, buttoning his suit jacket and ignoring the questions shouted at him by the press pack. He was clean-shaven but his eyes looked as though he had not slept since yesterday.

'I'll talk to them later,' he told DCS Swire.

His sister got out of the car and the mob charged forward, screaming her name. Charlotte Gatling had a face that was as near to perfect as I had ever seen. Yet grief and shock were etched deep on that face, and the effect was hypnotic.

'Scout,' Mrs Murphy said from the back of the black cab. 'Come, little darling.'

I crouched down to ease Scout safely into the back of the cab. When I straightened up, Charlotte

Gatling was staring at me through the crowd with an unnerving intensity.

As if she had never seen a father carrying his daughter before.

CHAPTER 6

'The cattle gun,' said Sergeant John Caine of the Black Museum. 'Also known as the captive bolt pistol and the stunbolt gun. Farmers call them stunners, as though they are very attractive young ladies. Primary use is stunning cattle prior to slaughter. Also quite effective on goats, sheep, horses and of course human beings.' He took a sip of tea from a mug that said, BEST DAD IN THE WORLD. 'You ever see that movie *No Country for Old Men?*'

'Tommy Lee Jones was the cop,' I said. 'He was good.'

'And Javier Bardem was even better,' John said. 'He was the villain with the cattle gun, remember? *Anton Chigurh.* Having a bad hair day. Remember his cattle gun?'

'He used it to open doors. Blew the lock out. He killed a man with it once but mostly he used his shotgun. The cattle gun was on this big carbon-dioxide canister. Looked like an oxygen tank.'

'Cattle guns don't look like that any more,' John said. 'What old Anton Chigurh had, that's the Model T Ford of cattle guns. I don't know what

63

the filmmakers were thinking. The modern cattle gun looks more like a hand drill.'

'Do you have one I could see, John?'

He laughed. 'We've got the lot in the Black Museum. You know that, Max. Shall I put the kettle on?'

'No, I better get cracking.'

He took out his key and unlocked the door to the Black Museum. I followed him into a Victorian drawing room that was stuffed full of deadly weapons.

The Black Museum in New Scotland Yard looks like a boot sale for psychopaths. Weapons everywhere. Most of these weapons have either killed or wounded policemen or civilians. But I couldn't see what I was looking for.

'At the far end,' he said. 'I've only got the one.'

He led me to a distant corner of the Black Museum that I had never noticed before.

The cattle gun sat on a small card table. John Caine was right. It looked like a hand drill. Or maybe some kind of sophisticated nail gun. It was scarred and rusting, as though it had seen a lot of service. Above it there was a yellowing newspaper article in a dusty glass case.

'That's him,' I said. 'The Slaughter Man.'

RITUAL SLAUGHTER ON ESSEX FARM
Slaughter Man executes father and sons in midnight killing spree

A killer was jailed for life yesterday for murdering a father and his three grown-up sons with a bolt gun used to slaughter livestock.

Peter Nawkins, 17, had been engaged to the only daughter of Ian Burns of Hawksmoor Farm, Essex. When the engagement was ended, Nawkins broke into Hawksmoor Farm and slaughtered Farmer Burns and his sons Ian Junior, 23, Martin, 20, and Donald, 17, before setting fire to their home. Mrs Doris Burns, 48, and her daughter Carolyn, 16, were present but escaped unharmed by the killer the press have dubbed the Slaughter Man.

There was more but I was looking at the article's two photographs. One showed a man who looked like a large, overgrown boy being led away in handcuffs by a uniformed officer, the boy-man's face smooth and unlined and totally empty, as if he was thinking of nothing at all. He was strikingly handsome, in a way that seemed from another time. The mass of black curls pushed back from a Roman profile, like the head on a coin, the picture somehow not marred by a nose that had been bent by man or nature.

The other picture showed a family laughing under a Christmas tree. The father dark and beefy, his three boys the same, and his wife and daughter both slim and fair.

'Why do they give them these names?' John said, the anger suddenly bubbling up. '*The Slaughter Man!* As though he's some kind of superhero? Who put the idea about that these little men are anything special? This one – old Slaughter Man – was illiterate, as I recall. Couldn't even read and write.'

I was still studying the clipping.

'Nawkins got a life sentence with a minimum tariff of twenty years before parole could be considered,' I said. 'Is that all? Seems a bit of a slap on the wrist for four murders.'

'Mitigating factors, weren't there?' John said. 'Nawkins' IQ level was lower than his shoe size. Possibly not his fault. He never had much formal education – him being a Romany and all. He was seventeen years old – just about. Over eighteen, they would have hit him a hell of a lot harder. And he didn't bring the weapon with him. The murders were not premeditated – at least, that's what his brief got the judge to believe. He was a young simpleton who wouldn't hurt a fly. Until he killed four men.'

'So Nawkins was a gypsy . . .'

'Came from a long line of colourful travelling folk.'

'Sentenced to a minimum tariff of twenty years in 1980. Is he out? Is he still alive?'

'No idea. You'll have to ask HOLMES. You don't like him for this Highgate turnout, do you?'

I shrugged. 'Same MO.'

'But Nawkins didn't steal a child, did he?'

'No, he didn't.'

'And the killings he did – they were *personal*. Farmer Burns didn't like his only daughter going out with a gypsy. Made her break it off. I mean, Nawkins was a murdering scumbag, no doubt about it. But he was a murdering scumbag with a genuine grievance.'

'We're just looking for leads. I know murders happen with cattle guns, but not often enough for us to discount someone like Nawkins. Was this the weapon he used?'

John nodded. He picked it up.

'It's a cordless, gas-powered captive bolt tool. You get a thousand stuns out of one gas canister, so it gives you plenty of firepower. Primary use is on-farm culling.'

He handed the cattle gun to me. It felt strange in my hand. Somewhere between a tool and a weapon.

'How does it work?'

'It's not complicated. A pointed bolt is fired into the skull by pressurised air. It destroys the animal's brain but keeps its heart beating. This is the older, meaner type – the penetrating stunner. These days they use a non-penetrating stunner with a mushroom-shaped tip. Causes concussion rather than brain damage. Less effective, but brain matter doesn't enter the bloodstream the way it does with this type here, so there's less risk of contamination with mad cow disease. What did they use in Highgate?'

'No idea. But they made a mess. How easy is it to use?'

'Easier to kill a man than stun a cow. And you need contact pressure to activate the thing. You can't shoot anything with it unless you've got it pressed right in there. So – if you're stunning a cow or topping your girlfriend's dear old dad – you have to stick it right against the flesh and bone, or it doesn't fire. You're meant to shoot down at a 45-degree angle to penetrate the brain with enough concussive impact to produce instant unconsciousness. But that's with pigs and cattle. I imagine you don't have to be quite so fussy when you're killing human beings.'

'Why kill anyone with a cattle gun? Why not just stab them? Or shoot them?'

He shrugged. 'As a general rule, the amateur kills with whatever's handy.'

I was looking at the face of Peter Nawkins. Seventeen in 1980. He would be a middle-aged man now, if he was still alive. He was a big, good-looking lad before he went inside. I wondered what twenty years of hard time had done to his looks.

I took a step back, still hefting the cattle gun in my hand, struggling to believe that it could be used to wipe out a family. I was in a corner of the Black Museum that I had never noticed before. Apart from the Slaughter Man, most of the exhibits in the dusty corner seemed to date from the founding of the Black Museum in 1875.

There was a display of Victorian mugshots,

brown with age, the faces of these long-dead villains seen facing forward and also in profile, just like today, except their profiles were all reflections in a mirror when they were facing the camera. They all posed with their hands resting on their chest and their expressions looked like villains throughout the ages. Resigned. Defiant. Some of them trying to look amused. Some of them trying to look hard. Many of them bearing the scuffs and bruises that come with resisting arrest. There were women on display, plenty of them, but for the most part they looked as cold and hard as the men.

Apart from one.

She was young, plain, and among that wall of Victorian mugshots she was the only one who looked as if she had been crying.

'Maisy Dawes,' I read. 'What did Maisy Dawes do?'

'Maisy Dawes wasn't a villain,' John said. 'She was a blind.'

'A blind?'

'A blind was a false trail left to deceive the law. An unwitting decoy. A distraction. Some poor sucker who is used to mislead the police. Maisy Dawes was an innocent young woman who was used by villains to send investigating officers off on a false trail. See the date on her picture?'

'1875. The year the Black Museum opened.'

'Maisy was a maid in Belgravia back then. Scrubbing toilets for some Lord and Lady in Eaton

Square. Then one night there was a burglary. Those Victorian burglars called themselves the Dancing Schools of London. They would go on the rob at dinnertime because that was when the entire house was eating their dinner, upstairs and downstairs. What they would do is slip into one of the higher floors – dancing inside, they called it – and lift the jewels at the top of the house. But before they danced out again they often left a souvenir under the mattress of some poor little cow like Maisy Dawes.'

'So when detectives searched the premises they found the jewel under Maisy's mattress. And they stopped looking for the real thieves.'

'Exactly. And Maisy Dawes did hard time. Ten years for lifting some lady's bauble. Maisy came out, went on the game and died of smallpox in some East End gutter.'

'How do you know so much about her?'

'Because they found the real jewel thieves after Maisy died and she became famous. And because Maisy Dawes fascinates me, young man. In this temple of human cruelty, what they did to Maisy Dawes takes some beating.'

I looked around the room, the cattle gun feeling suddenly heavy in my hand.

'You think we might be following a blind now?' I said. 'That someone might be setting up the Slaughter Man?'

'No idea, son,' John Caine sighed. 'But I leave Maisy Dawes up there so that the boys and girls

70

from Hendon will learn to distrust their first impressions.' He took the cattle gun from me and put it back on its little display table, carefully adjusting it so it was exactly where it was before.

'In answer to your question – Maisy Dawes didn't do anything,' he said. 'That was her tragedy, son. All she did was die.'

CHAPTER 7

'It's really not a big deal,' Mary Gatling said, twenty years old in 1994, a beautiful young woman in a Team GB tracksuit, her face flushed with embarrassment, serious exercise and all that mountain air. Then she smiled awkwardly at a press conference full of camera crews and journalists who were about to make her virginity the biggest deal in the world.

The camera briefly cut to the reporters, all wrapped up warm enough for Norway in the middle of winter, and you could see some smirks that registered – what? Disbelief? Cynicism? Envy? All of the above, I thought, as that long-lost girl squirmed before a forest of microphones, her blonde hair falling in front of her face.

I hit the pause button and stood up, stretching.

It was after midnight and I had been looking at these clips on YouTube for two hours. I still hadn't learned a thing.

Out in the street I could hear the quiet roar that Smithfield meat market makes through the night. Stan stirred in his basket and stared at me with bleary eyes, checking to see if I might be planning to give him some food. He settled back into his snoring slumber as I went to look in on Scout. She was sleeping peacefully but had kicked all her bedclothes off. I pulled the duvet back over her and quietly slipped out. I knew I should turn in and try to sleep, but I felt that I was missing something that was just out of reach.

I came back into the main space of the loft and stared at Mary's face on my screen. She looked like a daughter of privilege, one of those rich English kids who grow up on ski slopes.

I hit play.

Mary sat before a poster that said LILLEHAMMER '94, a flurry of white lines on a blue background, and it took me a moment to understand that they were meant to represent the Northern Lights. There was a man with her on stage, same kind of coach, middle-aged, also wearing a Team GB tracksuit. He covered the microphone with his hand and whispered to Mary. She nodded, composed herself and spoke.

'Look – when I gave that interview to *Ski Monthly* I thought that we were talking about my fantastically slim chances of a medal. Right at the end of the interview, the journalist asked me if I had a boyfriend and I answered honestly – I *don't* have a boyfriend and I don't *want* one until I meet . . . someone special.'

'The love of your life, Mary?' a woman shouted, the question laced with mocking laughter.

Mary looked at her coldly, her white teeth bared

in a thin smile, and I saw the fighting spirit in her.

'The love of my life? Why not? It would be nothing less than what I deserve. And now – well. All this.'

Then there was a CNN reporter on screen.

'But Mary Gatling, the Ice Virgin of Lillehammer, may have found love in the snow of Lillehammer.'

There was some footage of Mary coming a spectacular cropper on the slopes, and then CNN cut to the Olympic village, where Mary was being pushed in a wheelchair by a grinning young man – although Brad Wood was not as young as her. He was ten years older than Mary and looked it. The presenter on CNN could hardly contain her excitement.

'After withdrawing from the downhill event following a nasty fall, the young Brit was consoled by American biathlete, Brad Wood – who was just out of the medals in the biathlon but has perhaps been luckier in love.'

The film cut to the closing ceremony. There were athletes everywhere. The Olympic flag was being passed from the mayor of Lillehammer to the mayor of Nagano. And Mary was out of her wheelchair now but walking with a cane in one hand and Brad's meaty paw in the other.

'It looks like the Ice Virgin of Lillehammer has finally found her Prince Charming.'

The film stopped with a close-up of Mary and Brad looking up at the fireworks of the closing ceremony, his arms wrapped around her tight. Wrapped up warm like a couple of kids at a bonfire. The clip had over a million hits. And there was more, much more. *Mary Gatling 1994 Olympics. Mary Gatling 1994. Mary Gatling Ice Virgin. Mary Gatling Brad Wood 1994. Ice Virgin XVII Olympic Winter Games.*

But I kept staring at the frozen frame before me. Brad Wood with his large hands placed protectively on Mary's stomach. And they had that look I remembered. The delighted surprise of a man and a woman who can't believe their luck in finding each other.

It might have been all the gear they had on.

Because I could have sworn that the Ice Virgin looked as if she was already pregnant.

An early morning mist hung over The Garden.

At the far end of the gated community two uniformed officers stood either side of the crime scene tape that still surrounded the Wood house. Our people were knocking on doors of the other five houses. I watched one door opened up by a Filipina maid who we had already talked to.

Edie Wren cursed. 'The door-to-door is a total washout,' she said. 'All we've had are housekeepers and cooks who were all off on New Year's Eve.'

'Good time to kill someone,' I said.

'Six houses and five of the owners are away on New Year's Eve? It doesn't make sense.'

'They're rich,' I said. 'Seriously rich. And the

seriously rich have always got other places to be. Only the poor stay home.'

But it felt like the holidays were over. The gates of The Garden were open and there was a steady flow of vehicles arriving. A pool guy. White vans. Live-out housekeepers and cleaners walking from the bus stop on the other side of Waterlow Park.

'The security guard was quite certain the gates were closed on New Year's Eve,' I said.

'Why would he lie?' Wren asked.

'The same reason they always lie,' I said. 'Because he was scared. Maybe he was asleep. Maybe he had slipped off to see in the New Year with his family. Maybe he was in on it, if only to open the gates. But if the gates weren't open, then they came over the wall.'

'There's a lot of traffic now,' Wren said. 'Maids. Cleaners. Gardeners. Builders.'

'The rich take a lot of looking after.'

'We're compiling a list of everyone who's had access to The Garden over the last six months. It's not easy with casual workers who like cash in hand.'

'Saves on the paperwork,' I said, and we started walking towards the twelve-foot wall that surrounded The Garden. Beyond it the wood that almost consumed Highgate Cemetery stretched off into the mist. The search teams had gone and stone angels peeked half-hidden from the trees.

'If he – or they – came in over that wall, he – or they – didn't go back over it,' I said. 'Not carrying a four-year-old child.'

'Not if the kid was alive,' Wren said.

'But if he was dead – why take him?'

A big Lexus pulled into The Garden. A deeply tanned man and woman of about fifty were in the front seats. A teenage girl, her face hiding behind long hippy hair, was slumped in the back, plugged into an iPod. The driver's window slid down.

'Miles Compton,' the tanned man said. 'We live next door to the Woods. Heard the news just as we were leaving St Lucia.' His eyes left me and stared with horror at the tape around the murder scene. 'Is it really true?'

'I'm afraid it is, sir,' Wren said.

Next to him, the woman's hands were pressed to her mouth.

The man nodded grimly. 'I always knew he would push his luck too far,' he said.

'Who?' I said.

'The boy. Marlon Wood. That arrogant little shit.' He shook his head with real regret. 'Bloody shame about the rest of them, though. Bloody shame.'

He drove off to the house next door to the Wood property. 'I'm on my way,' Wren said, and started walking towards them.

I walked to the wall and followed the perimeter around The Garden. At the back of the house next door to the Comptons, workmen were taking down some scaffolding.

'Stop that!' I called.

They stared at me for a moment and then carried on dismantling the scaffolding.

77

'*Zatrzymać!*' I shouted, and my Polish was good enough to get them to stop immediately. '*Policja,*' I said. 'Let me try something, men. *Jing kweer.*'

As they conferred in Polish, I climbed up a ladder on the scaffolding and then another to the point where it was above the top of the wall. I walked to the end of the plank. The branch of a tree that grew inside the cemetery hung close to the house, brushing the top of the scaffolding. Some of the branches had been cut back, but it must have been a while ago now. I looked up at the branch above me and then jumped up and gripped it, hanging there for a moment, checking it wasn't going to break any time soon. It seemed strong enough to hold me so I swung my legs up and caught it. The Polish builders had lit cigarettes and were enjoying the show. Sweating now, I shuffled down the branch, passing over the top of the wall. I kept going until my shoes touched the trunk of the tree. I clambered upright and started edging down the tree. I couldn't see the Polish builders any more but I could hear them applauding. Coming down was easier, although there was a sheer drop for the final ten feet or so. How could you do it with a child?

With a child that was still alive, I thought.

I dropped into the cemetery.

I hit the ground and caught my breath, staring into the thick wild wood of Highgate Cemetery. There was a stone angel next to me. The features of its face had been worn completely smooth by weather and time. In the distance I could see glimpses of giant crosses and strange memorials. Massive stone animals. A lion. A dog. All curled up with their eyes closed, sleeping for eternity. It was like leaving the world behind and stepping into a dream. The silence was total. It did not feel like the heart of the city. It felt like another planet.

Then suddenly Mary Wood was walking towards me through the mist, watching me every step of the way, just the two of us in that silent place.

I held my breath, flashing back to when I had last seen her on a stainless-steel table at the Iain West, and when I had first seen her dead in her marital bed.

And I realised it was not Mary Wood.

It was her sister, Charlotte Gatling. And she was looking at me with the same watchful intensity that I had seen when I was with Scout in Savile Row.

'Please don't give up on him,' she said. 'Don't give up on Bradley. My nephew.'

I shook my head.

'Never,' I said.

'I know you think he's probably dead,' she said, raising a hand before I could say anything. 'I know that's what the statistics all say – you find the child immediately or you never find the child at all. But he's not dead, Detective. I don't give a damn about the statistics. I can feel it. That little boy is alive.'

There was something in her hand.

A small toy. A cowboy. One of those eight-inch

plastic figures. Boots, waistcoat, white shirt. No, not a cowboy. Han Solo from *Star Wars*. Of course – the space cowboy. Her nephew's toy, I thought. Bradley's favourite toy.

Then there were more people coming out of the trees and the day suddenly felt even more like a dream. There was her brother and a camera crew. The Media Liaison Officer and the Family Liaison Officer were trailing behind Nils Gatling and the camera crew, flustered and ignored, their high heels unsuitable for Highgate Cemetery in January.

'What's happening?' I said.

'We're doing a reconstruction,' Charlotte Gatling said. 'For *Crimewatch*. They want me to be my sister arriving home so we can perhaps jog a few memories.'

'Did we set this up? The Met?'

'My brother set it up. It's good, isn't it? Exposure is the key. That's what Nils says.'

'Exposure can be counter-productive,' I said, as gently as I could. 'Because every nut comes out of the woodwork. We can get so many false leads that we miss the real leads. Exposure needs to be carefully managed.'

There was a flash of irritation in her eyes and I remembered her sister staring down the mocking reporter in Lillehammer.

'But it's better than just being ignored,' she said. 'Like the families of most missing children.'

'Yes,' I said quietly. 'It's better than that.'

Then I saw something inside her start to crack.

'So where is he?' she said, her voice strained with distress, as though her throat wanted to choke down all the terrible questions. 'What's happening to him? What are they doing to Bradley?'

Thinking that way did no good, I knew. Thinking that way just paralysed you. But I couldn't say that to her.

'I'm going to find Bradley,' I said. 'I promise you.'

She stared at me as if she could see into my soul.

'You really promise me?'

'Yes.'

Her brother approached us.

'They're ready for you, Charlotte.'

'My brother, Nils Gatling,' she told me.

I held out my hand.

'DC Wolfe of West End Central,' I said. 'I'm so sorry about—'

But Nils Gatling was not interested in any more sympathy from strangers, and he had looked away before we had finished shaking hands, his face set and his eyes cold.

'Just start doing your job,' he told me.

'HOLMES gives us six men who have been convicted of murder with what the law calls a captive bolt pistol over the last thirty years,' Wren said. 'It's a very small club. Three are dead, two are doing time and then there's the Slaughter Man.'

81

She hit a button on her laptop.

A good-looking man in his middle years appeared on the big plasma screen on the wall of Major Incident Room One. He wore shabby, threadbare clothes and looked as though he cut his own hair. In his large hands were two plastic supermarket bags. But he was still recognisable as the young man who had been locked up in Belmarsh in 1980. There was more than just a shadow of that seventeen-year-old. Because Peter Nawkins still looked as though he was thinking of absolutely nothing.

'*That's* Peter Nawkins?' I said. 'That's the Slaughter Man?'

'Handsome devil,' Wren said.

'But this was taken when he got out. It's the most recent image I could find. Got it from Reuters. He probably doesn't look as lovely as he did ten years ago.'

'Who does?' Whitestone laughed.

The door to MIR-1 opened and a tall man of about sixty came in wheeling a suitcase. He smiled shyly at our applause, running a hand through his snowy-white hair.

'Dr Joe!' DCI Whitestone said, happily adjusting her glasses. 'Fresh off the Heathrow Express! Thanks for coming in.'

Dr Joe Stephen, Forensic Psychologist at King's College, slumped at a workstation, foggy with jet lag. Gane stuck a mug of black coffee in his hand and he nodded gratefully.

'Four dead and a missing child,' he said, the

California accent smoothed by thirty years in London. 'I wanted to get started.'

He took a file out of his case and spread it before him. Crime scene shots. Autopsy pictures. The usual blank-faced catalogue of gore.

'What do you make of it, Dr Joe?' Whitestone said. 'The abductors of children don't spree-kill. Mass murderers kill everything that moves but don't steal kids. We've been struggling to make any kind of sense of it.'

Dr Joe seemed very tired. And it wasn't just because of the night flight from JFK.

'It feels like the deliberate destruction of happiness,' he said.

Wren shot me a look. That had been her theory from the start. The Woods had been killed because they were a happy family.

'What about the missing boy, Dr Joe?' I said. 'Do you think there's a chance he's still alive?'

Dr Joe ran a hand across his face. 'Four days into your seven-day window? There's still a chance, isn't there? But time's running out fast now. Have you come up with any leads?'

DCI Whitestone turned to the uniformed officer who was at one of the workstations. Carrot-haired and gawky, he looked like an overgrown kid dressed up as a copper. You would never guess that he had a QPM, the police medal for conspicuous valour.

'How you doing, Billy?' she said.

PC Billy Greene held up his hands and I saw

the blackened burns on his palms that would probably keep him on desk duties for the rest of his career.

'Bradley Wood was seen in a department store on Oxford Street in the company of a man and woman,' Billy said. 'The child was crying. The man was angry. Bradley was also seen at a service station on the M1 in the company of a man who was buying him a sandwich in a coffee shop. Bradley was also seen on the swings in a park just outside Leeds. He was apparently happy. A young woman was with him. And he was seen in the café at Legoland.'

'These sightings, are they all since last night?' DI Curtis Gane said.

'No – this is just the last hour,' Billy said. 'And it's going to get a lot worse when this *Crimewatch* thing goes out tonight.'

'Can't the MLO rein in Nils Gatling?' Gane said. 'Can't the Chief Super have a word?'

'Apparently not,' Whitestone said. 'Mr Gatling treats the MLO like a very junior and extremely stupid member of his personal staff.' She shook her head. 'You get families who don't know how to play the media. And you get the ones who do. And that kind never makes our job any easier.'

There was a set of keys on Whitestone's work-station. She picked them up and held them out to me.

'The Financial Forensics Unit dug this up – a property Brad Wood owned that we need to check out,' she said. 'It's your neck of the woods, Max. An apartment in the Barbican.'

'The family owned a flat in the Barbican?'

'Not the family. Just the father.'

'FFU traced it through direct debits on Brad Wood's bank accounts,' Wren said.

'Rental property?'

Wren shook her head. 'As far as we can make out, it was for his own personal use. The utility bills are next to nothing. Doesn't look as if anybody was living there.'

I thought about that for a while.

'The apartment's been processed by forensics, so you can touch what you like,' Wren said. 'See if you feel a tremor in The Force.'

I slipped the keys into my pocket.

Whitestone turned to Dr Joe. 'What do you make of the sexual assault on the mother? Is that significant? Should we be looking at known sexual offenders?'

Dr Joe's mouth tightened with something that I could not read.

'I wouldn't place great emphasis on the rape of Mary Wood,' he said. 'Sex and violence are almost always interchangeable in the mind of a psychopath. The choice of weapon is, I would suggest, more significant. The use of a cattle gun to slaughter a family indicates a wish to make the victims less than human.'

'Any joy with the neighbours in The Garden?' Whitestone asked Wren.

'Mr Compton says his wife and daughter are too distressed to talk to us right now,' she said. 'But he's not shedding any tears over young Marlon Wood. The phrase "degenerate little scumbag" came up, but he wouldn't be more specific. Closed the door in my face with some force.'

'Talk to him again,' Whitestone said. 'Get him to be more specific, tell him we can do it at his place or at West End Central. But first we need to talk to Peter Nawkins.'

We all looked in silence at the old man on the screen.

'I know,' Whitestone said. 'Nawkins feels like a waste of our time, doesn't he? But he's in a category of one – the only living cattle-gun killer who's not doing time. So the TIE process demands that we talk to him. It's not optional.'

TIE means trace, interview and eliminate any individual who could have realistically committed the offence under investigation. It is not the same as being suspected of the crime, but we had to cross the Slaughter Man off our list.

'Where is he?' Gane said. 'We have a release address for when he came out of Belmarsh?'

'Oak Hill Farm. On the border of the East End and Essex.'

'Oak Hill Farm? The gypsy camp.'

'The travelling community camp – and it's more than a camp,' Whitestone said. 'It's the largest concentration of travellers in Europe. There are some permanent settlements there. Not all of them legal.'

'You don't really like him for this, do you?' Gane said. 'This sad old man with his plastic shopping bags?'

Whitestone shrugged. 'He's been out for nearly ten years,' she said. 'I bet he has people showing up from time to time. And they might be of interest to us.'

'You mean journalists?' I said.

'I mean fans,' she said. 'I mean obsessive nutcases. I never saw a multiple killer yet who didn't have a sizeable fan club.'

Dr Joe was on his feet, staring at a family photograph of the Woods on the whitewall of MIR-1.

'She was so beautiful, wasn't she?' he said. 'Mary, I mean.' He saw us watching him and shook his head, embarrassed. 'I don't mean because she was conventionally good-looking – although there's that, of course. But there was a radiance to her beauty. The kind of beauty that you so rarely see, inside and outside. She had both.'

'I guess a lot of us feel as though we knew Mary,' Whitestone said.

Dr Joe smiled, and behind his glasses I saw that his eyes were shining with tears.

'Of course,' he said. 'Although she was more complicated than her public image suggests.' He hesitated for a moment. 'She was in therapy with me for a number of years,' he said.

We let that sink in.

Whitestone took a step towards him.

'Recently?' she asked.

Dr Joe shook his head. 'I stopped seeing her ten years ago. When her children were small. The first two children, I mean. Marlon and Piper.' He was still staring at the family photograph.

'Is there a problem here, Dr Joe?' Whitestone said. 'Do we have to worry about therapist–patient privilege?'

'There's absolutely no problem, Pat,' Dr Joe said. 'Because I'm not going to tell you what we discussed during therapy. It is simply not relevant. And there's no problem because, if anything, knowing Mary makes me even more determined that you nail him.'

He could not control the anger in his voice. I had never known this mild-mannered man to sound so angry.

'Let's just find the rotten bastard that did it,' he said.

And the first thing next morning Curtis Gane and I drove out to meet the Slaughter Man.

CHAPTER 8

Oak Hill Farm was built on the vague border where the end of London meets the start of Essex, a place of fields and warehouses, ancient farms and new houses, concrete and grass, where every colour is either grey or green.

Just beyond Gallows Corner, I turned the BMW X5 off the A127 and we could see it in the distance.

'What's the history of this place?' Gane said.

'It was an illegal scrapyard for years,' I said. 'There was actually a farm – I think there still is – and the farmer sold two plots of land to a pair of travelling families in the Eighties. They built a couple of homes and the council told them to tear them down. They fought it in the courts and won. More travellers came. And they kept on coming. Now there are around a hundred families on ten acres.'

'Looks like a small town built upon a rubbish dump,' Gane said.

'That's exactly what it is,' I said. 'And for about five hundred people – it's home.'

There were two walls around Oak Hill Farm,

and within the second wall the white caravans were parked nose to tail. There was only one way in, under some giant scaffolding with hand-painted signs that said WE WON'T GO and NO ETHNIC CLEANSING surrounded by children's paintings of brightly coloured caravans.

I drove slowly inside. Eyes watched us all the way.

Dead washing machines, fridges and TVs were scattered between neat little chalets with net curtains. A grubby-looking white horse grazed on a scrap of grass. A dog defecated beside a brand-new Audi. Oak Hill Farm was a strange mix of suburban gentility and unapologetic squalor.

'I like what they've done with it,' Gane said.

There were no street names so I stopped and Gane opened his window. A woman and a teenage girl were walking by, perhaps a mother and a daughter, holding hands.

'We're looking for Mr Nawkins,' Gane said.

They stared at Gane's black face for a while and then gestured vaguely to deeper inside the camp where a lone girl was walking with a pack of dogs. She had long straight dark hair and pink hot pants, despite the weather hovering just above freezing. She was around fifteen years old but anxious to be grown-up. High on one cheekbone she had the yellows and purples of a fading black eye. Her dogs were a mixed pack of Staffies and mongrels with a magnificent Akita walking by the girl's side.

The dog paused to lick his testicles.

'I wish I could do that,' Gane said.

'Maybe you should buy him dinner first,' I said.

The Akita was the pack leader and he considered me with his pale blue eyes as I got out of the car. I stood there and did not move while he tasted the air.

'Lots of people,' the girl said, 'they hold out the back of their hand so the dog can smell it.'

I laughed. 'But there's no need, is there?' I said. 'He can smell me all right.'

'That's right. You don't need to hold out your hand. He already knows what you had for breakfast.'

'He's magnificent. What's his name?'

'Smoky,' she said, and when she ran her fingers through her hair I saw the tattoo of a dog on her inner wrist. It looked like a German Shepherd, although it might have been an Akita. Maybe the body artist couldn't do an Akita.

'Do you know Mr Nawkins?' I said.

'My dad,' she said. 'I'm Echo Nawkins. I'll show you where we live.' Then she looked at us doubtfully, as if she couldn't decide what we were. Gane was in one of his Savile Row suits.

'You the lawyers or the council?' she said.

'We're the law,' Gane said.

She nodded, suddenly cooler.

'And you're a traveller,' I said, trying to restore relations. It didn't work.

'Our Lord was a traveller,' she said, as if I had attempted to insult her.

I got back in the car and we followed Echo Nawkins and her pack of dogs.

'Do you think people would like them a bit more if they cleared up their trash instead of chucking it out the window?' Gane said.

'This is it,' I said.

She had led us to a caravan and a chalet, both twice the size of anything else in the camp. There was a skip on the drive, overflowing with junk, and the acrid black smoke of burning plastic was rising from it. On the patch of grass in front of the chalet, a man sat reading the *Guardian* and drinking tea at a small table where breakfast was set for one. He was tall and lean, around fifty, and his rimless spectacles gave him a studious air. He poured milk from a bottle that said 'Oak Hill Farm Dairy' into a cereal bowl. Gane and I looked at the burning skip and then at each other. They were clearly not big on recycling in these parts. We got out of the car.

'I'm Sean Nawkins,' the man said. 'Who are you?'

Our warrant cards came out.

'DI Gane and DC Wolfe,' Curtis said. 'I believe we want the other Mr Nawkins. Peter Nawkins.'

'My brother,' Sean Nawkins said, shaking his head and looking at us as if he wanted to rip our throats out. 'You'll never leave him alone, will you? You'll never let him get on with his life. He did his time. A lot of time. The best years of his life. What do you want with him? These London murders, is it?'

'A few routine questions,' Gane said easily. 'Where is he?'

But Sean Nawkins was building up a head of steam.

'Can't you let him die in peace?' he said.

We let that settle for a while.

'What's wrong with your brother?' I said.

'Pancreatic cancer.'

'Terminal?'

'He has months rather than years.'

'Is he having chemotherapy?'

Gane gave me a look. As if we were not actually here to discuss anyone's medical problems.

'Peter doesn't want chemo,' Sean Nawkins said. 'He saw what chemo did to both of our parents. He just wants to enjoy whatever time he has left.' He softened. 'Please – can't you let him be? Can't you just get off his back?'

'Yeah,' came a voice from somewhere behind and above us. 'Get off his back.'

We turned to look at a man on a large white horse. The man was dark and bearded, and the horse looked like the one we had seen grazing on the scrap of grass. But I was no expert. It might have been a completely different horse.

'Tell the bastards about your wife, Sean,' the man said.

'They don't care about my wife,' Nawkins said.

'What happened to your wife, sir?' I said.

'Do you really want to know how she died?' he said.

93

'Dad,' the girl said.

'Shut up, Echo,' he said, not looking at her. 'Townies set fire to our caravan. Ten years ago. Gunnersbury Park. Remember that riot?'

'There was an illegal traveller settlement in Gunnersbury Park,' Gane said. 'Some of the locals took matters into their own hands.'

'That's the one,' Sean Nawkins said. 'Why did you never catch *them*? Why is it always *us* who get the strong arm of the law?'

I turned at the sound of a large amount of animal moving towards me. The man and horse were edging forward, sideways on, although I couldn't quite work out how he was doing it. He had no saddle or reins. It was as if he was moving the horse through some act of will.

I turned back to look at Sean Nawkins.

'This really doesn't have to be difficult, sir,' I said. 'We just need to ask your brother a few questions.'

'Or stitch him up.' The bearded man was off his horse and staring at Gane. 'Look at you,' he said. 'Walking on your hind legs and everything. Got many coloured chaps in your line of work?'

Gane let it go. You would be amazed how much of this stuff we have to let go. Every day of our lives we let stuff go. And it is worse for the guys like Gane. I looked at the horseman and then I looked at Sean Nawkins.

'As I say, this really doesn't have to be difficult,' I said. 'But it can be – it can be as difficult as you want to make it – but it doesn't have to be. We just need to eliminate your brother from our enquiries.'

'Fitting him up!' said the bearded man. 'Those London murders! That family! Pinning it on him, they are! Because they always have to nick someone for the big ones!'

'Dan,' Sean Nawkins said quietly. 'Get my brother, will you?'

The bearded man snorted, but went away.

'Doesn't look like you do a lot of travelling,' Gane said. 'Considering you're travelling folk, I mean.' He gazed around, nodding at the dozens of new chalets. 'You look quite settled.'

Sean Nawkins folded his copy of the *Guardian* and spoke to DI Gane as if addressing a simple child.

'Our people never travelled all year round,' Nawkins said. 'Not in this country. In our family the year began with potato planting and ended with hop picking. And in the winter months we were off the road. Do you know what they did to him?'

'Your brother?' I said.

He laughed with genuine pleasure. 'Yes. Peter. My brother. Do you know what they wanted to do to him? The farmer he killed? His sons? *They were going to nut him.* The way you nut a horse. That's what they tried to do.'

'You mean – they tried to castrate him?' I said.

'That's exactly what I mean, Detective. For

touching the girl. For getting her in the family way. No way that old farmer was going to tolerate a posh-rat in his family. Know what a posh-rat is, do you? It means half-blood. People think a posh-rat is a gypsy who lives in a house. But it means that our mother was not a traveller. They hated him so much and he is not even a full-blooded traveller. They picked up Peter when the girl was away with her mother. Took him down some lane. Had his trousers off. *Going to cut his fucking balls off, they were.* But he fought them off. Big, hard lad, he was. Then he went back. And he made sure they would never do it again. Now you tell me, detectives – what the hell has any of that got to do with those murders in London?'

We were silent for a moment.

'Does your brother ever have visitors?' Gane said.

'You mean outsiders who are obsessed with what he did? Fans, obsessives, stalkers, the like?'

Gane nodded. 'Like that.'

Sean Nawkins shook his head. 'Not any more. It's all a long time ago. You still think of him as the Slaughter Man, don't you? To me he was a boy with learning difficulties who made a mistake after some dreadful, terrifying provocation. To you – he's just some old lag. To me – he's my brother.' He was looking over our shoulders and his voice dropped low. 'He did the crime and he did the time and he has earned the right to die in peace.'

Then he was suddenly there.

Peter Nawkins.

The Slaughter Man.

I tried to see the violence in him. I tried to see the dark shadow of the past. But he did not look like a man who had taken the lives of four other men. He was large, much larger than the bearded horseman who walked beside him, and Peter Nawkins' face was still a fading photocopy of the matinee-idol looks he'd had as a young man. But he seemed far older than his years. That was prison, I thought, and that was cancer. And as he wiped dirt from his hands on to his tracksuit, I believed that I could tell he was dying.

'Been working on your allotment?' his brother said gently.

'Lots to plant in January,' Peter Nawkins said, looking at Gane and me. 'Aubergines. Leeks. Cauliflowers, of course.'

'Peter Nawkins?' Gane said, and we produced our warrant cards and made the introductions again.

Peter Nawkins looked at his brother.

'I didn't do anything, Sean.'

'It's all right, Peter. They just want to ask you a couple of questions and then they'll go back to their holes in London and you can get back to the garden.'

We were drawing a crowd. They gathered between us and the car and I wondered how much of a problem this might be.

'Where were you on New Year's Eve, Mr Nawkins?' Gane said.

Peter Nawkins looked at his brother.

'Just tell them,' Sean Nawkins said, with a hint of irritation.

'I don't know,' Peter Nawkins said.

We let that sink in.

'You don't know where you were on New Year's Eve?' Gane said.

'He was in camp,' Sean Nawkins said. 'I can get witnesses.'

'Yeah, I bet you can get five hundred witnesses,' Gane said.

The bearded horseman had acquired a little rat-faced friend.

'Don't get smart, black boy,' rat-face said to the back of Gane's head.

I smiled at him but he kept looking at the back of DI Gane's shaven head, muttering to himself and the horseman, working himself up into a frenzy. That's what people who were not drunk or stoned had to do – they had to work themselves up to the violence. More bystanders arrived to gawp, gossip and give advice. A woman with a baby in her arms spat on the ground behind Gane's muddy Italian shoes.

'I pay your wages,' she said.

'Were you here on New Year's Eve?' I said.

Peter Nawkins nodded. 'I guess. When was that? That was last week, right?'

'Have you ever met any member of the Wood family, Mr Nawkins?' Gane said.

'He's never met any member of the Wood family,' Sean Nawkins said.

'Please, sir, I would rather talk to your brother,' Gane said.

The rat-faced man said, 'And he'd rather talk to the organ grinder instead of the monkey.'

It got a laugh and I knew they did not fear us.

'No,' Peter Nawkins said. 'No to all of the questions. I wasn't there and I don't know them and I didn't do anything wrong.' His breathing was becoming more shallow. He was old and he was sick but he was big enough to be a handful if he lost it. *And I'm not going back to prison.*'

Gane and I looked at each other.

Something passed between us and we knew it was time to go.

By now the crowd had got bigger and there were more of them between us and the car. If anything was going to happen, it would happen over the next sixty seconds. We thanked Peter and Sean Nawkins for their time. We turned away. And then it happened.

'You black—'

It was rat-face.

And before he had finished, Gane had picked him up by the collar of his shell suit and slammed him with maximum force against Sean Nawkins' caravan.

I don't think he was aiming for the window. But there was an explosion of glass as rat-face's head went clean through the caravan's window. I picked up the milk bottle from the table and in one smooth move I brought it down on the ground and then offered its broken end to the men who were coming for us.

'Now it has to be difficult,' I said.

They stopped. Rat-face was on his knees, blood all over his verminous features.

We paused, giving them their chance to make their move. But nobody stepped up, so we walked slowly to the car. The bearded horseman thought about it more than the rest. I dropped the broken milk bottle into an overflowing rubbish bin.

'Catch you later,' I told him.

We took our time getting in the car.

But we didn't take our time getting away.

'Hit it,' Gane said.

I hit it.

For several minutes the green fields of Essex flashed past.

'Pull over,' Gane said.

I pulled over.

He was still shaking with adrenaline.

'That went well,' I said.

'I wasn't aiming his head at the window, Max.'

'I figured.'

'Sometimes they go too far.'

'I know,' I said. 'I get it. People think the police are racist. But we just hate the people who give us the most trouble. That doesn't make us racist,' I said. 'It makes us human.'

We sat in silence for a bit. The heavy traffic to London roaring by, the tension draining away.

'What do you make of him?' Gane said. 'Peter Nawkins. The Slaughter Man.'

'If he killed anyone, I reckon it would have to be personal.'

'It was personal, wasn't it? They tried to cut his balls off.'

I closed my eyes and steadied my breathing. It had been a busy morning.

'That's quite personal,' I agreed.

'They tried to castrate him because he fell in love with some girl he shouldn't have fallen in love with. You can see how that would make you reach for the cattle gun. The poor simple bastard. He's not a hitman. He never was a hitman.'

'And it's probably too late to start now,' I said, sticking the X5 into drive. 'He's too busy dying.'

CHAPTER 9

I t was a beautiful apartment.

A seventh-floor penthouse in the Barbican. Light, airy, modern. Lots of white walls, not much furniture. A table for two, a white leather sofa, music system, elliptical trainer. The bare necessities, but all very tasteful. I opened doors. Just one bedroom. It was a bolthole, but a very luxurious bolthole. Brad Wood wouldn't have got much change out of a million. Wren said there was no mortgage.

There were a couple of paintings on the wall of the living room and they were the only real splash of colour. I peered at the signature. Patrick Caulfield, they both said. They were paintings of cool modern rooms that looked a lot like this one. There was a desk where a computer had been, but forensics had taken it away.

I stepped out on to the south-facing balcony. There was a courtyard with a small lake and private gardens seven floors below, and above the rooftops there was the dome of St Paul's, looking very close, and on the far side of the river, the Tate Modern and London Eye. It was late afternoon and the sun was setting in a cloudless and freezing cold sky, the brilliant blue streaked with rivers of red.

I couldn't see it from here but Smithfield meat market and our loft was almost next door, just the other side of Aldersgate. We were practically neighbours.

The doorbell rang. I answered it. It was a young woman in her mid-twenties, pretty and short and a shade too blonde to be believed, slowly smiling as if we shared an innocent secret.

'Hello,' she said.

'Hello,' I said.

'May I come in?'

Her English was pretty good, but not so good that it wasn't charming. I stood aside and she walked in, taking her time, not sure which way to turn. So it was her first time here too. She was wearing shiny black heels, very high, and they were the kind with the red soles. Christian Louboutin. My wife had liked those shoes, too. Ex-wife, I mean.

'This is such a cool area,' she said.

'It used to be Cripplegate,' I said. 'One of the oldest parts of London.'

She looked surprised. 'Cripplegate? That's a funny name.'

'From Roman times,' I said. 'It was a gate in the city wall. Then in the war, the Germans bombed it flat.'

'Oh,' she said. 'Sorry about that.'

'I'm sure it wasn't you personally.'

'Could have been my grandfather. Perhaps both my grandfathers. Have you lived in the area long?'

I thought about it. I had been single and married and divorced in this area. I had been childless and a father here. I'd had a dog and I'd had no dog.

'For years,' I said, but by then she had wandered off.

She was making herself at home. I heard water running in the bathroom. I went back out to the balcony. If you get up high enough, I thought, then London has the greatest sunsets in the world.

'Sir?' she said behind me.

She was still wearing her Christian Louboutin shoes but that was all. She had a dancer's body – small-breasted, not tall although the heels gave her some height, but with strong quad muscles in her thighs and what looked like a very hard abdomen, the kind of stomach you can't get without ten thousand sit-ups.

As I wondered what kind of dancer she had been she held her hands up, palms facing me, as if we had to decide something very soon.

'And should I keep my shoes on, Mr Wood?' she asked me.

My new friend – Claudia – was on the edge of tears from the Barbican all the way to Gerrard Street in Chinatown. I parked the X5 in the big multi-storey behind the fire station and looked at her over the bonnet. She suddenly seemed very young.

'Hey,' I said. 'Claudia.' She stared at me, wiping her nose with the back of her hand. 'You haven't done anything wrong,' I said. 'You don't have to be scared of me.'

'I know,' she said. 'It's not you I'm scared of.'

We walked through the great gate at the start of Gerrard Street. Chinese New Year was coming soon and thousands of red lanterns filled the evening sky. The smell of roast duck reached us and made me feel giddy with hunger.

'So you were a dancer?' I said.

'How did you know?'

'Wild guess. What kind of a dancer were you?'

She almost laughed. 'I've been every kind of dancer there is,' she said. 'This is the place.'

We were halfway down Gerrard Street, between a restaurant where Cantonese in their late teens and twenties were queuing for a table and a Chinese medicine shop where two middle-aged women in white lab coats were playing mah-jong. There was a code box by the door and a buzzer. Claudia went to press the buzzer. I stopped her.

'You know the code?' I said.

She thought about lying and decided against it. 'Yes.'

'Then use the code,' I said.

She tapped in four numbers and the door opened. We went up a narrow flight of stairs. A young black man was leaning against the wall on the landing, fiddling with his phone. He looked at me with disbelief as he got out of his seat.

'Claudia,' he said. 'What's he doing here?' He placed a hand on my chest. 'No, no, no,' he said. 'Looking for trouble, are you?'

I smiled pleasantly. 'I am the trouble,' I said.

He was smart enough to let me pass.

I opened the only door on the landing and stepped into a small white room where a woman of about thirty was sitting behind a desk, staring at the biggest iMac I had ever seen. She wasn't Chinese but she looked as if she had some Asian blood and she was peering at me from behind black-rimmed spectacles. The room was perfumed by a scented candle, probably in an effort to disguise the smell of roasting duck that drifted up from downstairs.

'DC Max Wolfe,' I said, holding out my warrant card. 'Claudia here paid the late Mr Brad Wood a visit. She found me instead.'

'That appointment was *cancelled*, Claudia,' the woman behind the desk said, an American accent grafted on to something else. She took a very deep breath. 'Didn't you receive my voicemail cancelling your appointment in the Barbican?'

'No.'

'My text message? My email? My DM?'

Claudia sniffed. 'Lost my phone,' she said.

The woman behind the desk shook her head and then looked at me with a strange mixture of fear and defiance. It struck me that she had been expecting this moment, or something like it, for years.

'Where's the boss?' I said.

'You're looking at her,' she said.

'And what's your name?'

'Ginger Gonzalez. This is my company. Sampaguita Ltd.'

'Sampaguita?'

'National flower of the Philippines.'

'You Filipina?'

'Not any more. My father was a US serviceman stationed in the Philippines. My mother was a dancer.'

'Like Claudia.'

'Yes. That kind of dancer. Exactly that kind of dancer. In Angeles. Where the Americans were stationed. Then they went home. And when I was sixteen, I went looking for my father.'

'You find him?'

'No. But after a few years I got a US passport. Even better.'

I looked around the bare white room.

'And what do you trade in here at Sampaguita, Ginger?'

'Sampaguita is a Social Introduction Agency,' she said with a straight face.

'Social Introduction Agency?' I smiled. 'Is that what they call it these days?' I nodded at the black kid. 'Who's he? The Pound Store Al Capone?'

'That's my Security Director.'

I shook my head.

'It's all euphemisms with you people. Why do you need a bouncer – sorry – why do you need a Security Director at a Social Introduction Agency?'

'The locals. The gangs here in Chinatown. Sometimes they ask for rent when absolutely no rent is due.'

I nodded. The Triads would need a bit of scaring away if you set up shop around here. Although they tended to prefer waving their machetes in the faces of members of their own community.

'Give your Security Director the rest of the night off,' I said. 'Claudia too. We need to talk.'

Ginger dismissed the pair of them with a curt nod of her head. We heard footsteps scrambling down the narrow staircase. There was one chair opposite her desk. I took it.

'So how does it work, Ginger?'

She took a breath.

'I introduce affluent, high-achieving men to educated, beautiful younger women.'

'What should I Google? How do they find you? All those high-achieving men?'

'It's strictly word of mouth. Personal recommendations only. Sampaguita is not online. We're totally discreet. Nobody wants to leave a digital fingerprint these days.'

'Until one of the girls loses her iPhone,' I said.

She bit her lower lip.

'The prostitution laws in this country are interesting,' I said.

'Aren't they?' she said. 'They seem to come down hardest on soliciting. In my experience.'

'True. The exchange of sexual services for money is legal. But if you run a brothel, or if you pimp, or if you coerce, or if you solicit, then the law comes down on you like a ton of bricks. In my experience.'

She waited.

'I'm not going to bust you,' I said.

'Thank you.'

'But I will if you don't help me. I'm looking for a murderer, Ginger. And I'm looking for a missing child. And if you make me slow my pace then I will close this place down in my tea break and get you locked up without hesitation.'

'I understand.' She paused. 'It's terrible, what happened to that family, to that little boy.'

'Tell me about Brad Wood,' I said.

'Mr Wood was a regular client.'

'How often did he use your services?'

'Once a week. For two years. A different girl every time.'

'That sounds like an awful lot of girls.'

'It mounts up.'

'You've got over a hundred girls on your books?'

She shook her head. 'Nothing like that number. They tend to come and go. Get married. Go home. Go back to school. Rethink their career. But there are always new faces. There are always new girls in town.'

'How long was the booking for?'

'Never more than a few hours. They never stayed the night. Mr Wood had to get home.'

I thought about it.

'And he let you choose who to send round to his flat in the Barbican?'

'He trusted my judgement. And Mr Wood was quite conventional in his tastes. Young. Blonde. Non-smoking, of course – he was an elite athlete, you know. No tattoos or piercings.' She raised her eyebrows. 'I prefer to employ young women with no tattoos or piercings, but they're not so easy to find these days, believe me. But most men are attracted to younger versions of their wife. And that's what Mr Wood liked. Younger models of Mrs Wood.'

'Why did he never want the same girl twice?'

'My theory is that it was the fear of an inappropriate attachment. He didn't want to like any girl too much. He didn't want to get involved. And of course there's the sexual novelty factor. What Mr Wood liked – if I may use a technical term – was *strange*. I prefer that term – *strange* – to *fresh meat*, which I find demeans both the man and the woman.'

I thought about all this for a while.

'And how did you meet him?'

'I met him in the bar of the Connaught.'

'So when you say word of mouth and personal recommendations, what you mean is that you pick up rich men in swanky bars?'

'That's a very crude way to put it, Detective. But yes – that's often how initial contact is made with my blue-chip clients.'

'Always the Connaught? For your fishing expeditions?'

She smiled.

'Not always. Although the Coburg Bar at the Connaught has been a happy hunting ground for me. But I also use the American Bar at the Savoy. The Rivoli Bar at the Ritz. The Fumoir at Claridges. The Promenade Bar at the Dorchester. Although I tend to steer clear of the Dorchester as I prefer not to do business with some of our more devout Arab friends. But we all have our prejudices, don't we? Prejudice is the wrong word. Think of it as a preference.'

'So not always the Connaught, but always five-star.'

'Yes.'

'What happened with Brad Wood?'

'He asked if he could buy me a drink. We had dinner a couple of times. I saw how lonely he was and I made my suggestions as to how he could remedy that situation.'

'With Sampaguita.'

'Yes.'

'You sleep with him?'

She shook her head.

'I met him three times. That was it. Two years ago. Everything else was done by text message on two BlackBerrys that were used for the sole purpose of our communications. Nothing else. We both understood the importance of discretion. On the third and final occasion we met I convinced him that I wasn't what he needed. And I told him that an affair with someone he really liked was not the answer to his problems. Affairs are incredibly destructive, Detective. They destroy marriages. They destroy families. They destroy lives. Affairs are never worth the trail of tears they leave behind. Sampaguita offers a healthy, danger-free alternative and Mr Wood took it. He was a wise man and a pragmatic man, a generous man and a decent man.' Tears shone in her eyes and they seemed to be genuine. 'And I can't tell you how incredibly sad I am that he is dead,' she said. 'He was a good guy. And for all their money and education and beautiful homes to go back to, they are not all good guys, Detective.'

I wondered how much of this I could believe.

'I'll tell you something else about Brad Wood,' Ginger Gonzalez said.

'What's that?' I asked.

'That man loved his wife,' she said.

CHAPTER 10

With our breath making clouds in the freezing morning air, Scout guided Stan through the early morning crowds of Smithfield. The streets were covered with the refuse of another busy night and St Paul's Cathedral stood against a sky that was grey with the prospect of snow. Scout was wrapped up for the worst of the winter, her perfect face circled by woolly hat, school scarf and a jacket that was zipped right up.

Scout was very good with the dog.

She smiled politely at the compliments the little red Cavalier received from the bleary club kids emerging from Fabric and the meat porters at the end of their long night at Smithfield, but she was alert to sudden bursts of traffic, wrapping the dog lead around her wrist one extra turn at the first sign of danger. Stan trotted happily by her side, the feathery plume of his tail erect and his tiny snout savouring the morning air.

We crossed Charterhouse Street, skirted the market and reached the open space of West Smithfield, where Stan liked to inspect the markings of other dogs before doing his business. He sniffed the dark splashes on the stone chairs that skirted the black statue of a woman that stood in the centre of the square.

While Stan checked his pee-mail, I looked at my messages. My heart took that lurch it always did on those rare occasions when my ex-wife got in touch.

I want to see her.

When I looked up, Scout was slowly mouthing the words that were carved into the stone chairs of West Smithfield. Stan crouched for his toilet, ready at last, turning his bulging eyes towards me for a pleading moment and then shyly looking away. I put my phone in my pocket and took out a small plastic bag.

Scout looked at me, her face lit with delight.

'It's a story!' she said. 'The words in the stone! Do you see?'

'And I bet you can read some of it, can't you?'

She nodded once. 'But you read it to me, Daddy.'

I scooped up Stan's mess, tied the top of the plastic bag and dropped it in the bin. Dog owners can do it in one smooth move. And then I leaned in to the words that were cut into the stone chairs.

'*It was market morning,*' I read. '*The ground was covered nearly ankle-deep with filth and mire; and a thick steam perpetually—*'

'Perpetually?' Scout said.

'Always,' I explained. The words spun out across the stone chairs and I had to slowly walk around the square to read them. '*And a thick steam perpetually rising*

114

from the reeking bodies of the cattle, and mingling with the fog, which seemed to rest upon the chimney tops, hung heavily above.' I straightened up. 'Charles Dickens, *Oliver Twist*.' I indicated the square. 'Dickens was writing about Smithfield, Scout.' I spared her the stuff about Bill Sikes dragging young Oliver through Smithfield on the way to commit a burglary. 'Dickens was writing about where we live. A long time ago. When they still brought cattle to the market.'

'Once upon a time?'

'Yes,' I said. 'Once upon a time.'

I crouched down so that I was level with my daughter.

'Scout,' I said. 'Your mother would like to see you.'

Scout blinked at me. We were not like other divorced families who effortlessly handled the new arrangements. The breaking of our family had been brutal and we all still reeled from the shock of the ending, even as we got on with our lives, Scout and I in the loft high above Smithfield, Anne in a new house in Richmond, with her husband and young son, and another baby growing inside her. Anne's contact with Scout had been sporadic. My ex-wife was always looking for a window, she told me. She had apparently found a small window before her due date rolled around.

'But school starts today!' Scout said, immediately anxious.

'You would stay at the weekend. Friday night,

Saturday night. Something like that. I would drive you down there. Collect you.'

'But what about my stuff? I don't have any of my stuff there!'

I placed a gentle hand on her shoulder. 'Scout, you can take what you need. It's just for a night or two. You know your mother loves you, don't you?'

'But what about Stan?' Scout said, wringing her hands now, on the verge of tears. 'The weekend is when Stan goes off-lead! You know that, don't you, Daddy?'

It had become our habit to take Stan up to Hampstead Heath on the weekends when I wasn't working. Our little red Cavalier was not the easiest dog to let off-lead – he would stick with the pack until something more interesting came along, like a rabbit or a bird or, increasingly, a female dog of round about his own size. When that happened it felt like he would gamble with his life and home for one brief sniff of paradise. But he needed that time to run loose. We had to learn to let him go. Just as I had to learn to let Scout go.

'I can walk Stan alone,' I said. 'And – if you think it's not safe to let him off-lead when you're not there – then we can just go for a walk in the woods behind Jack Straw's Castle and save the Heath for when you come back. Then we can do it together. OK, angel?'

She sighed with all the world-weariness she could muster.

116

'OK, Daddy.'

Scout turned quickly away, Stan following her, but before she dipped her head, all wrapped up for winter, I saw it in her five-year-old eyes.

The flash of joy.

'So it was about the father,' DCI Whitestone said. 'It was always about him.'

We stared at the images of Brad Wood on the whitewall of Major Incident Room One. Brad Wood with his eyes blown out on the bedroom floor. Brad Wood on a stainless-steel slab at the Iain West Forensic Suite, the bloody pulp of his eyes expertly cleaned up now, but those empty sockets still seeming to stare at death itself. He looked very different from the rest of his family.

'Mary, Marlon and Piper,' I said. 'They were all violently murdered. But it was more than that with Brad Wood. He was slaughtered.'

'A different prostitute every week for two years,' Gane said. 'Even assuming time off for Christmas and all the major holidays, that's still knocking on for a hundred different hookers.'

'All of them with boyfriends,' Wren said. 'All of them with a motive to blackmail a wealthy man. And despite what the lady pimp told Wolfe, I doubt if every single one of them had a PhD and a heart of gold.'

'And no tattoos,' Gane said. 'I bet some of them had a few tattoos.'

'What about Marlon and Piper?' Whitestone said.

'Piper had a long-term boyfriend,' Wren said. 'Ashley Cooper. Lives with his mum and dad in a big gaff on Winnington Road. Parents both doctors. He's in bits, poor kid. They were quite keen on each other, Ashley and Piper. That explains the sperm that Elsa found inside Piper.'

'What's long term these days?' Whitestone said.

'Six months,' Wren said. 'He's a boy from her brother's school.' She consulted her notes. 'Same age as Piper. They had a row on New Year's Eve – a former girlfriend sent him a text message wishing him a Happy New Year – and Piper came home from the party early. Want me to have another word with him?'

'Not right now. What about Marlon? You said that the neighbour – Miles Compton? – seemed to hate his guts.'

'Young Marlon played the field,' Wren said. 'Like his father. No regular squeeze, but he liked the ladies. Sounds like he had been sniffing around Compton's teenage daughter a bit too enthusiastically. Compton's dislike feels more like a daddy looking out for his girl than a motive for murder. Another word?'

Whitestone shook her head.

'Let's just keep an eye on the neighbour,' Whitestone said. 'And the boyfriend.'

We sipped our coffee and let it settle. All four members of our MIT had got in early, only to find PC Billy Greene already there in his quiet corner of MIR-1, mugshots of known offenders flickering on his screen, logging calls from the public, trying to wade through false leads to find the trail that would take us to a stolen child.

'Think of the lies that bastard Brad Wood told,' Whitestone said. 'The risks he took. Just to get through the working week.'

She shook her head with a sense of wonder that was edged with real anger. I knew she had a fifteen-year-old son she was bringing up alone and for the first time I wondered what had happened to her husband.

'Hey, Billy,' Wren said. 'How would you like to trace, interview and eliminate a hundred escort girls? Might spice up your social life.'

Billy Greene was the only one not laughing. He looked as though he hadn't slept for a week. On his screen the faces of blank-faced men scrolled by, banal and endless. Always the two shots, profile and mug, the eyes dead, the images in black and white, the name and numbers at the bottom of the screen.

The large club of convicted paedophiles that is called 'known offenders'.

'There's another kid missing,' Billy said, and it killed our laughter stone dead. 'This morning. Another boy. Another four-year-old. Just like Bradley. Taken from his bed in the night.' Billy consulted his notes. 'Off Electric Avenue. Down there in Brixton.'

Whitestone cursed. She looked at me and I nodded. Another abduction of another four-year-old boy in the middle of the night was close enough to our case for me to drive across the river to check it out.

'Anybody dead?' Whitestone said.

'Nobody dead,' Billy said, and seemed to flinch as it hit him that he had no idea if the child was still alive.

Then we all looked up at the massive flat-screen TV on the whitewall as it suddenly cut to show the front gates of The Garden.

A little girl of around three was being held by the hand by her mother as she placed a small bouquet with the rest of the floral tributes. They were piled up against the security gates, a great tidal wave of flowers that made it feel as though Bradley Wood was already being mourned.

'Turn that thing off,' Whitestone said, and then to me: 'What can we bust her for? The lady pimp?'

I shrugged.

'Causing or inciting prostitution for gain. Controlling prostitution for gain . . .' I hesitated. 'She would be looking at six months inside. We'd be looking at a pile of paperwork and not a lot to show for it. Wouldn't you prefer to keep her in play? She could be a lot more use to us as an informant than doing six months under the Sexual Offences Act.'

Whitestone thought about it. And perhaps she

also gave a passing thought to the man she had once been married to.

'No,' she said. 'Let's bust the bitch.'

But Sampaguita was gone.

The room above the duck restaurant on Gerrard Street was empty now. The only sign that Ginger Gonzalez and her Social Introduction Agency had ever been here were the cables for a broadband connection snaking out of the wall and the rectangles of dust where her desk had stood. A glass that contained the remains of a scented candle sat in the corner. Whitestone picked it up and sniffed it as an old Chinese gentleman entered the room lugging a vacuum cleaner.

'The lady who was here,' I said to him. '*Ng-goy bawng bawng mawng?*' My Cantonese was rusty and it had never been that sharp to begin with. 'Can you help us, sir?'

'Gone, gone,' the old man said. 'All gone, gone.'

Two much younger Chinese men staggered into the room with a massage table. The old man barked at them in Cantonese and they stood it up against the wall. Gane appeared in the doorway as the old man turned on his vacuum cleaner.

'Ma'am, you want me to keep this room clear?' Gane shouted above the racket.

Whitestone shook her head impatiently. She joined me at the window. The red lanterns of the Chinese New Year bobbed in the late morning gloom.

'Any ideas, Max?'

I thought of the Coburg Bar at the Connaught. The American Bar at the Savoy. The Rivoli Bar at the Ritz. The Fumoir at Claridges. The Promenade Bar at the Dorchester.

'She could be anywhere,' I said.

Electric Avenue, Brixton. Wren and I walked between market stalls piled high with Caribbean fruit and vegetables. Guava berry, sugar apple, milk fruit. Yams, plantains, papaya. Mangoes, paw-paw, nutmegs. And plenty of things we had never seen before – red bananas, giant cherries and strangely shaped peppers.

We turned into Coldharbour Lane and followed the blue lights of our cars to a block of grey, sullen flats called Southwyck House, known locally as the Barrier Block. A few kids who should surely have been at school sat around on their bicycles waiting for something to happen.

Something else disturbed me about the scene, but it was just out of reach.

The Barrier Block looked like a high-security prison, with tiny windows cut into the high flat slabs of wall. We showed our warrant cards to the young uniformed officer at the taped perimeter and signed in.

'What you got?' Wren said.

'Michael McCarthy, male, black, four years old,' the young PC said. 'His mother woke up this morning and the boy was gone. They're up on the second floor.'

We went up two flights of stairs to a tiny flat where a woman was crying hysterically in a back room. I caught a glimpse of her through a half-open door. An overweight young black woman who was not quite twenty years old sat on a child's bed. A female uniformed officer was kneeling before her, holding her hand.

'My baby . . . my baby . . . my baby . . .'

A detective came out to meet us and we shook hands. He looked as though he had been a copper in Brixton for too long.

'West End Central?' he smiled. 'What you doing down here?'

'Bradley Wood,' I said. 'You've got another four-year-old boy missing, right?'

'Please . . . please . . . please . . .'

The woman choked with shock and grief. The detective lowered his voice. 'It's a different sort of four-year-old boy. This family are known to social services. The mother has convictions for substance abuse. The little boy – Michael – has already been taken into care twice.'

'Father?' I said.

His smile grew wider.

'Father? You're a long way from West End Central, friend. A few miles, one river and several hundred light years. What's a father? Look – if you want to stick around – that's fine. We're about to put the kettle on. But between you and me, you're wasting your time down here.'

I nodded and suddenly realised what was wrong

with this picture. There were no journalists at the Barrier Block. Not one.

There was no recognition in the wider world that Michael McCarthy was gone from his home.

I thought of Nils and Charlotte Gatling refusing to let the world forget their nephew and I wondered who was going to care that much about Michael McCarthy.

'We got it,' the detective told us, stifling a yawn.

CHAPTER 11

Saturday morning. We parked across the street from Anne's house and I turned to look at Scout in the back seat, her fingers scratching in the fur behind Stan's ears, her face pale with thought.

'You're going to have such a good time,' I said, so jolly that I sickened myself. And then, in my own voice, 'Your mother loves you, Scout. She never stopped loving you. You know that, don't you?'

Scout nodded once and we got out of the car. Apart from Stan. The dog kingdom held no charms for my ex-wife. Stan would have to wait in the car.

'Stay, Stan,' Scout told him. 'Good boy.'

As we got out of the car, Stan was already whimpering for Scout, knowing something was up because of her backpack and this strange destination at London's green and leafy end.

The entire family came to the door. The new man. *Oliver*. I was going to have to start thinking of him as Oliver. He wasn't really the new man any more. Oliver was the man. And their little boy, hanging back shyly. And Anne – very heavy, about eight months along now. She held her arms wide.

'Scout! So grown up!'

Scout bumped awkwardly against her mother's pregnant belly.

I always expected waves of grief to drag me down when I saw Anne in her new life. But the handover was smooth, brief, and I felt nothing much at all as Scout was led inside, smiling tightly at all the fuss, unused to being treated like a visiting head of state.

The door gently closed on me – Anne smiling, not unfriendly, just distant – and I knew that the grief was still out there, and that I would mourn for my dead marriage for a long time, but not here, and not today. The grief of bereavement would ambush me when I was least expecting it. I went back to the car and put Stan in the passenger seat. He smacked his lips with anxiety.

'It's OK, Stan,' I told him. 'This is what normal looks like.'

Midnight came and went and I was still sleepless.

I prowled through the loft, our home feeling the size of a planet without Scout in it, and stood at the window watching the lights of Smithfield blazing far below. Their night was just beginning in the meat market and it made it easier to admit to myself that sleep would be impossible tonight.

I went to Scout's bedroom. Stan was curled up in the centre of her pillow. His huge round eyes glittered in the darkness.

'I'm going out for a while,' I told him.

He lifted his head with interest.

Where we off to then?

'Just me,' I said.

I went to my room and started getting changed. Shirt. Tie. Stan was in the doorway, watching me suspiciously.

'No dogs where I'm going,' I said. 'Sorry. They don't let dogs in, OK?'

He cocked his sleepy head to one side, as if he found that impossible to believe.

Saturday night in the West End. I thought of the Coburg Bar at the Connaught. The American Bar at the Savoy. The Rivoli Bar at the Ritz. The Fumoir at Claridges. The Promenade Bar at the Dorchester. All the strangers meeting in bars tonight. Eye contact. Drinks. Deals struck. I thought perhaps I would start with the Connaught, as that was where Ginger Gonzalez had met Brad Wood.

Stan watched me expectantly with huge bright eyes. I knew I would not be able to close the door on that face.

'If you come with me you've got to stay in the car, OK?'

Stan stretched and yawned as he watched me putting on my wedding suit.

Ginger wasn't at the Connaught on Carlos Place and she wasn't at the Ritz on Piccadilly. But I found her at a small corner table of the American

Bar of the Savoy. The man she was with was around fifty, sleek and prosperous and slightly more drunk than he should have been. He was tracing an index finger on her wrist as if about to tell her fortune. I picked up a stool from a neighbouring table and sat down with them. The man stared at me.

'And who the bloody hell are you?' he said.

I ignored him and looked at Ginger. 'I thought you were picking up the children, darling?'

The man abruptly stood up. When he was gone, she smiled at me.

'I like it when you call me *darling*,' she said. 'It makes me think that you're less likely to arrest me.'

'I wouldn't count on it. You left Chinatown in a hurry.'

'It seemed like the smart move. You don't like me.'

The waiter approached our table and I shook my head.

'I don't like what you do. You can dress it up how you like – call yourself a businesswoman, make like you're some entrepreneur – but it's still the same old game to me. And I've seen too many poor little cows come to this country thinking they were going to be nannies or dancers or waitresses only to find themselves having sex on some stinking mattress with twenty men a night.'

Her mouth tightened. 'Not my girls.'

'I've seen too many of them on drugs, too many with their front teeth knocked out and too many with no idea whatever happened to their passport – or their lives.'

'That's *not* what I do.'

'But I don't chase pimps. That's somebody else's job. I hunt killers. That's my job. And it's my boss who wants to bring you in.'

Ginger sipped her drink. Mineral water with ice and a slice of lemon. She was working.

'Anything I can do to stop that happening?' she said.

'Help me,' I said.

She shook her head. 'I told you all I know about Brad Wood.'

'I want to know about the rest of them,' I said. 'The others. You said that they're not all good guys.'

'No. They're not.'

'I can't believe that it's as straightforward and wholesome as you make it out to be. Consenting adults, stimulating conversation and consensual sex where nobody gets hurt. No tattoos? No tears? There's more. There has to be.'

'What are you asking me?'

'You must get special requests.'

She looked around the bar.

'It happens.'

'What do they want? What do they want you to set up? What are their fantasies?'

'You can't imagine what they want.'

'But I bet I can. Some want cruelty of one kind or another. Some want a bigger party than one-on-one.

129

Some want all the stuff they've seen online. Some want underage. And some of the bastards want children.'

She was rattled for the first time.

'I don't do any of that stuff,' she said.

I pushed my card across the table.

'I know,' I said. 'If I thought you did, we would be sitting in an interview room.'

She took my card.

'I see there's another little boy gone missing,' she said.

'That's right.'

The waiter came back.

'If you're not going to order anything, sir, then we need the table.'

Rather than start throwing my weight about, I ordered a beer I didn't want. Ginger studied my card. When my beer came I sipped it slowly.

She smiled at me.

'You don't have anyone to get back to, do you?' she said.

'Not quite true,' I said. 'My dog's in the car.'

'I'm not sure a dog counts,' she said.

'He counts to me.'

'What happened? You break up with your girlfriend?'

I hesitated. Did I really want to share my secrets with a woman who ran a Social Introduction Agency?

'Wife,' I said.

'Anything else I can help you with?' she said, playing with me now.

'You think I need a younger version of my wife?'

'I think you look lonely, Detective.'

'Everybody's lonely,' I said, standing up to go.

Her face became serious. 'You know, there's something far worse than the stuff they see online,' she said.

'And what's that?' I said.

'The stuff they see in their head,' she said.

Sunday morning at Fred's.

With my hands inside big eighteen-ounce Lonsdale gloves, I threw hooks to the heavy bag. Bam-bam-bam, on and on, the lactic acid building in my arms and making them feel heavy and aching. I was determined to exhaust myself so that I would sleep better tonight.

'Punch from your shoulders, not your hands,' Fred was telling the young man in the ring with him. When the buzzer went for the end of my three minutes I stood and watched them. Other people were pausing in their workouts to watch.

The kid was that good.

Fred was taking him on the pads. Calling the shots.

'Double jab. Double jab. Come on, Rocky! Double jab – right cross – left hook. Good. Don't worry about power. Worry about speed. Punch from your feet! Get your whole body behind it! And now our seven-punch combination.' The punches rattled out in a perfect blur. 'Good, Rocky,' said Fred, his pirate's face splitting into a wide grin.

The young man was lean and very fast, with the kind of fitness level that only comes when you are very young and very serious. And you have to be good to call yourself Rocky. I watched his jab pop out and slap hard against the pads, the stinging sound of leather hitting leather. There was something Mediterranean about the way he looked, dark-haired and sallow-skinned, Italian or Spanish maybe, and if he wasn't a professional boxer already then he was thinking about it.

Fred set down the pads. He put in his mouthguard and pulled on his headguard and fourteen-ounce gloves. Then they sparred for a few rounds, Fred fighting on the back foot, flicking his jab out, staying away from the kid's big right hand. What shocked me was that only Fred wore a headguard. After three three-minute rounds they climbed out of the ring.

'You don't spar in a headguard?' I asked the kid.

He grinned. 'Never use them,' he said. 'Makes me too willing to get hit.'

'These travellers like to fight,' Fred laughed. 'It's in their blood.'

So Rocky was a gypsy.

'You a pro?' I said.

'Thinking about it. Might be getting married soon.' He couldn't have been more than eighteen. 'Working on the black stuff right now. You know. Laying driveways.'

I nodded. 'Good luck with it all.'

'Thanks, man.'

We touched gloves.

I was back banging the heavy bag when the news on the TV cut to The Garden. Nils and Charlotte Gatling were looking at the flowers that were piled up at the security gates. He had his hands behind his back with all the self-consciousness of visiting royalty. She stood nervously twisting her right hand over her left wrist, as if the gesture gave her comfort, as if she was holding hands with herself. Together brother and sister read the messages, exchanged a few words, watched from a respectful distance by what felt like the entire nation. I waited to see if there was anything about Michael McCarthy of Brixton.

But they cut to the sports desk, as if the other boy had already been forgotten.

After training at Fred's I went home and got clean and caffeinated. Then I drove up to Hampstead Heath, Stan over-excited in the passenger seat, panting with anticipation, knowing exactly where we were going.

The ground was rock hard and glittering with ice, and under the blood-red sky we ran past ponds where fishermen slept in their tents and we walked down lanes where foxes watched us with mild contempt and we crashed through thickets of bare winter trees into unexpected meadows that we would never find again.

We were on Kite Hill, looking down at all of London, when my phone rang with a number that I didn't know.

133

'It's Oliver,' said the new man. 'We're at the hospital.'

The celebrations had already begun.

Oliver had the look of a man who had been up all night but found a happy ending waiting for him in the morning. He was talking excitedly with an older, affluent-looking couple who could not be anything but his dear old mum and dad. The woman was holding two bouquets of flowers. More were arriving.

Scout sat quietly at the centre of it all, drawing on her iPad.

I shook hands all round.

'Congratulations,' I said. 'Mother and baby doing well?'

'Just a bit early,' Oliver said, and for the first time something passed between us. I understood exactly how he felt. The mixture of relief, pride and unalloyed joy. It stuck in my heart. Because I remembered it well.

I held out my hand for Scout.

Oliver's parents exchanged anxious looks. Everyone was very friendly but there was no denying that Scout and I were part of the abandoned past. And at that moment I think I understood my ex-wife a little better. It is all so much easier if you can pretend that you never loved before.

'Anne,' said Oliver's mother.

'Sleeping,' Oliver said.

'Exhausted,' said his father.

'Of course,' I said, and we were free to make our escape.

Oliver looked at me and smiled with something that I could not quite read. Perhaps he was truly seeing me for the first time, too.

I smiled back. There was no reason to prolong their agony. We just wanted to get out of the way of their happiness.

My daughter's hand was tiny in mine.

The Sunday traffic was light and we were soon crossing Blackfriars Bridge for home.

'When she gets out of hospital,' I said, 'and when the baby comes home—'

Scout cut me off. 'It's OK, Daddy,' she said, with a maturity that I had never seen before. She looked out at the river, the streets of Farringdon Market, old London closed up for its one day of rest.

'I like it here best,' Scout said.

At some point near the end of the night Scout awoke and I stumbled to her room.

'The cool side of the pillow,' she murmured, her eyes still closed with sleep. 'Make it the cool side of the pillow.'

I gently eased her into a sitting position as I turned her pillow over. Then she lay back down and within moments she was sleeping again, her head now resting on what she called the cool side of the pillow.

CHAPTER 12

In Room 101 of New Scotland Yard, Sergeant John Caine unlocked the door that led to the Black Museum and the police cadets filed inside.

There were a dozen of them down from the Peel Centre, the Met's principal training centre that we simply call Hendon. They went inside laughing and happy, like big kids on a field trip, and that lasted until they reached a display case of firearms that had been used to kill a police officer.

John and I followed them from a distance, me with a triple espresso from Bar Italia and him with a half-pint of builder's tea in his BEST DAD IN THE WORLD mug. The cadets' next stop was the collection of pots that Dennis Nilsen had used to boil the flesh off the heads, hands and feet of his victims. They were no longer laughing. They were no longer talking. They were starting to understand that any day of their career they could leave home in the morning and never come back.

'How many out there, John?' I said.

'How many did Nilsen kill?' he said. 'He couldn't

remember, could he? They reckon fifteen or sixteen. More than enough to clog up his neighbours' drains.'

'No,' I said. 'I mean how many are there make a living at it? Not the nut jobs like Nilsen. Not the cowboys and gangsters, the ones who will do anyone for a few grand. And not the crimes of passion committed on the spur of the moment with a kitchen knife because someone saw a text message they were never meant to see. I mean the real pros who treat it as a job. Killing for a career. How many of them are out there?'

'The ones who get away with murder?'

I nodded.

'We don't know, do we?' he said. 'We can never know. By definition, they're under our radar. But my guess? There are no brilliant pros or genius hitmen. They are all dull little toerags, full of rage, looking for an easy buck. All of them. The ones who do it for money, and the ones who do it because some woman hurt their feelings. The answer to your question, son, is – none.'

I thought about it.

The cadets were passing the display of Maisy Dawes, the victim of a Victorian blind, the girl who didn't do anything but die. They did not even glance at her.

She didn't do anything. That was her tragedy. All she did was die.

'I think it's more, John,' I said. 'A little bit more than none.'

My phone began to vibrate and I went back inside his office to answer it. Edie Wren was calling.

'We found the murder weapon,' she said.

It was cold in the catacombs of Highgate's West Cemetery.

'At the far end, sir,' a uniformed officer told me at the perimeter. I ducked under the tape. There were black figures at the far end of the catacombs and I began walking towards them. I could hear low voices, the cackle and crack of our radios.

The catacombs are nearly one hundred yards long with almost a thousand individual recesses, each one just large enough to contain a single coffin. And although the catacombs are above ground, they are cut from a hillside, and the cold of the grave seems to cling to the brick and iron.

A light came on. Beyond a final tapeline, I saw the suited SOCOs. Whitestone was talking to the Crime Scene Manager. Gane was on his knees, peering into one of the recesses that still held a coffin. Wren took notes as she interviewed a couple of terrified boys, shaking her head at their stupidity, her red hair falling over her face.

I ducked under the tape.

'These two found it,' Wren said. 'Climbed over the wall. Poking about where they shouldn't be.' She glared at them. 'And it's not even Halloween.'

'We weren't going to steal anything,' one said, close to tears.

'Just having a look,' said the other, dry-eyed. 'We

did good, didn't we? Found important evidence, like.'

I knelt by Gane's side. He shone his torch into the coffin. A skull grinned back at us.

'Apparently the Victorians liked the head at this end,' he said. 'So they could have a nice natter with the dead.'

I couldn't see a thing. 'Where's the weapon?'

'Halfway down. In the ribcage. So these two herberts reckon.' He nodded at the boys. 'They pulled the body out and shoved it back inside when they saw what was in there. Told one of their mums and she called it in.'

'If we hadn't been in here—' the dry-eyed boy began.

'Just shut your cakehole,' Wren told him.

Gane and I stepped back to let the Crime Scene Photographer do her work. When she had finished, DCI Whitestone gave me the nod.

'Who's got the longest arms?' she said.

'Me,' Wren said.

'Fish it out, Max,' Whitestone told me.

I snapped on blue latex gloves and reached my hand inside the coffin. My fingertips felt the smooth edge of a skull. They ran down the knobbly bumps of the neck and the start of the spine. I leaned forward, shutting my mouth tight, trying not to inhale the dust of the ancient grave. I felt the curve of ribs that were powdery with time. Some of the ribs were sharp and broken. And that was recent.

I reached inside the dead man's ribcage and felt the cold of modern steel. My fingers felt the short barrel, the thick body and the three letters of the manufacturer's name.

My fist closed around the handgrip.

Very slowly, I began to pull out a cattle gun.

'How'd they get it in there?' Wren said.

'Broke the ribcage,' I said, feeling the sharp edge of the dead man's ribcage cut through the glove and fleshy part of my thumb. The warm blood oozed down my wrist.

My knuckles brushed the side of the coffin. The wood was rotten with age. Something slimy slithered away from my presence.

I pulled the cattle gun from the coffin.

The Crime Scene Manager was waiting with an evidence bag. As I dropped it inside I saw a single blond hair clinging to the muzzle. The photographer began to take more pictures.

'When I hold it, I can see the attraction,' I said. 'Lightweight. Portable. Legal.'

We watched the cattle gun lit up by the photographer's flash. It was silver and grey, more like a heavy hand drill or a nail gun than a firearm. But there was a brute force about it. It looked effective and deadly.

'It's still a strange choice for a murder weapon,' Wren said. 'I mean – why would you? It's a big ask to use that thing to take out an entire family.'

'Not if you fill them full of Rohypnol,' I said.

'Or if you're trying to set somebody up,' said Gane.

'Done,' said the photographer, and DCI Whitestone took the evidence bag and held it in her hands, feeling the weight of the cattle gun.

'Or if it's what you know,' she said.

Wren and I walked back to The Garden through Highgate Cemetery, wild nature pressing in on all sides, this secret place feeling more like a jungle than a graveyard. Even without their leaves, the great trees crowded in on us and covered us in their shade. I didn't know what they were but I knew they were the kind where the leaves are sticky when they are green in summer and slimy when they fall in autumn. A city tree, although the city felt light years away in here.

Then I saw him.

Moving between the shadows of the trees, disappearing around the corner on one of the rising, winding paths, the hoodie he wore pulled over his eyes.

'This part of the cemetery is closed to the public, right?' I said.

Wren nodded. 'Guided tours only. You told me, remember? The west side is always closed to the public.'

'Then who the hell is he?'

We found him sitting by an ancient tomb in a wild tangle of undergrowth, his hand resting on the massive statue of a sleeping dog that lay beside it. The tomb itself was plain, but the stone dog was enormous, ten times life-size.

Rocky smiled at us from under his hoodie.

'What are you doing here?' I said.

'Visiting my hero,' he said, patting the dog's head. 'You heard of Tom Sayers? He was a boxer, too. The big star of bare-knuckle boxing in the middle of the nineteenth century. This is where he's buried. Tom Sayers was the Floyd Mayweather of his day. The Muhammad Ali. The Sugar Ray Leonard. He was little – like me – but he fought much bigger men. No weight divisions, see. Not in those days.'

Wren narrowed her eyes at Rocky.

'You know this gentleman?' she asked me.

'From the gym,' I said. 'Rocky's a boxer. How do you know this place, Rocky?'

'Did some work up here. For one of my dad's mates. On the black stuff. You know – laying drive-ways. I told you, didn't I? I thought I told you.'

'What's the name of your dad's mate?'

'Sean Nawkins.'

Wren and I exchanged a look. And I did not let the jolt of shock show on my face but I thought of the caravans and chalets of Oak Hill Farm out in the wilds of Essex and I thought of the Woods' beautiful home on London's highest hill.

Different worlds, I had thought.

But I was wrong.

'You ever do any work in The Garden?' I asked, my voice harder now.

His eyes were wide with innocence.

'Which garden might that be?' he said.

'The Garden is the gated community the other side of that wall,' I said, feeling that he already knew the answer. 'Six houses.'

He shook his head. 'No, this was further out. Hadley Wood. But I heard that Tom Sayers was buried here and I wanted to pay my respects. Do you know how many people went to his funeral? *One hundred thousand.* They followed his coffin up here from Camden Town. Imagine that . . .'

'You shouldn't be in here,' I said. 'You know that, right?'

But Rocky just scratched the giant stone dog behind its ears and gave me his big easy grin, as if all my petty rules did not apply to him and his kind.

The bell in Mary Wood's Japanese garden moved with the freezing wind.

I was standing halfway down The Garden, our team going over the list of workers who had been admitted to the gated community over the last six months, working out who remained to be traced, interviewed and eliminated from our investigation when the toll of the bell made me look up.

There was a sergeant and a couple of uniformed PCs standing guard outside the Wood house. The POLICE DO NOT CROSS tape was already looking tatty. And I could hear the bell.

The house was speaking to me.

Trying to speak to me.

It was bitterly cold in the growing dark of late

afternoon, ice forming on the windscreens of the Range Rovers and Porsches and BMWs that sat on the driveways.

I took off, running towards the house. I ducked under the tape, hearing the bell quite clearly now, that pure ringing sound from the back of the house where the Woods had been happy.

'Sir?'

The sergeant was at my side, his breath coming out in steam. But I shook my head, not knowing what I was looking for, not understanding what the house was trying to say.

I was still standing on the driveway, listening to the bell, when Wren reached me.

'What is it, Max?'

I stared at her. 'I don't know.'

The last weak shards of winter sunlight died as the darkness fell and, as Wren and I stood on the drive, suddenly the ground beneath our feet lit up – two dozen lights built into the driveway, stretching from the road to the front door, either side of the path.

I crouched down and touched the surface, looking up at the other driveways with the ice glinting on the windscreens, then I touched the Wood driveway again. It was unbroken black asphalt. But on the other drives I could see wear and tear, marks from rubber and exhaust fumes, the scars of time and the weather.

But not here. I let my fingertips trace the smooth black surface.

'This is new,' I said.

'What?'

'The driveway. I reckon late summer, early autumn. Not long ago. Not long enough to mark it.' I remembered Rocky in the gym. '*Working on the black stuff right now. You know. Laying driveways.*' And at the grave of Tom Sayers. '*Further out. Hadley Wood.*'

Rocky, I thought. You lying little bastard.

Who was he trying to protect?

Sean Nawkins? His father? Himself?

The sergeant and his two men watched me as I crouched down, my fingertips touching the smooth black asphalt, our breath steaming. I looked up at Wren.

'The firm who laid this driveway,' I said. 'They're not on the list, are they?'

Wren looked at me, then at the driveway. She looked at the other driveways, and I knew she could see what I could see.

Only the driveway of the Wood home was pristine. Only the driveway of the Wood home was new.

Wren consulted the printout in her hands as the wind stirred the trees beyond the wall and was answered by the bell. She cursed quietly, crumpled the list in her fist and then she was running towards Whitestone and Gane, her red hair flying in the growing dark.

CHAPTER 13

'Laying a driveway like the one outside the Woods' house is a two-day job,' Wren said in MIR-1 late the next morning. 'The contractors turn up with the hot-mix asphalt. It's a mix of sand, stone and gravel held together by asphalt cement. Pour. Level. Trowel. Forty-eight hours, in and out.'

'The security at the gate should record every entry and exit to The Garden,' Whitestone said.

Wren nodded. 'But early in the morning – residents off to work and school – the gates are left open. And it seems they didn't get round to recording whoever put down the black stuff on the Woods' drive.'

'Paper trail?' Whitestone said. 'Invoices? Bills?'

'We can't find anything,' Wren said. 'And no digital trail. I looked on the search history of the Woods' computers.'

'Cash in hand, saves on the paperwork,' Gane said.

I stared at the huge map of London on the wall of MIR-1. The Garden was on the west side of Highgate West Cemetery – the highest point in the city. You could approach it north from Finchley, south from Kentish Town, west from Hampstead, east from Holloway. If the contractors came off one of London's orbitals, the North Circular or the M25, then they would have come from the north.

'Nobody remembers anything?' Whitestone said. 'Security? Neighbours?'

Wren consulted her notebook. 'The security guard remembers the Woods parked their cars on the road for a few days at the tail end of last summer. Late August, early September, he thinks. And nobody ever parks their cars on the road in The Garden. That must have been due to the hot-mix asphalt. You have to let it set before you can park on it. So we are looking at late last summer.'

'Cameras,' I said. 'The cameras might have them.'

Gane laughed. 'You know how many CCTV cameras there are within a mile radius of the murder scene?'

'Not the CCTV cameras,' I said. 'The ANPR cameras.'

The public call them speed cameras. But we call them ANPRs – for Automatic Number Plate Recognition. Because it's not just your speed they clock. That's just the start. What ANPRs are really interested in is your identity.

'The CCTV cameras are no good because none of them have footage going back that far,' I said.

'But it's different with the fixed cameras. It's different with ANPRs. They keep data for a lot longer.'

Wren's fingers were flying over her keyboard. 'There's a fixed camera on the hill outside Highgate Cemetery,' she said. 'Another one on The Grove just before you turn into The Garden. Two – no, three – on Spaniards Road if they came from the west.'

'They didn't come from the west,' I said. 'They came from the north, off the North Circular or the M25.'

'How do you figure that?' Whitestone said.

'Laying driveways,' I said. 'It's a suburban trade. They're out-of-towners.'

'And the ANPRs,' Whitestone said. 'How long would the DVLA keep data?'

'Depends,' I said. 'If a car doesn't have MOT, insurance, vehicle registration. If the car is owned by a person of interest. If it is doing something illegal. The DVLA would pass it on to the enforcing agency but keep it on their own database.'

'How long?' Whitestone said, her eyes suddenly fierce behind her glasses. 'Potentially?'

'Forever,' I said.

When we knew we were going to pull an all-nighter we ordered food while we still had the chance. Even Soho shuts eventually. Then we all called home.

Scout was long in her bed and Mrs Murphy told

me it was no problem, she would sleep on the couch and see me early in the morning.

I was vaguely aware of the others talking quietly at their workstations. Whitestone Skyping her teenage son. Wren on her phone talking low, I guessed, to her married man. And Gane putting off whoever he was meant to be seeing that night.

Then their voices faded away, and all I was aware of was the soft Irish voice in my ear, telling me about what Scout had drawn at school, MIR-1 fading away while all I heard was the sound of home.

But my eyes drifted back to DCI Whitestone and the face of the thin, tousle-haired teenage boy in glasses on the computer screen before her. The son. And while I could not hear what they were saying, somehow I recognised the fierce bond that exists between a lone parent and their child. I saw – or at least I imagined I saw – something that I knew so well, an unbreakable bond of love and blood, the feeling that there is you two and then there is the rest of the world.

For the very first time, I looked at my boss, that quiet, unassuming woman in glasses with ten years in Homicide and Serious Crime Command and a kid at home, and I believed that I saw myself.

All night long we looked at the black-and-white images of the ANPRs.

We saw no faces. That's how people swap points, deny they were at the wheel, pretend they were home in bed, allege that the missus was driving, Your Honour.

Because it's the plate the ANPRs clock.

I sat at Gane's workstation as he scrolled through the still images of the camera on the hill, of the traffic in the summer sunshine, crawling to the top of London. We worked in silence, my nerves rattling with too many triple espressos from Bar Italia. When I finally spoke the sun was high over the rooftops of Mayfair and my voice was hoarse with the long slog of the night.

'Stop,' I said.

A white open-top pickup truck was struggling up the hill.

A distinctive car. A Ford Mustang. You could not see what they were carrying in the back and you could not see the driver. But you could see the words sharp and clear printed in black on the doors.

Premium Blacktop.

I looked over at Billy Greene.

'Premium Blacktop, Billy?' I gave him a car registration and the make.

'Wouldn't they have a concrete mixer?' Gane said. 'Steamroller? Heavier kit?'

'You would think so. But the ANPR wouldn't have kept this image if they were kosher.'

Billy Greene swivelled in his chair.

'That vehicle had no MOT – that's why it's still on the database. Premium Blacktop has no website, no Facebook page, no Twitter account. No digital presence at all, as far as I can see. They're a firm from Essex registered at Oak Hill Farm. Managing director is a Mr Sean Nawkins.'

Billy hesitated now, choosing his words carefully. We can't just say what we like these days. It's not allowed.

'Travelling people,' Billy said.

CHAPTER 14

Sixty minutes later I turned the BMW X5 off the A127 at Gallows Corner and there was Oak Hill Farm waiting in the distance, the white caravans parked back to back on the perimeter, making the camp look like a wagon train waiting for the Apache.

'I'd feel better with the heavy mob,' DI Gane said.

It was just the four of us in the car. Me at the wheel with Whitestone in the passenger seat, Gane and Wren in the back. Just our MIT.

'No hats and bats,' Whitestone said. 'No ghosties. Not for a chat.'

Hats and bats are officers in helmets with riot sticks. Ghosties are officers with a steel battering ram – the ghostbusters.

We were silent as we approached the camp. Ragged flags flew high above the scaffolding that served for the gateway. NO ETHNIC CLEANSING, said the signs, and WE WON'T GO, and THIS IS OUR HOME.

Then we were inside that place of rural squalor and suburban gentility, the neat little chalets at odds with the fridges and washing machines with the doors pulled off, the busted TVs and ancient computers with their shattered screens.

I slowed the car, careful among the children and dogs that milled around. A fifteen-year-old girl emerged from the pack.

'Hello, Echo,' I said. 'No school on a weekday?'

'Is it a weekday?' she said.

'Is your dad home?'

She looked over my shoulder at Gane in the back.

'He shouldn't have come back here,' she said. 'None of you should have come back.'

With an escort of children and dogs, I slowly drove to where the large chalet and the caravan stood side by side. Sean Nawkins was sitting outside his chalet, and he frowned at us from behind his spectacles. He put down his *Guardian* and stood up, jabbing a finger at Gane as we got out of the car.

'I'm talking to my lawyer about you,' he said.

The caravan still had a broken window where Gane had put rat-face through it.

'DI Gane,' Whitestone said. 'Have a look for that car, would you? Go with him, DC Wren. Mr Nawkins?' Whitestone had her warrant card in her hand. 'I'm DCI Whitestone. I believe you've met DC Wolfe.'

The crowd parted for Gane and Wren. Echo appeared by her father's side, slipping her arm through his, and I couldn't tell whether she was trying to restrain him or seeking protection.

'Do you know what they did to my brother?' Nawkins asked Whitestone. 'Those farmers? They stripped him naked and held him down and they were going to cut his nuts off. They weren't just trying to scare him. The father wasn't man enough to take him alone, so they did it mob-handed. I'm glad he killed them. They deserved to be killed. And it has nothing to do with anything else, all right?'

'Do you own a Ford Mustang pickup truck, Mr Nawkins?' Whitestone said. She consulted her notes and read out a registration number. Then she stared at him and waited.

'I own a lot of cars,' Nawkins said. 'A Ford Mustang, you say? I've owned a few of those. Good for building work. You know – laying the black stuff.'

'Did you lay any of the black stuff in North London? Highgate way?'

'Plenty,' he said, and his face twisted in a sneer. 'What's this? You're going to stitch up my brother just because I did some work in The Garden? That was six months ago!'

Peter Nawkins appeared in the doorway of the caravan. He looked at his brother.

'They came back!' he said to his brother. 'You said they wouldn't come back any more! And they have!'

The dogs and children were now being joined by adults. A dozen men and women, watching us, their arms folded, talking among themselves, and then twenty, and then more than I could count, coming out of their neat chalets and the white caravans, and among them I saw the large bearded man and rat-face, his forehead still bandaged from when Gane pushed it through a window.

'So you don't deny you did work at the Woods' home in The Garden?' Whitestone said.

Nawkins laughed. 'Why should I deny it? I didn't even meet them. I spoke to him – the man of the house – on the blower and the housekeeper – some kind of Eastern European who had an envelope with the cash – plus a little drink for a job well done.' He laughed with real amusement. 'You really going to try to parlay that into a murder charge, are you?'

Whitestone looked at me. I was looking at the crowd.

'We're here because a vehicle from Oak Hill Farm was at The Garden,' Whitestone said. 'And we need to eliminate the owner of that vehicle from our enquiries.'

'That's me, all right? Christ – we were up there half a year before they were topped! Is that really the best you can do?'

Laughter in the crowd. That's OK, I thought. When they are laughing they are less likely to rip your throat out. But I saw Whitestone's face flush red and I watched her mouth tighten. One fingertip pushed her glasses up her nose. It was amazing how much emotion she could put into that gesture.

She looked hard at Peter Nawkins.

'Where were you on New Year's Eve?' she asked.

'Your coppers asked him that already,' said Echo.

'I believe they asked about the other Mr Nawkins,' Whitestone said, not looking at the girl. 'Now I'm asking this Mr Nawkins. And he still hasn't given me a satisfactory reply.'

'We've done this already,' Sean Nawkins said. 'And we're not doing it again. Knock on somebody else's door. I was away on business on New Year's Eve. In Ireland. I can get you as many witnesses as you need. My brother was right here. Like it or lump it, lady. Either way, you can sling your hook. Go inside,' he said to his brother. 'Go inside and calm yourself down.'

Peter Nawkins went into his caravan. Whitestone gave me the nod and I followed him.

Inside it was like being on a boat. Every inch had been utilised as if there were many miles to travel. I found him leaning against the sink in the kitchen, his huge shoulders juddering with fear.

'You want to put me away!' he said.

'Not if you haven't done anything wrong.'

'But you do! You want to lock me up so you can say you solved it! You have to lock someone up or you'll get in trouble! And it's easy to lock me up because of what I did all those years ago.' He looked at me with fierce eyes. 'That's the way it works, isn't it?'

'Sometimes,' I said. 'It has worked that way some-times in the past. Innocent people got locked up – for bombings, for murders – because somebody

156

had to get locked up. But that's not happening here. That's not happening now. You don't have anything to fear if you haven't done anything wrong. But you have to help us. There's a boy missing. There's a family dead.'

'I'm *ill*.'

'I know.'

'I've got the cancer. The kind you can't cure.'

'And I'm sorry.'

He nodded, apparently satisfied. I could hear the voices of the crowd outside. I glanced at the window but I could see nothing. I didn't like leaving Whitestone alone.

'You understand why we're here, don't you?' I said. 'You know what happened to that family? They died the same way Farmer Burns and his three sons died. With a cattle gun. And you killed those four men, didn't you?'

'Because they were going to *cut me up*!'

I took a step towards him.

'Is Premium Blacktop your brother's firm?'

A pause. Then Peter Nawkins nodded.

'You help him?'

'Sometimes.'

'Were you with him last summer at The Garden?'

'I didn't do it,' he said. 'I didn't meet that family. None of us did. You know that, don't you?'

I stared at him for a moment and then I nodded once.

It was true what his brother had said.

We were getting desperate.

157

Peter Nawkins turned away and went into his bedroom. Ahead of me I could see a large bed occupying most of the floor space in the small room. He threw himself on the bed and filled it entirely, his massive limbs spilling over the side.

I stepped into the room and stood by his bedside, staring down at him.

Then I followed his gaze and looked up at the ceiling.

And the same woman's face smiled back at me a thousand times.

Pictures of Mary Wood covered the ceiling of his bedroom.

They had been printed off the Internet and most of them seemed to feature Mary as a much younger woman during the winter of her fame.

Mary in her ski gear. Mary smiling in Lillehammer. Mary troubled and thoughtful in her Team GB tracksuit as she faced the press. And Mary smiling on the arm of her future husband, although some careful scissor work had removed Brad Wood from the picture.

I found that I wasn't breathing.

'Peter?' I said.

'Yes?'

'What the hell happened at The Garden?'

His eyes were closed now, as if he refused to look at the dead woman staring down at him while I was looking at her. As if he did not want to share Mary Wood with anyone.

'Nothing happened,' he said. 'I just liked her,

that's all. I liked the way she looked. She looked kind. She looked like a kind lady. Didn't you ever like someone you never met?'

'You met her at The Garden, didn't you? Stop lying to me!'

'I *didn't* meet her! I didn't speak to her. I could never speak to a lady like that. But I saw her.' He opened his eyes and looked at me. 'You can't imagine how perfect she looked.'

Then I was in the doorway of the caravan, and I was breathing again, and the crowd was by now a hundred strong, maybe more. Whitestone was listening to Nawkins lecture her about police brutality and human rights.

There was no sign of Gane and Wren.

'You need to see this, boss,' I said.

Whitestone came into the caravan and followed me into the bedroom where Peter Nawkins was still lying on his bed. Then she followed my eyes to the ceiling. She stared at the pictures for a long time and then at the big man sprawled across the bed.

'Where's Gane and Wren?' she said.

There was a black nylon pouch on Whitestone's belt and she opened it without a sound and took out a pair of ASP handcuffs, black and steel, chain-linked.

I went to the window. All I could see was the crowd.

'They can't be far,' I said.

She nodded and I knew exactly what she was

going to do now because they hammer it into us in our training days. *A formal arrest will always be accompanied by physically taking control.* You don't nick someone when they still have the option of running away.

'Peter Nawkins, you are under arrest for the murder of Mary Wood,' Whitestone said calmly.

Nawkins opened his eyes and sat up.

'What?' he said, but by then the ASP cuffs had already secured his hands behind his back. We gently helped the big man to his feet. He stared at us with wild eyes, as if his worst nightmare was coming true.

'You do not have to say anything,' Whitestone said.

I could hear jeers and catcalls outside and I guessed that Gane and Wren were returning.

'But it may harm your defence if you do not mention when questioned something you later rely on in court,' Whitestone continued. 'Anything you do say may be given in evidence. OK, let's go.'

I went first.

When I got to the doorway of the caravan I saw Gane and Wren in the middle of the crowd, being jostled as they tried to get through. Then Whitestone and Nawkins came out of the caravan behind me and a moan of outrage rose from the crowd. All at once they pushed forward and I saw Wren go down. Someone swung a fist at Gane's head and he flinched as the blow caught him in the ear.

But the car was not far. And I had the keys in my hand.

I was not aware of the bottle being thrown but it suddenly exploded in the middle of Whitestone's forehead.

The sound of breaking glass and the sight of livid blood were simultaneous. Whitestone half went down, more from shock than pain – the pain would come much later – and I saw Peter Nawkins stumble into his brother's arms.

The blood sent them wild.

Suddenly I was fighting for my life, and I understood how you died, how the mob kill you, how that copper had died in Tottenham, how those soldiers had died in Belfast, how the mob can get you down on the pavement and then rip you to pieces.

I felt a flurry of fists in my face, wildly hitting my neck and my ears and the back of my head as much as my mouth and nose and chin and eyes, and trainers catching me on my shins, my thighs, my buttocks, some of them aiming for my balls and missing, and the faces of the men and the women were so close that I could smell the stink of food and cigarettes on their breath.

Whitestone called my name for what felt like the last time and I fought my way towards her.

She was on her knees. Her glasses were hanging from her face. She desperately pushed them back on and they stayed there even as the women around her rained kicks into her small figure, and

Whitestone was not reacting, the shock of sudden violence setting in, just touching the wound in the centre of her forehead and marvelling at the amount of blood on her hands.

Then all at once they were backing off.

I saw Gane, his nose possibly broken, staggering towards us, and Wren, getting to her feet, screaming at the crowd – holding her fist out, pointing something yellow at them, backing them off. The Taser in her hand.

'I'm warning you!' she said. 'I'm warning the lot of you!'

It was a Taser X2, compact and lightweight and canary yellow. For a long moment it seemed to have done the trick.

Then the bearded man stepped forward. The twin lasers of the X2 were bright red on his filthy vest.

'Yeah, and I'm warning you, none of youse are getting out of here alive, you little whore!'

Wren shot him with the Taser. The X2 is double-barrelled, with a backup shot making it harder to miss.

And she didn't.

The bearded man screamed as his muscles contracted with involuntary spasms. Neuromuscular incapacitation, they call it. It really screws you up. He was still on the floor surrounded by his friends as we helped Whitestone into the car.

'Nawkins?' she said.

'We'll get him,' I said.

162

There wasn't room to turn the car around so I stuck it in reverse and floored the pedal. I fishtailed at the entrance, under the great scaffolding gateway, and pointed the car towards London.

My phone began to vibrate and I let it ring until we were at Gallows Corner and I could see we were not being followed.

It was Ginger Gonzalez.

'I know where they're keeping the boy,' she said.

CHAPTER 15

'What happened to you?' Ginger said.

My face had some of those red scuff-marks that you get when you have been punched by people who don't really know how to throw a punch.

I actually got off lightly. I had come straight to see Ginger while the other three went to A&E. Whitestone with mild concussion, Wren with strained medial ligaments in her left knee from when she went down and Gane with a broken nose. But what hurt us most of all was that Peter Nawkins was on the run.

'Day-trip to Essex,' I said.

We were in St Augustine of Canterbury, a Catholic church so deep in the East End that the streets outside looked as though they had not changed for sixty years.

I slid along the pew to sit next to Ginger.

'Is that him?' she said. 'The man on the news? Is he the one who killed that family?'

I nodded.

'How do you know?'

'He ran,' I said.

'They said that you had him and then you lost him.'

'And now we're going to get him again,' I said. 'Is that her?'

There was a girl praying by the altar. A slim, slight figure with her head bowed to the Virgin Mary. She looked very young. Her mousey-brown hair was pulled back into an untidy ponytail.

'Yes, that's her,' Ginger said.

'We need to get moving,' I said. 'Now.'

Ginger nodded. 'She's just saying a prayer for the little boy.'

When the girl got up I saw that she was older than I first thought. She looked like a very tired sixteen-year-old. She stopped dead when she saw me but glanced at Ginger and joined us, taking the long way round the pews so that she could sit with Ginger between us.

'This is Paula,' Ginger said, and I saw that she had some kind of Asian symbol tattooed on her wrist.

'Tell me about the child you saw,' I said.

'He was at a house on The Bishops Avenue,' she said.

I took a breath.

The Bishops Avenue was known as Billionaires' Row. Running between Highgate and Hampstead, and acting as the border between Highgate Golf Course and Hampstead Golf Course, The Bishops Avenue was famous for two things – some of the most expensive houses in the world and some of the most tasteless architecture, which tended towards the Saudi Arabian vision of beauty and splendour.

There was a lot of foreign money on The Bishops Avenue. In fact, it might all have been foreign money.

'Address?' I said.

'I don't know,' Paula said.

I felt my mouth tighten.

'I don't care what your name is,' I said. 'I don't care what you've done. And I don't care about your visa status. All I care about is the child. But if you lie to me then I will suddenly start caring about all of these things. Do you understand?'

'I don't know the address! Please – I don't know the address. It was one of those big houses on The Bishops Avenue. A party. A man took me there. A man I met in the West End.'

She named a lap-dancing club.

'What were you doing there?'

'Working.'

'OK,' I said. I nodded at Ginger. 'And how do you two know each other?'

'Paula was briefly employed on a freelance basis by Sampaguita,' Ginger said. 'But it didn't work out.'

'Why not?' I said. 'Because she's got a tattoo?'

Ginger shook her head. 'Sometimes I overlook the odd tattoo.'

'I thought you might,' I said. 'So why'd you kick her out?'

'Too young,' Ginger said.

I stared at her for a moment then turned back to Paula.

'What's the man's name? The man who took you there?'

'Fat Roy,' she said. 'Can we make sure—'

'I'm not going to let anyone hurt you,' I said. 'Not this Fat Roy guy or anybody else. Tell me about the party.'

'He drove me up there from the West End. There were men. Older men. And girls and boys. Younger than me. A lot younger.'

I took a breath.

'Children?' I said.

'Yes, children,' she said.

'You see the boy?'

'They kept him out of sight. In a room. They called it the VIP room. I heard him crying.'

'Were the men filming?'

'They were using their phones to film. Does that count?'

'That counts.'

'I wasn't there long. They sent me away. Some men – they told Fat Roy they didn't want me there. They gave me £200 and kicked me out. I went to see Ginger. I knew it was wrong.'

My phone vibrated. A message from Wren. DONE, it said. They were all out of the hospital and ready to roll.

I turned to Ginger's girl.

'Why did they kick you out, Paula?' I said.

'I'm too old,' she said.

PC Billy Greene had sent me an old mugshot of known offender Fat Roy from when he had gone down for trespass with intent to commit a sexual offence.

The man gawping at me on my phone was a chubby twenty-year-old with an Eighties mullet and a baggy white 'Frankie Says No War' T-shirt. But the Fat Roy now disappearing into the toilet in the crowded Shoreditch pub was a morbidly obese man of unknowable age, his head shaved bald and his one nod to fashion a small gold ring through the side of his nose.

Or maybe the head wasn't shaved.

Loss of body hair is just one side effect of chemical castration.

The others are an increase in body fat, a decrease in bone density and, weirdest of all, a discoloration of the lips. I had clocked that Fat Roy looked as though he was wearing a particularly garish lip-gloss. It wasn't a great look. Chemical castration does things to a man.

None of them are good.

But the judges like chemical castration. And the parole boards like chemical castration. And all the great and the good want to believe that chemical castration really does stop the sickness. Reduce sex drive, lower testosterone and kill the compulsion to hurt the vulnerable and the weak and the very young. If a known offender agrees to be chemically castrated, they usually give him back his lousy life.

Not that they literally castrate anyone. They just give them drugs. MPA in America, cyproterone acetate over here. That's meant to do the trick and make all the cruel dreams go away.

They don't literally cut their nuts off. More's the pity.

I got up and followed Fat Roy into the toilet.

He was washing his hands.

'Any parties tonight, Fat Roy?'

A quick glance, the lizard tongue flicking out to touch those purple lips.

'I don't know you,' he said. It wasn't a question.

'I'm the guy who's looking for a party,' I said.

He took his time drying his hands. A big man, not rushing, and this was far from the first time that he had been cornered by the hand soap. He was still not looking at me. But he was thinking about it. Wondering if he would have to put me down before he walked out of there.

'I'm looking for the party on The Bishops Avenue,' I said, and I saw him flinch. 'Billionaires' Row. And you're going to take me there.'

Now he looked at me. And at the warrant card that I was holding in my left hand. Keeping my favoured hand free in case he tried to do a bunk or went for my throat.

'Sorry,' he said. 'I'm not taking you anywhere. Take me in, if you like. Knock me about while resisting arrest if you want. But I'm not taking you to The Bishops Avenue tonight or any other night.'

'Is the boy there?' I said.

He did not reply. Instead, he leaned over the sink, scrubbing his hands, rubbing at something that would never come off.

I saw that he was scared. His hands were shaking. But it wasn't me that he was scared of.

There was a messenger's satchel over his shoulder. I indicated it with a nod.

'I bet if I looked on your laptop I'd find some nasty stuff,' I said. 'If I got one of my clever tech mates to dig deep enough. Get past all the layers of encryption that hide your grubby little secrets.'

The judges might believe that chemical castration can change a man's heart.

But not me.

I don't believe it for a second.

Fat Roy tugged self-consciously at the shoulder strap. The gold ring in his nose glittered in the harsh light. The door opened and a half-cut City boy staggered in, singing a popular tune.

'Not now,' I said. And after taking a moment to think about it, the drunk City boy went away.

'You're more frightened of them than you are of me,' I said. And that wasn't a question either.

The tongue lapped quickly on the purple lips.

'Did you ever see what a very small amount of sulphuric acid does to someone's face, Officer?' he asked me.

I nodded. 'Once or twice.'

'Well,' he said.

'Is that how they keep the party polite? Burning faces? Or threatening to burn faces?'

'You have no idea. This is not some bunch of losers sharing images on the Dark Web. This is the hard core. These are the extremists. They'll burn your face off with one hand and pass the Play Gel with the other.'

'Still a bunch of losers,' I said. 'A bunch of grown men torturing little children. Biggest bunch of losers on the planet. Bradley Wood is up there, isn't he? They've got him at the private party on The Bishops Avenue.' Then I was right in his face. *'Haven't they?'*

He backed off, maintaining the space between us, keeping me out of range. He was a man who understood violence.

'I never saw the boy,' he said. 'I never touched him.'

'But he's there, isn't he?'

He nodded briefly, hanging his head.

Then he held out his wrists, waiting to be cuffed, the lizard tongue wetting purple lips.

'But I still can't take you there,' he said. 'You're just some ten-a-penny tough guy and they're killers. *They burn faces.* Go ahead. Beat the shit out of me. But why should I be scared of you?'

I almost smiled.

'Because I have a daughter,' I said, starting towards him.

Fat Roy came out of the pub ahead of me, half a roll of kitchen towel pressed to his face.

I gave him a little push in the back and said, 'The old silver BMW X5,' and he stumbled towards the car.

In the passenger seat, Whitestone was buzzing down the window.

'Fat Roy here doesn't know the address,' I said. 'But he's going to show us the house. Aren't you, Fat Roy?'

'Yes,' he said, the words muffled behind the layers of kitchen towel, and hoarse with shock.

'And you've seen Bradley Wood?' Whitestone asked him.

Fat Roy shook his head, not looking at us.

'I only heard him,' he said. 'That's the truth.'

'What did you hear?' Whitestone said.

He took a breath. He would not meet our eyes.

'I heard him crying,' he said.

Wren got out of the car so that Fat Roy could get in between her and Gane, and I climbed into the driver's seat.

'You'll want hats and bats for this one,' Gane said to Whitestone, his phone already in his hand. 'And you'll want SFOs.'

He meant Specialist Firearms Officers from CO19, Scotland Yard's specialist firearms unit.

Whitestone nodded.

'But we're not waiting for anyone,' she said. 'We'll see them in The Bishops Avenue. Edie, call in our exact location when we get there. Let's go, Wolfe.'

I hit a switch on the dashboard.

The siren howled and two blue lights began to flash inside the BMW's grille.

As I pulled into traffic I tossed something from

the window. A small gold ring that still pierced a bloody clump of white flesh. The nose ring shone for a moment in the Shoreditch street lamps and then it was lost to the gutter.

We lit up the night.

CHAPTER 16

The Bishops Avenue.

I drove slowly down that tree-lined avenue of rich men's dreams, grille lights off and siren silenced now, past sprawling mansions where no expense had been spared and no taste exercised.

The big houses of The Bishops Avenue were set well back from the road, on the far side of electrified fences and high walls and security gates that bristled with CCTV, but they were so massive that they were still clearly visible.

The Bishops Avenue was unlike anywhere else in London. It made you believe that planning permission had never been invented. There were spirals and turrets and towers on houses that looked as though they had been built by Walt Disney on bad acid. This was where the Arab oil money ran to back in the day when Saddam Hussein was on the march. It showed.

There were acres of golf courses on either side of The Bishops Avenue and the houses sat in the surrounding darkness like islands of impossible privilege. From the street you could see the lights of crystal chandeliers twinkling prettily in the distance. Then the security lights on the gates blazed on to acknowledge our passing, blinding us, and hiding the lives inside. I could see endless luxury but nothing that was human, nothing that was living, nothing that was worth having.

'This is it,' Fat Roy said.

I stopped the car. We were at the far end of The Bishops Avenue, where the opulence starts wearing thin, just before it hits the main road that separates it from East Finchley.

I could see only tall iron gates, set into a brick wall topped with ancient razor wire and, just visible at the end of a long sweeping drive, the huge house in total darkness. It looked as though nobody had lived there for years.

'What's this place?' Whitestone said.

'It's one of the wrecks,' Fat Roy said. 'There's maybe twenty of them on The Bishops Avenue. All derelict. Most of them are owned by Middle Eastern gentlemen. The Saudi royal family has got a collection. They let them fall to bits and they're still worth another ten million every year.'

And I saw in the moonlight that the grand house was in ruins. There were metal grilles over the windows but vandals had still managed to smash them all. The great walls were seared with cracks and covered with ivy. I squinted into the blackness. The roof appeared to have a hole the size of a car.

'And they use this place for their parties?' I said.

Fat Roy nodded.

'I don't see any lights,' I said.

'They're on the far side,' Fat Roy said. 'Away from the street.' He dabbed at his nose. The kitchen towel was sopping wet with blood that was pitch black in the moonlight. 'Nobody can see them if they stay over there. They use the rooms at the back.' A pause. 'There are plenty of rooms to choose from.'

'Where's the boy?' I said.

He didn't look at me. 'They were keeping him in a room on the first floor.'

'When?'

'Week ago. A bit less.'

'How do you get past this gate?' I said.

'Code key. Changes once a month. There's a panel on the side there, see it?' He told me the six digits. 'Can I go now?'

'No,' I said. 'You're coming with us.'

'Leave him in the car,' Whitestone said.

'In the boot?' I said.

'Jesus Christ!' said Fat Roy.

'The back seat will do,' Whitestone said. 'Lock him in.'

We got out of the car and left Fat Roy inside. As I locked the doors I saw total loathing in his eyes. Then his gaze slid away, and he dabbed again at his nose. We stood outside the iron gates as Wren called in our location to CO19.

'They're coming up the Holloway Road,' she said. 'Maybe ten minutes away.'

'Are we waiting for them?' Gane said.

'We can't wait,' Whitestone said. 'Not with the boy inside.'

There was a sign on the gates.

AMBASSADORIAL RESIDENCE FOR SALE ON BEHALF OF THE RECEIVERS

I tapped in the code key and the gates clicked. We went through, the only sound our footsteps treading lightly on the gravel drive. The ruined house rose before us. Now I saw cars parked on the lawn on one side of the house, not visible from the road. One of them was a large van with blacked-out windows. There were lights on in the rooms at the back. As we got closer, I could hear voices, low music. There was a swimming pool containing nothing but dead leaves.

'Burglar's route?' Whitestone said.

I nodded and picked up a brick. Burglar's route meant the front door – the entry point for most burglars.

I stepped up to the ornate door with its rusting lion's head and I brought the brick down on the handle as hard as I could. It came away clean. I kicked at the door. No deadbolt. The door swung open and we went inside and then we just stood there for a moment, trying to understand what we were seeing.

It was a palace that had been left to rot.

Either side of the front door, a double staircase

swept up to the second floor where it abruptly ended just before reaching the top.

At the top of the staircase there was only a gaping black hole.

What remained of the staircase was covered in shattered tiles and shredded plaster and the torn branches of a very large tree, suggesting the top had been demolished when a tree caved in the roof. Something black flew out of the hole at the top of the staircase and flapped wildly into the higher reaches of the house.

'I bloody hate bats,' murmured Wren.

Everywhere you looked, nature was taking over the derelict mansion. There was an old bird's nest in the velvet curtains. Weeds and ferns and moss grew all around, and dead leaves from the fallen tree skittered down the staircase. Under our feet was a white pile carpet stained brown by the weather and covered in the droppings of birds and rats and foxes.

There was hardly any furniture, just a mattress in a darkened corner covered in stains, a velvet chair covered in mould and a grand piano that had been dragged from some other part of the house, and then smashed to pieces with a sledgehammer.

Water streamed down walls two storeys high and collected in paintings that were peeling with damp and decay, giving the faces in the old portraits the look of a leper colony. There was a crystal chandelier in the ceiling, half of its bulbs dead now, but still working, and it threw out light like a dying sun.

Suddenly I was aware of a flurry of wetness on my face. I looked up and I saw that snow was falling hard through the gaping black hole in the roof. A single snowflake settled on the back of my hand and then was gone.

The voices coming from the back of the house were a lot closer now.

'Upstairs,' Whitestone said. 'Get the boy.'

But by now they had heard us.

At first there was just the girl.

Perhaps twelve years old, painfully skinny and pale with lank brown hair. Someone had given her a short dress that was too small and high-heeled shoes that were too big.

She held a paper cup and stared at us in amazement.

'Do you speak English?' I said, and then the first man was there, shoving her aside and coming toward us. He was heavy and middle-aged and his face was covered in a film of oily grease.

Wren stepped forward.

'You're under arrest,' she said, and he punched her in the face with all his strength, and his fist must have connected with her chin because Wren went down very hard, unconscious before she hit the floor.

I felt a flame of pure fury rise in me that anyone would dare to lay their hands on her.

The man kept coming.

179

Stepping over Edie Wren's prostrate body, fists by his side, showing his teeth to me, snarling something obscene.

He just kept on coming and that was perfect because he walked straight into the big right hand that I threw, a punch that was hard more than accurate, full of my suddenly boiling blood, my anger throwing my aim way off, missing his chin by six inches, but it still connected with the tip of his nose and it gave way with a sharp crack and there are very few men who can take a broken nose in their stride.

This bastard wasn't one of them.

Gane kicked the man's feet from under him and Whitestone got down to cuff him as I bent over Wren, saying her first name – *Edie, Edie, Edie* – and feeling terrified when she did not respond to the hands that I pressed against her pale face.

Then I felt eyes on me and I stared up at the child in the mini dress and I wanted her to know that she was safe now. But there was no time because there were more men coming for us.

Some of them were armed with hammers. I saw Gane raise his hand and catch a hammer blow high on his arm, and lash out with the side of his foot, a side-thrust kick, some muscle memory from a martial arts class, and he caught the man at the soft spot where the top of a shin meets the bottom of a knee.

The man dropped his hammer. Gane got him in a headlock. The man's fingers reached up for

Gane's eyes, clawing for them as he screamed abuse. Locked together, they stumbled around in the pale light of the old chandelier.

Then one of them had something small and yellow in his fist and I saw him point it at the side of Whitestone's face as she stood up, her right foot resting on the back of the neck of the man on the floor. I shouted at her and threw myself at the man as he squirted her with acid.

There was a moment when she burned and her clothes burned with her, skin and flesh and nylon jacket and fake fur all hissing and burning and dissolving in the stream of sulphuric acid.

Then Whitestone screamed, holding her neck, hideous steam rising from the scalded flesh just above the neckline of her jacket and the man was below me on his back and I could feel his front teeth cutting into the knuckles of my hand as I knocked them into the back of his mouth.

I looked up.

I saw the skinny legs of girls in shoes that were too big. And boys too – the boys younger, and all of them standing there with the paper cups in their hands and staring at us in wonder.

'Water!' I was screaming at Whitestone, and she howled with agony and clutched her neck. 'Water on it! Now!'

The men were running.

I saw Gane still grappling with one of them, and then the man broke free and ran into the back room they had all come out of, and I heard cars starting up, voices full of panic and fury, engines being gunned and tyres skidding on the wet grass.

They were getting out of here.

Whitestone had disappeared, looking for water. Wren was still out cold.

And through the falling snow, heavy inside the house now, I saw Gane slowly climbing the staircase.

Gane was going to get the boy they kept upstairs, and I saw he was dragging one of his legs as if he had done something to his knee, and I didn't see how he could get across the destroyed staircase with a leg that bad.

And then I saw the man who followed him.

Fat Roy was doused in blood. It still poured from his nose where I had ripped out the ring and now it covered his hands where he had beaten out the window of the BMW X5.

Tiny shards of broken glass covered the arms of Fat Roy's jacket, catching the light of the crystal chandelier that shone like the last rays of some fading sun.

And I knew that Gane had not seen him.

I got up and went after them.

Gane had stopped at the top of the stairs, staring into the black hole, and I called his name.

'Curtis!'

They both turned. Gane at the top of the smashed double staircase and Fat Roy just behind him now, and it was only then that I saw the knife in Fat Roy's hand.

A black carbon lock knife.

Aluminium-handled.

With a blade somewhere between three and four inches long.

I looked up at him as he stabbed me in the stomach.

A stab like a punch. The way a good teacher will show you how to punch. The hand snapping back as fast as it snaps out.

Because then you are ready to do it again.

I sank to my knees, the shock kicking in but the pain still some distance away, touching my side as he took half a step towards me, telling me what he had wanted to tell me all along.

'You stupid flat-footed bastard,' he said, not loud, this between the two of us. 'What the fuck do you think we do with them when we've sucked out all the juice? Let them go home to Mummy and Daddy?'

He turned away.

I was on my knees. Not falling, not getting up. Stunned, looking with wonder at the palm of my hand.

Nothing but fresh blood.

I looked up and saw Gane back away from the blade in Fat Roy's hand, and I saw him step backwards into nothing and fall away into the blackness.

And then I was on my feet and climbing the last few stairs, Fat Roy looking down into the space where Gane had fallen, the knife by his side, still slick with my blood.

'Hey,' I said, and he turned towards me.

And as we were facing each other, and I was a few steps lower, my right fist was on a direct line to his heart.

It was one straight punch. Full force. In the heart.

Fat Roy staggered backwards and his eyes were wide with horror as he stepped into nothing.

He screamed all the way down.

I clutched my side, still not feeling the pain as I stared into the black hole and at the two bodies that lay in the darkness two storeys below.

They were not moving. Gane opened his mouth as if to say something and I stopped and saw the black blood come spilling from his mouth. Then I kept going, gripping the broken banister and edging as far as I could around the rim of the smashed staircase before throwing myself over the distance that was left.

Then I was running down an empty corridor, the destruction in the house not so pronounced up here, the paper peeling and cracks showing and moss on the carpet but no weather damage, no animals using it for a toilet. My left hand on the stab wound in my gut, feeling the warm blood pulsing out against my palm.

And I called his name.

I kept calling his name.

'Bradley! Bradley! Bradley!'

I threw open doors.

Empty rooms.

The rooms all the same. Swag velvet curtains limp with age and the only furniture the odd bare mattress. But rubble everywhere. Smashed bits of plaster and tiles and bricks, as though a war had passed through this luxurious wasteland.

'Bradley! Bradley! Bradley!'

And then I was in the room with the bodies.

They lay entwined, half-sleeping, half-naked, the mattresses pulled together, waiting for some terrible call, and as I stood in the doorway they stirred and I recoiled at the sound of all that shifting flesh.

It was like a pit of snakes that had been disturbed more than a room full of children who had been woken from their fitful dreams. They moved at the sound of my voice and my flesh crawled at the sound of that slow, slothful movement.

'Police officer! I'll be back! You're safe now!'

The boy was in the room at the end of the corridor.

The last room.

Locked.

I kicked at the lock. That is what you must do. You must bring the full force of the heel of your strongest foot to bear on exactly the spot where the door is locked.

And then it will fly open.

The boy was lying face down on a single bed with just an old white sheet beneath him.

He was wearing a T-shirt and pants and there was a single streak of blood towards the top of one thigh.

And I knew the boy was dead before I felt the pulse in his wrist, before I felt the pulse in his neck.

I knew he was dead before I looked into his open eyes.

I sank to the floor beside the bed, suddenly too exhausted to remain standing, and I hung my head as the tears came, all those useless tears of rage and grief that change nothing.

'Please God. Please God. Please God.'

I might have said it or I might have thought it. I don't know. And I wondered what exactly I was asking God for because it was too late for Him to help me now.

Or the child.

And I choked on the thought of the mother waiting for her son in the block of flats they call the Barrier Block, just around the corner from Electric Avenue, as with one hand I stemmed the blood pumping from my stomach and with the other I held the lifeless hand of four-year-old Michael McCarthy of Brixton.

FEBRUARY

KNOWN OFFENDERS

CHAPTER 17

'Your family are here,' the nurse said.

I stared at the open door until Scout appeared. She hovered there uncertainly for a moment, wearing her school uniform but matched with her favourite trainers, the ones with the lights in the heels that flashed when she moved. They sparkled green and blue in the hospital gloom. She walked to the bed where I was sitting as the Murphys piled shyly into the room behind her.

They were all there. Mrs Murphy and Big Mikey. Little Mikey in his work clothes leading Shavon and Damon by the hand. Siobhan holding Baby Mikey.

My eyes stung with relief and gratitude.

What the hell would I do without them?

Then Scout was by my side, not quite touching me, but leaning in, a five-year-old girl with something urgent to say.

I leaned towards her.

'I don't want you to get hurt any more, OK?' she whispered. 'Is it a deal?'

My heart filled up with guilt and shame and a

terrible helplessness. I believe it was shame more than anything. Scout's words choked my throat and stung my eyes and for long moments I could not speak. I held her close so that she would not see my eyes shining. She deserved a far better father than me.

'It's a deal, Scout,' I managed, and I knew the raw terror of the lone parent, the terrible knowledge that you are the last line of defence between your child and all that is rotten in the world.

I kissed her on the top of her head and she smelled of shampoo and sugar and felt-tip pens and that fresh biscuit smell that you get on young dogs. In response she placed her small hands on my face and stared at me hard. I hung my head, choking down the feelings that threatened to overwhelm me.

Live, I told myself. Just live. You have to live for long enough to raise this beautiful child. Don't you know that much, you stupid man? There's nobody else to do it.

Then it was time to stop whispering. Scout and I moved away from each other. The Murphys had gifts – fruit, chocolate and a small bouquet – and as I thanked them they stared at me with real concern.

'I'm sorry for all this,' I said to Mrs Murphy, feeling that I owed her an explanation. 'It comes with the job.'

'I understand, sweetheart,' she said, but with a tiny flinch that made me feel my job was becoming harder for her to understand.

Because she loved Scout, too.

My mouth twisted into what was meant to be a reassuring smile.

'You should see the other guy,' I said, and that got a nervous laugh from Little Mikey and Big Mikey, although Mrs Murphy and Siobhan didn't smile.

They all watched me as I gasped with a sudden jolt of pain. Mrs Murphy placed a hand on Scout's shoulder and my daughter looked up at her.

My side hurt about as much as flesh always will hurt when a piece of sharpened steel has been stuck into it. It was a heavy, throbbing pain than spread out from the small wound into the rest of my torso, making it feel as if it was made of some material so dense and heavy that I felt I would never be able to walk properly again.

But I knew I had been lucky.

If you have to get stabbed, then the stomach is one of the better places for it to happen.

Because blood loss and organ failure are what kill stab victims. If your attacker doesn't slice an artery, and if there is no internal bleeding, and if you don't bleed out – and if the shock doesn't kill you with a heart attack or stroke – then you just have to sit around eating grapes for a day or so while they monitor your blood pressure and core body temperature, sucking up the pain as you count your blessings. There are worse things that can happen to a copper than getting stabbed in the stomach. I considered myself lucky that Fat

Roy didn't know enough to stick his knife in my heart or my neck or my lungs or my eye – in one of the places where if the haemorrhage doesn't kill you, then the shock will.

'How's Stan?' I said. It was strange how much of our conversation revolved around that small red dog.

'He's in my van!' Big Mikey said, stunned at this unexpected turn of events.

'I love Stan,' little Mikey said.

'He's a good boy,' said Mrs Murphy.

'But he's started jumping on other dogs all the time,' Scout said, laughing and frowning with concern at the same time. *'I'm Stan! Who are you? I'm Stan! Who are you?'*

We all laughed. That's exactly what he was like.

'I think he's reaching sexual maturity,' Scout said, and the Murphys all immediately stopped laughing and didn't know where to look. She leaned in to me again.

'Listen,' she whispered.

'I'm listening,' I whispered.

'I want to help you with your work.'

'Listen. You do help, Scout. By being a good girl for Mrs Murphy and by keeping an eye on Stan and our home. By trying hard at school. And I'll be out of here tomorrow.'

She shook me with all the ferocity of a five-year-old who demands to be understood.

'I want to be with you always,' Scout said.

'And you always are,' I told her, tapping my heart. 'In here.'

She copied me, tapping the badge of her school blazer.

'Don't forget our deal,' she said. 'OK, Daddy?'

'Come here, you.'

I held out my hands and Scout came to me and I hugged her as hard as I dared.

My beautiful, smart, deal-making daughter at five years old.

There was almost nothing of her and she was my world.

The real pain came in the night and it felt exactly like the thing that had made the pain. The real pain was like a few inches of good steel cutting through that exact amount of fragile human meat. The real pain was a blade that cut through flesh and veins and muscle and then spread out through the rest of my body and into my head and into my dreams.

The sleeping pills they had dosed me with were not nearly enough to stop me waking with a gasp. Edie Wren was sitting in the little room's only chair.

'It's a mess,' she said. 'A bloody shambles.'

I couldn't tell if she was talking to me or herself. The sleeping pills were a thick fog in my brain.

But I remembered when we were at Oak Hill Farm. I remembered the pictures of Mary Wood, young and beautiful and dead, above the bed in the caravan. I remembered the fists and the boots and the fury of the mob. I remembered Peter Nawkins being arrested, and getting away.

'Did we get him yet?'

She shook her head.

'Not yet. But every copper in the country is looking for him. The big lump can't run for long.'

And as a wave of nausea swept over me and the fog in my head seemed to clear, I remembered the house on The Bishops Avenue, Wren being knocked out with one punch, the hiss of acid burning Whitestone's clothes and flesh and the way Gane had looked after falling two storeys.

I remembered holding the hand of the dead child.

I swallowed the sickness that made me feel like gagging and I blinked, trying to understand what was happening as Wren, as if in sympathy, retched noisily into the wastepaper basket. Nothing came up.

'Sorry,' she said, wiping her mouth on the back of her hand. 'I don't know what's wrong with me. You get hit in the head hard enough and you feel like someone pressed the pause button on time.'

'You feel really sick, don't you?'

'Do you think that might be a really stupid question?'

'Seeing little black stars?'

She nodded.

'You shouldn't be walking about alone,' I said. 'It's *concussion*, Edie.'

She cursed me in the darkness and I saw that her eyes were wet with tears.

'You shouldn't be going home alone,' I insisted. 'We can get you a ride . . .'

'I've got a ride,' she said, and I now saw the man beyond the doorway, waiting for her.

He was a good-looking man in a suit and tie, like a politician on the campaign trail, but a lot older than I had expected, maybe the far side of forty. With his shock of black hair, neatly trimmed, and the fitness of the college athlete who stayed in shape for the next twenty years, he was undoubtedly a handsome man, and he knew it. He's no stranger to a jumbo-sized bottle of male moisturiser, I thought. When he looked at his watch, I saw his wedding ring glint in the strip lighting of the hospital corridor and I wondered what lies he had told to his wife back at home tonight.

Edie Wren's married man.

She was staring at me defiantly.

'How's the boss?' I said.

'Lucky. If you can call getting battery acid on the back of your neck lucky. DCI Whitestone is tough. She'll have a scar for life, of course. But the collar of her coat took most of it. She's going to need a new coat.'

I swallowed hard.

'And Gane's dead, isn't he?'

'No. Fat Roy was DOA – but not Curtis.'

'But . . . I saw him fall.'

'He's alive.'

We were silent in the darkness. The hospital made no sound but not far away I could hear the heavy traffic around Archway.

'Gane broke his spinal cord,' Wren said. 'But he's not dead.'

I could hear her trying to sort out her breathing. 'It's a bit worse than that,' she said.

Daylight.

The prettiest girl I had ever seen was standing by my bed. Not a girl – a woman. But a woman who had all of her life ahead of her. A blonde in a red coat. For the rest of my life I knew I would always look twice whenever I saw a blonde in a red coat.

'Who was he?' Charlotte Gatling asked quietly, her right hand nervously twisting over her left wrist, that strange gesture, as if she was holding hands with herself.

The fog was still in my head but I knew who she was talking about. I closed my eyes and I could see him. I knew that I would always see him now.

'His name was Michael McCarthy,' I said. 'He was four years old. He lived with his mum in South London. Brixton.' I opened my eyes and looked at her. 'He was a little boy who never stood a chance.'

She sat on the bed.

'You thought they had my nephew,' she said. 'You were looking for Bradley.'

I nodded. I felt like I had failed everyone. Especially Michael McCarthy and Bradley Wood.

'The man on the news,' she said. 'The man they

are hunting – Peter Nawkins. Is he the one who killed my sister?'

'We found evidence that connected him to her.'

'What evidence?'

'You don't want to know.'

A flash of impatience in the blue eyes.

'Believe me, Detective Wolfe – I want to know.'

'Peter Nawkins was obsessed with your sister. We discovered pictures of her – I don't know, hundreds of images, maybe thousands – above his bed. And then he ran. He's running still. The innocent don't run.'

'Will you catch him?'

'Catching him is an absolute certainty.'

'Anything – any sign – my nephew . . .'

Her eyes were pleading with me and I knew she wanted me to tell her something reassuring.

'We'll keep searching for Bradley,' I said. 'And we will never stop until it's over.'

She nodded, satisfied. And then something inside her seemed to collapse and she covered her face with her hands. I watched her sobbing with her face hidden.

'That poor child,' she said. 'Poor little Michael. What he must have suffered . . .'

She wasn't crying for her nephew. She was crying for a child she had never known and that stirred some feeling inside me that I thought had gone forever.

I touched her arm lightly.

She composed herself.

'The nurse said you had a knife wound,' she said. 'Are you in pain?'

'The pain's getting better,' I said.

'Have you been stabbed before?'

'This is a first. And also a last, I hope.'

'The men you found – the ones that did this to you – they're nothing to do with what happened to my sister and her family?'

I shook my head.

'Thank you,' she said. 'You were looking for Bradley. You were risking your life to find him. You were putting your life on the line when I know you have a family of your own. And I can tell you – he's not dead. *Bradley's not dead.* Do you believe me?'

'Sure.'

She squeezed my hand.

In her perfect Grace Kelly face I could see the ghost of her sister and I could understand how Peter Nawkins would look up from his labours and fall in love with that face.

Just one look. That is sometimes all it takes.

I could imagine Nawkins looking up outside her home and being poleaxed by all that smiling blue-eyed perfection. I could see it so easily, and understand how that lonely, simple-minded man could look at Mary Wood's face in the dying light of the summer and believe that she was the best thing he had ever seen in his life. What I could not understand was why he would want to destroy something he loved so much.

I placed my free hand on top of Charlotte's hand. I realised I had stopped breathing.

'Let me hold you for a moment,' she said, and looked at me for some response, but I could not come up with anything, I was completely out of responses.

So she wrapped her arms around me and held me in an awkward embrace. I could smell her perfume and, beyond that, the beautiful fact of her existence. Her head was close to mine and when I turned to look at her she pulled away.

I watched her smooth her red coat and do up a button that had somehow come undone.

'My brother's waiting for me,' she said.

CHAPTER 18

I saw her again when I went back to work. I looked up from my workstation in MIR-1 and there she was on the big flat-screen TV, her face pale and impassive, and one hundred cameras clicking like crazy every time she raised her head.

It was late afternoon and they were having a press conference down on the second floor of West End Central. Charlotte Gatling settled herself at a long table next to her brother Nils with Detective Chief Superintendent Swire next to him, the Chief Super's hand covering the microphone in front of her as a Media Liaison Officer leaned in for a few last words.

'Thank you for coming, everyone,' the MLO said. 'DCS Swire will be making a statement about recent events. We will not be taking any questions. Thank you.'

Charlotte turned to look at the MLO as she stepped away and the battery of cameras clicked in a furious attempt to capture the moment.

'Grief and beauty,' Wren said to herself. 'They love it, don't they?'

The door of MIR-1 opened and Dr Joe Stephen walked in, and when I saw how the forensic psychologist looked at us – a mixture of shock and pity – I knew our MIT had taken a real beating.

Wren was still muttering to herself, displaying all the classic symptoms of concussion, and the million nerve cells in her brain that were never coming back. I looked all right but the bandages that covered my stab wound were wet with the slow warm ooze of fresh blood, leaving a growing stain on my shirt. And on one side of her neck, Whitestone had a livid pink acid burn.

I suddenly wondered if she had had the same kind of conversation with her son that I had had with Scout. Did the boy dream of protecting his mother? Did he want her to quit her job? Was he afraid of what would become of him if his mother were gone? And was she? I wanted to talk to Whitestone about all of these things, but I did not know where to start.

Dr Joe touched the back of the empty chair at DI Gane's workstation.

'Did we pick up Nawkins?' he said.

'Not yet,' I said. 'Where will he run to, Dr Joe?'

He thought about it.

'Where is he loved?'

Wren laughed bitterly.

'Nowhere,' I said.

'Then he'll just run,' said Dr Joe.

'They're starting,' Whitestone said.

'First of all, our condolences to the family of

Michael McCarthy,' DCS Swire began. 'I can confirm that the recent operation on The Bishops Avenue was not – as we first believed – related to the investigation into the murder of the Wood family and the abduction of Bradley Wood.' She paused, making eye contact with the room. She was a fine public speaker, moving at exactly her own pace. 'Arrests have been made. Charges will follow.' A glance down at her notes. 'Fifteen children, ranging in age from nine to fifteen, have been taken into the care and custody of social services.' Another pause. 'We remain totally committed to finding those responsible for the murders of Brad Wood, Mary Wood, Marlon Wood, Piper Wood and the abduction of Bradley Wood.' Her mouth set in hard lines. 'We are confident that Peter Nawkins can assist us with our enquiries and would ask anyone with knowledge of his current whereabouts to contact the number behind me. Do not approach this man. He is a convicted killer and quite capable of killing again. Thank you.'

They got up to leave. Scarlet Bush, the chief crime reporter of the *Daily Post*, was on her feet.

'Charlotte! Charlotte!'

She instinctively turned to the sound of her name. The cameras clicked with excitement.

The MLO was holding up her hands.

'We're not taking questions!'

Scarlet Bush ignored her.

'Charlotte, what would you say to the people who have taken Bradley?'

There was silence in the room. Even the cameras were still as Charlotte stared at the reporter and then beyond her, to something only she could see.

'Please,' Charlotte said. 'I would say – please.'

Her brother had her by the arm. He appeared to be trying to get her to move away. But she did not move and for the first time I saw the steel in her.

'I would say – *please don't hurt him,*' she said. 'I would say – whoever you are – whatever you have done – please see that Bradley is just a little boy who never hurt anyone and who does not deserve to be hurt . . .'

She lowered her head. Nil Gatling's face was a mask. He was no longer trying to pull her away.

'I would say – please let Bradley come home.'

Then the press conference was over and DCS Swire came up to MIR-1 to explain to us why that was never going to happen.

'You've been in the wars,' DCS Swire said, coming into MIR-1. 'Let me have a look at you, Pat.'

DCS Swire inspected the burn on Whitestone's neck. A layer of skin about the size of a saucer had been scorched away behind her left ear, and the raw angry pink mark would be there for the rest of her life. Swire hugged her and Whitestone winced with what looked like a combination of embarrassment and physical pain.

Wren and I exchanged a look. We had never seen DCS Swire hug anyone before. Wren grinned nervously, as if she might be next in line for a hug.

Whitestone's arms hung awkwardly by her side but after a while she gently patted Swire's back, as if at once thanking her and telling her – enough.

Swire stepped back.

'How's DI Gane?' she said, staring hard.

'It's not great,' Whitestone said.

Swire nodded grimly. She was a cold, controlled woman, not easy to like. But I thought I saw for the first time how much she cared about every one of us.

'And how are you doing, Pat?' she said.

Whitestone pulled a face, and I saw her fight to control her emotions. She did not say that she should have waited – for more backup, for the hats and bats, for the guns. But DCS Swire knew that was exactly what she was thinking.

'You made the right call, Pat,' she said quietly.

Whitestone swallowed hard, and tried for a smile that would not come.

'Did I?' she said, a glint of tears behind her glasses, which she removed, angrily wiping her eyes with the back of her hand, looking half-blind and easy to hurt until she had jammed her spectacles back on. She sniffed once and blinked at DCS Swire, waiting for the rest of it, her face expressionless.

'There could have been greater loss of life if you had waited,' Swire told her. 'There could have been more than one dead child. You did the right thing. But maybe if you had waited you wouldn't have got so knocked about.'

'Knocked about,' Whitestone said flatly.

We were all masters of understatement. But *knocked about* didn't quite say it this time. Not with Gane in the hospital.

DCS Swire nodded. She wasn't giving Whitestone a line to comfort her. This was what she believed. Whitestone had made the right call and we had done our job.

'We'll take good care of DI Gane,' Swire said. 'That's what we do. We take care of our own. You know that, don't you?'

'Yes, ma'am.'

Swire turned to look at the rest of us.

'You smashed one of the biggest paedophile rings in northern Europe. A lot of evil men are going away for a very long time. And a lot of children have been saved.'

I thought of Michael McCarthy. I knew I would always think of Michael McCarthy.

'You all understand our priority now?' Swire said.

'Find the boy,' Whitestone said. 'Find Bradley Wood.'

Swire shook her head.

'The boy is dead,' she said quietly.

We let it sink in.

'*What?*' Wren said.

'Bradley Wood must be dead by now,' DCS Swire said. 'He's gone and he's never coming back. Maybe he's within a mile of his home in Highgate. Maybe he's in a river or a skip or a sewer out in the wilds of Essex. *But how can he possibly be alive?* What conceivable scenario encourages us to believe that child is still alive?'

We were silent.

Because it was true.

It was impossible to see how Bradley Wood's life could have been spared.

Charlotte and her brother might want to believe that Bradley was being taken care of by someone kind. Perhaps they had to believe it because it was the only way they could stay sane. Perhaps holding on to that belief was the only way that they could snatch a couple of hours of sleep every night.

But it didn't happen in the real world.

In the real world children were taken for sex and then they were disposed of.

Or children were taken to shut them up and then they were disposed of.

They were never stolen to be given a happy, loving home. The people who are desperate to love a child do not steal somebody else's child. That is a straw that desperate families cling to. And I understood why.

I would have clung to that straw myself.

'Bradley is never coming home,' DCS Swire said. 'Bradley Wood is gone. If he was lucky, it was over quickly. And if we're lucky, we'll find a body to give to the family. But let's not kid ourselves. There are no happy endings for children that are lost for this long. So just nail the perp. Just get Peter Nawkins. Dead or alive, it makes no odds to me.

Just get the bastard so we can shut this circus down.'

So we drove out to Oak Hill Farm.

And we tore that place apart.

CHAPTER 19

The thousand faces of Mary Wood smiled down on the single bed of Peter Nawkins. A SOCO on a stepladder photographed the shrine on the caravan's ceiling while another SOCO filmed it. As they finished their work, the photographs started to slowly come down, and were carefully placed in evidence bags. All those smiling faces captured forever behind cellophane and a file number.

Sean Nawkins stared up at the shrine with a sick look on his face.

'I don't believe it,' he muttered to himself, in the tone of a man who believes the truth at last.

'And you're telling me that you didn't know this was here?' I said.

He kept looking at the pictures of Mary.

'How would I know?' he said.

'You never came into this room?'

'He was my brother, not my wife.'

'But you've lied about everything else,' I said. 'You didn't tell us you'd done work for the Woods. You didn't tell us that your brother was at The

Garden. You didn't tell us that your brother had met Mary Wood. *Look at me.*'

He tore his eyes from the shrine. And for the first time I saw something like resignation in his eyes.

All around us a Specialist Search Team were removing the panels from the caravan walls, pulling up the floorboards, removing light fixtures. Whitestone and Wren crouched in a corner of the crowded caravan, watching the SST unscrew an electrical socket.

'I was trying to protect him, that's all,' Nawkins said quietly.

'You were perverting the course of justice,' I said.

He snorted, the old defiance coming back. 'At worst I'm a reluctant witness.'

'Reluctant witness? What are you – a lawyer now? Your firm did work for the family!'

'Months ago! Six months before . . . it happened.'

I took half a step closer to him. With the SOCOs and the Specialist Search Team and what was left of our MIT, Peter Nawkins' little bedroom was fast resembling the Black Hole of Calcutta.

'You – and your brother – met the Wood family and withheld that information from our murder investigation,' I said.

'We met her once!' he protested. 'And only her. *Not* the father. *Not* the children. Just the mother. Mrs Wood. Mary. On a very hot day in August. She brought us lemonade. And most of them don't. These rich London types.' His eyes clouded with resentment that was old and deep. 'They would give a dog a drink before they'd give it to a gang of men.'

In my mind I saw them on the drive, the crew of men, sweaty and shirtless over the boiling black tarmac, and Mary Wood coming out with a tray of lemonade, and Peter Nawkins looking up and staring at her as if she was the most beautiful woman he had ever seen in his life.

'Did your brother Peter interact with Mrs Wood?'

'No,' he said, then shook his head, as if he was finally anxious to hold nothing back. 'She held the tray while Peter took a glass of home-made lemonade. He thanked her. She smiled at him.'

I waited.

'That's it?'

'Yes.'

'Did your brother ever mention her?'

'We never saw her again. He never mentioned her. A woman – some housekeeper – collected the glasses later.'

'How were you paid?'

'Cash. In an envelope Mr Wood left for us. All fifties. The housekeeper gave it to me on the last day.'

'Did you see the child? Bradley Wood?' I took a photograph from my wallet and showed it to him. A passport-sized photograph of a smiling little boy. Sean Nawkins did not look at it. He stared past my shoulder.

'I've seen it already,' he said.

'Look at it again,' I said. 'I'm asking politely.'

He looked at it, his mouth twisting.

'The little boy was with her,' he said. 'What can I tell you? That's it. Just a little boy with his mother as she gave a drink to a gang of men.'

He hung his head.

'Have a look at this, Max,' Whitestone said.

The electrical sockets were all off the wall and scattered across the floor. The SST had found something behind one of them. There was a matchbox and a set of keys on the latex-gloved palms of DC Wren. I picked up the matchbox and turned it in my own latex-gloved hand. Red words on a white background.

The Full English
Holloway Road, Holloway, N7
'Good' food. 'Healthy' too.

'Come over here,' I told Sean Nawkins, and I held out my hand to him as he crossed the wreck of the caravan.

'You know this gaff?' I said. 'The Full English on the Holloway Road? Where's that? Around Highbury Corner?'

Nawkins looked as though he was going to throw up.

'The Full English is at the other end of the Holloway Road,' he said.

'Around Archway?'

'Yes.'

'You could walk to it from The Garden, then?'
He nodded.

'And you did,' I said. It wasn't a question.

'We would stop there on our way to the job,'
Nawkins said.

I opened the matchbox. Inside there were four
figures scribbled in biro. I showed them to
Whitestone and Wren.

1 0 1 0

'One thousand and ten?' Wren said.

'Ten-ten,' I said.

'When was Mary Wood's birthday?' Whitestone
asked.

Wren consulted her phone. Tapped a few keys,
waited a few seconds. Then she had it.

'Tenth October,' she said. 'So it's a birthday.'

'It's more than that,' I said. 'What do most people
choose for a secret code? Their birthday. Get
Tactical Support to try the burglar alarm in The
Garden. I bet ten-ten still works.'

'Then this was how he gained entry,' Whitestone
said. 'He knew the code – guessed it or was told
it or most likely saw someone using it – and he
had a stolen set of keys.'

I held out my hand and Wren gave me the keys.
They weighed almost nothing in my hand. One
for the door and one for its deadlock. I looked at
them more closely. They were shiny and new.
Hardly a scratch on them.

'He probably borrowed a set for a few hours and duplicated them,' I said. 'These don't look stolen. They look like they're brand-new copies.'

'Were the men using the toilet in the house?' Whitestone said. 'It's not uncommon for these big houses to have some kind of Portaloo for the workers. But if that wasn't the case in The Garden . . .'

We looked up and saw Nawkins slipping out of the caravan. I followed him. A thin blue line of uniformed coppers encircled the outside perimeter of Oak Hill Farm, keeping back a crowd of locals.

Echo Nawkins paraded inside the camp, a pack of dogs barking furiously around her, as she exchanged furious abuse with the locals beyond the fence.

'I've seen this before,' Nawkins said, more to himself than me. 'I know what happens next. They always hate us. But then something happens. Some kind of spark that sets it all off. And suddenly people start dying.'

I knew he was thinking of his dead wife, burned alive in a caravan on the other side of the city.

'You have to get my brother soon,' he said. 'If you don't get him soon, they're going to torch this place.'

'Then you better hope we find him,' I said.

From the middle of the mob beyond the fence, someone chucked a brick. It shattered in the middle of Echo's pack of dogs and sent them into a frenzy of barking. Echo gave the crowd the finger and screamed a torrent of abuse. Then she picked up what remained of the brick and threw it back. The brick was answered with bottles.

And I watch a shower of broken glass spray across the boots of the young uniformed coppers who stood where they always stand.

Right in the middle.

I stopped at the hospital on my way home.

Even though it was nearly midnight, Gane's mother was there.

'Mrs Gane? I'm DC Wolfe. I worked with your son.'

The elderly West Indian lady adjusted her hat and carefully stood up. Then she took my hands and smiled. She had dressed in her best clothes to sit by the side of her son's bed in the Homerton. There were screens pulled around his bed. I thought I could hear him breathing behind them.

'His friend,' she said, the accent still more Trinidad than London after a lifetime in the country. 'You were his friend at work. His *good* friend.'

I smiled and nodded and had no words.

The truth was that DI Gane and I were never really friends.

When I joined Homicide and Serious Crime Command, DI Curtis Gane had looked at me as if I was fresh off the bus. And he was right. Gane had seen things that were still ahead of me. All the same, we were, I believe, on our way to becoming friends. This was true. But now that was all over. Now there was no time left.

'Would you like to see him, sweetheart?' Mrs Gane said, and I nodded mutely.

We slipped between the plastic screens and the sight of him made me gasp. His neck was in some kind of collar. A thick tube snaked into his throat. He didn't look like a man they were attempting to keep alive. He looked like a dead man.

'He's broken his first and second cervical vertebrae,' she said quietly.

I choked down the shock and grief.

'I don't know what that means,' I said.

'It means his spine and his head are no longer connected.' She touched his forehead very lightly. 'But it's still him, isn't it? It's still my Curtis. They are going to stabilise him and then they're going to see if there's anything they can do to fix it.'

I had no words. There were no words. And I suddenly saw that Mrs Gane was exhausted.

'If you need to go home,' I said, 'I'll stay with him for the night.'

She looked doubtful.

'I don't want to leave him, but there's Molly,' she said. 'I should see to Molly.'

I nodded. I had no idea who Molly might be.

'The cat,' she said, then she laughed. 'Ridiculous, really. My son has this happen to him and I worry about the cat.'

'It's not ridiculous,' I said.

'And it's difficult to wash here.'

'Go,' I said. 'Please, Mrs Gane. I'll not leave him until you come back. I'll be here all the time. I promise.'

She left us. I settled in a plastic chair. I felt like praying. I felt like weeping. I found that both were beyond me.

So I watched his face, and I closed my eyes, and the dream-like noises of a hospital at night seeped into my waking dreams.

He spoke at the end of the night, the hospital noises dying at last, and the washed-out grey of a February dawn breaking over the East End rooftops.

He said just four words, and I did not know if they were said to me, or himself, or the life that had been left behind. But those four words gripped my heart and made me fear for what the remains of his life would look like.

Because he was saying that his mother was as wrong as she could possibly be.

'This is not me,' said DI Curtis Gane.

CHAPTER 20

I left work early the next day so I could go to the Black Museum and stare at the unholy relics of the Slaughter Man, but the rusting cattle gun and faded newspaper clippings said absolutely nothing to me. Instead I found my eyes drawn to a display for police officers who had been killed in the line of duty.

OUR MURDERED COLLEAGUES, it said.

Inside the glass case there were more than a hundred years of faces, all of them official mugshots. Some of the faces were expressionless, and some of them were suppressing a smile.

There were faces from the early part of the twentieth century, the black-and-white grown grey with age, and there were more recent faces, with the haircuts and facial hair out of style but the colours still fresh.

Some of the names were famous, because some of the deaths were so shocking they had made front-page news.

WPC Yvonne Joyce Fletcher. 17 April 1984. Age 25. Shot.

It didn't say anything about the coward bastard gunman inside the Libyan Embassy.

PC Keith Henry Blakelock. 6 October 1985. Age 40. Stabbed.

It didn't say anything about the coward bastard mob that tried to decapitate him.

But then it didn't need to. There was one man I had known and loved. *DCI Victor Mallory.* And I saw him in the basement room with the screaming woman and the flames and the knife plunging into his neck about one fatal inch above the top of his Kevlar Stealth.

Age 50. Stabbed.

Yet most of the names were unknown. Perhaps they had been a headline for a day. Perhaps not. They had died in many different ways and yet the same causes came round again and again.

Shot. Stabbed. Shot. Stabbed. Run over. Run over. Rammed by vehicle being pursued. Bludgeoned during an arrest. Bludgeoned during an arrest. Shot. Stabbed.

'You done?' asked Sergeant John Caine.

He was closing the Black Museum down for the day and the weak winter sunlight glinted on the knives and swords and firearms that are piled up in Room 101 of New Scotland Yard like a boot sale from hell.

I turned once more to the exhibit for the Slaughter Man. The scratched and rusting cattle gun. The fading newspaper article.

RITUAL SLAUGHTER ON
ESSEX FARM
*Slaughter Man executes father and sons
in midnight killing spree*

A killer was jailed for life yesterday for murdering a father and his three grown-up sons with a bolt gun used to slaughter livestock.

Peter Nawkins, 17, had been engaged to the only daughter of Ian Burns of Hawksmoor Farm, Essex. When the engagement was ended, Nawkins broke into Hawksmoor Farm and slaughtered Farmer Burns and his sons Ian Junior, 23, Martin, 20, and Donald, 17, before setting fire to their home. Mrs Doris Burns, 48, and her daughter Carolyn, 16, were present but escaped unharmed by the killer the press have dubbed the Slaughter Man.

And the two photographs.

The Burns family laughing under their Christmas tree. The burly father and his petite wife. The three sons grown big on the farm.

And Peter Nawkins being taken down after being found guilty of murdering the father and his boys, the multiple murderer with the film-star looks and a natty nickname. I had stared at it all for a long time but it gave me no clues.

I found my mind drifting to Curtis Gane in the Homerton Hospital and my gaze to the glass case, remembering those who had died in the war we fight every day, the war without end, the war that could never be lost or won.

'Nothing for the ones who didn't die,' I said. 'The ones who were broken and have to find a way to carry on living.'

'No, there's nothing for them,' Sergeant Caine said with a flash of temper. 'But do you think that means they're forgotten?'

I shook my head, feeling a stab of shame. 'No.'

He began turning off the lights.

'And you still haven't got him,' he said. It wasn't a question.

'Where will he run to, John? Dr Joe – our forensic psychologist – said he would run to the place that he's loved.'

Sergeant Caine snorted.

'I don't know about that.' He thought about it. 'But it's true that most villains run to a woman. The woman *they* love. And what she might think about them usually doesn't come into it.'

I thought of Mary Wood smiling down on the lonely bed of Peter Nawkins and I saw her lifeless body on a stainless-steel table in the Iain West Suite.

'That's not going to happen.'

'Why not?'

'Because the woman Peter Nawkins loved is dead.'

John Caine snorted impatiently.

'I'm not talking about Mary Wood. He didn't love her. He might have been obsessed with her, but he didn't even know her. I'm talking about the farmer's daughter.'

'The farmer's daughter?'

'The one he wanted to marry until her dad and brothers decided they would rather cut his nuts off. That's what started the whole sorry mess, isn't it? Boy meets girl. Then the girl's father and brothers think that castration would make a nice engagement present.'

'John, that's half a lifetime ago. It was 1980 when Nawkins went down.'

'So what? What do you reckon he was thinking about for those twenty years inside? The woman he did it for.'

I smiled at him.

'What an old romantic you are, John. Do you really think a man can love a woman for so long?'

He looked affronted.

'I think if he loves her for anything less, then whatever it is, it sure as hell ain't love.'

We looked at the old newspaper article and the girl laughing with her family.

The girl that Peter Nawkins loved.

'*Carolyn Burns, 16,*' said John Caine. 'Whatever happened to her?'

Before going home I stopped off at the Smithfield ABC, knowing that I needed to exhaust myself to make sleep a possibility, happy to put on a pair of fourteen-ounce Lonsdale gloves and bang the heavy bag until my arms were sore.

Swinging from my hips, keeping the rhythm, keeping it neat, not hearing whatever was on the sound system. Not hearing the other sounds of the gym, hearing only the sound of sweat-slick leather striking leather until Fred said, 'Time.'

Smithfield ABC was filling up. A crowd of men – and they were all men – who had no intention of exercising were taking their place around the empty ring. This was always the way when some serious sparring was coming. The men wandered in off the street like a flock of birds responding to a signal that only they could hear.

'Do your stretching,' Fred said. 'Don't forget your abductors.'

Rocky strolled to the side of the ring.

He rubbed Vaseline on his face, stuck in his mouthguard and climbed into the ring. No head-guard. His opponent was a much bigger black lad. A bell rang and they began to dance around each other. And I saw now that it wasn't speed that made him so special. It was timing. Speed beats power. But timing beats speed. Rocky's opponent was strong and fast, a young pro with an unbeaten record. But he lacked Rocky's uncanny sense of timing. Rocky would feint a jab, draw the counter and then slip inside, throwing three-, four- and five-punch combinations and then getting out as his opponent swung at thin air. To hit without getting hit in return. It was almost impossible. You had to be dusted with magic. And he was.

Then suddenly Echo Nawkins was by my side.

'He's great, isn't he?' she said. 'Rocky.'

'What are you doing here, Echo?'

Then I saw the way she was looking at Rocky and I understood immediately. She was crazy about him.

'He didn't do it,' she said, not looking at me. 'My Uncle Peter. You've got every copper in the country hunting him. *But he didn't kill those people.*'

'What makes you think that, Echo?'

'Jab, Rocky! Jab! He's not in your league, sweetheart!'

She still wasn't looking at me.

'How can you be so sure?' I said. 'You saw the ceiling of his caravan, didn't you? Don't be so naïve, just because he's your uncle.'

'I just *know*. I do. Why do you think he did it? Because you found a few pictures?'

'More than a few! And everybody at Oak Hill Farm has lied to me right from the off. Your father. Your uncle. Your boyfriend up there in the ring. They all led me to believe they had never been anywhere near The Garden. It's not true, is it?'

'Rocky's not my boyfriend,' she said, blushing furiously. She leaned on the ring, her head resting on her arms, trying to hide her embarrassment. 'And nobody's lied to you. They just haven't told you the whole truth. But why would they? You're the law and you hate us.'

'I don't hate you, Echo. But your uncle is a convicted murderer. He had a thousand pictures of Mary Wood above his bed. And somebody killed

Mary Wood and her family with your uncle's weapon of choice. Doesn't look good, does it?'

'I bet a lot of men had pictures of her. I bet a lot of men liked her. Men who didn't even know her.'

'It's not the pictures,' I said. 'Or even that he had the alarm code and keys for the house.'

'What then?'

'He ran,' I said. 'Innocent men don't run, Echo.'

She shook her head, laughing bitterly.

'Now who's being naïve?' she said. 'They do if they're scared enough.' She gave me a cold glance. 'If they think they're being fitted up for something they didn't do.'

In the ring Rocky had his opponent backed up against the ropes. The other lad dug his elbows into his ribs as Rocky let rip with the body shots. Then Rocky swung a single short upper cut down the middle and the black lad's head jerked back so fast it made the watching crowd wince with shock.

His legs went – in that sickening way that legs go when something has been turned off in the brain – splaying at awkward angles, collapsing under the weight of a man who had been robbed of his consciousness.

Fred was climbing into the ring before he hit the deck, waving it off.

Rocky watched his opponent fall with the detached, dispassionate stare of a man who was born to beat other men into submission.

They can teach you many things in a boxing gym. But they can't give you that killer instinct in your heart. Because it's not natural, I thought.

Rocky gave me his big wide grin, showing his gumshield as my phone began to vibrate.

WREN CALLING, it said.

'We've seen Nawkins,' she said.

CHAPTER 21

You could see the blue lights from miles away.

They were flashing and swirling on a southbound service station on the M11, the long straight run from London to Cambridge, and in the gloom of the afternoon they lit up fields covered with unbroken snow.

Around twenty response cars were parked all over the service station, from both the Essex Police Force and the Met. I flashed my warrant card at the perimeter, signed in and ducked under the tape. Whitestone and Wren were inside, with three men who had recently taken a beating. They could have been brothers – three Asians in their twenties who looked like they worked out. Especially on the heavy weights. One of them had a broken arm. Another was dabbing a wad of kitchen towel on to his ruined nose. All of them had faces that were cut and bruised.

'Tell my colleague what you told me,' Whitestone said.

The one with the broken arm sighed. Witnesses think they can tell their story once and we will get it. But we like to hear it again and again and again. Just in case it changes.

'A man tried to do a runner late thith morning,' he said, lisping as if he was still adjusting to a mouth full of broken teeth. 'We tried to stop him.'

'We've got CCTV,' Wren said.

On the black-and-white screen Peter Nawkins stood stock-still, staring at the pump as he filled the tank.

'I can see the plates,' I said.

'Yes, we ran the plates,' Wren confirmed. 'Nissan Micra was stolen from a supermarket car park in Brentwood this morning. Lady had a full week's shop in the boot. So he had a car – and all the Pringles he could eat – but he didn't have cash for gas.'

On the CCTV Peter Nawkins finished filling his tank and made to slip into the door on the passenger side of the Nissan. The man with the broken arm came into view. In the hand of the arm that was broken, he was holding a hammer. I gave him a look.

'You play rough out here,' I said.

'We get boy racers from Essex clocking up a ton in their Escorts and Capris,' he said. 'We get all the Camden Town cowboys coming out to sell weed to the students in Cambridge. Don't let the sight of a few cows by the side of the road fool you. This is not *The Archers*. We have to play rough.'

In the footage the hammer swung at Peter Nawkins' head. He caught it on one of his massive arms and fell upon the man, spinning him round and twisting

227

his arm up behind his back until his face writhed with agony as the bone snapped. Then the other two men were on Nawkins, both of them swinging hammers. Nawkins punched the first one to the ground with a single blow that flattened his nose. Then he seized the last man standing by the scruff of the neck and slammed his face into the side of the car until his body was limp and a wing mirror was hanging off. Nawkins slipped into the car and it immediately sped off, leaving the three men motionless on the forecourt.

Wren pressed stop.

'The lengths some people go to for a free tank of unleaded,' she said. She indicated the garage workers who had taken a beating. 'These gentlemen didn't see inside the car.'

I stared at them. 'How could you not see inside the car?'

They looked sheepish.

'They were too busy getting their hammers,' Wren said. 'Not that they did them much good.'

We stared again at the CCTV screen.

'He got into the passenger side,' I said. 'Someone was driving him.'

Wren nodded. 'So he's not alone,' she said. 'Where's he heading?'

I stared out at the motorway. The M11 is a fast road. But if you are heading south, it only takes you to one place.

'London,' I said.

★ ★ ★

There was a copse in the field next to the service station. Just a thicket of small trees in the middle of nowhere. I walked out to it, the ground as hard as marble beneath my feet, and pushed through the tangle of trees until I found the remains of a campfire in a small clearing.

The skin and bones of a young rabbit lay next to the fire. I stood staring at it for a while, shuddering with the cold. The winter was harsher out here in the countryside.

I took out my iPhone and began taking photographs.

When I got back to the service station Whitestone and Wren were with an elderly white man in muddy waterproofs. He was complaining to them about something.

'I told the local station about the break-in but they say there's nothing they can do,' he said. 'They're useless. I saw your lights and I thought you might be able to help me. You're London coppers, right? Not the bloody locals?'

'This gentleman owns the farm down the road,' Wren said. 'He had a burglary yesterday.'

He looked at me as if I might be the answer to his problems.

'What was taken?' I said.

'I told them that already,' he said.

'Tell him,' said Whitestone.

'Clothes, cash, some cutlery,' he said. 'And my game gun.'

I felt myself shiver.

'What kind of game gun?' I said.

'Twelve-bore shotgun.' He warmed to his theme. 'Remington Model 1900 12-gauge. It was my father's gun, and my grandfather's gun. Been in my family for over a hundred years. The first hammerless double-barrelled shotgun that Remington ever made. It's worth a few bob. And what I want to know is – will you get it back?'

'Any shells missing?'

He looked offended.

'I keep my shells in the safe,' he said, bristling self-righteously. 'What kind of a moron do you think I am? No shells missing.' Then he thought again, looking sheepish. 'Apart from what was in it, of course,' he said.

'So it was loaded?' I said. 'Both barrels?'

'Not much good if it's not loaded, is it?' the farmer said.

Wren was already on the phone putting out a general alert that Nawkins was armed with a twelve-bore shotgun. And I felt myself shudder with a feeling that had nothing to do with the cold.

It was more like feeling footsteps on my grave.

CHAPTER 22

When the day was winding down, and the rush-hour traffic on Savile Row was finally easing off, Whitestone glanced at her watch, got herself a coffee and took her laptop to a quiet corner of MIR-1, where she Skyped her son.

I only glimpsed the kid on the screen – mid-teens, that carefully tousled hair they all like now, a sullen and good-looking boy – and I tried not to hear their conversation – mostly Whitestone asking questions about school, and dinner, and domestic arrangements, while her boy – Justin was his name – responded with weary, one-word answers that all sounded like a sigh.

When she had finished, Whitestone looked over at me at my workstation and adjusted her glasses, as if remembering that I was a single parent too.

'Enough for one day, Max,' she said. 'Go home to Scout.'

'No rush,' I said. 'Scout has a friend.'

Scout had one of those friends that you remember fifty years later, the kind of friend where the pair

231

of you spend all your time in helpless laughter at the rest of the world.

Mia was a fair-haired little girl with a light Australian accent and she was there one day when I got home from work, shrieking with delight as Stan chased her and Scout around the massive empty space of our loft, and after that she never really went away. I could not imagine that she ever would. I had only spoken to Mia's parents on the phone, but they were warm, friendly Aussies, with none of the frosty shyness of the English, and Scout was having a sleepover with Mia tonight.

'Scout is staying with her friend,' I said, and I couldn't keep the pride out of my voice.

I felt that Scout and I were more like other families now that she had a special friend. I felt that we were winning.

'I ran the murdered farmer's daughter through the PNC,' Wren said, meaning the Police National Computer. 'Carolyn Burns.' She tapped on her keyboard and I saw that her face was still white with the shock of violence. 'I've got you two images – same photograph – one from the Passport Office and the other from the DVLA. It took a while because she's never broken the law.'

'Thanks. Send them across, will you?'

A face appeared on the screen. A haggard woman who looked far older than her middle forties. Wren was staring at the same photographs on her work-station. There was no resemblance to the pretty, smiling sixteen-year-old girl whose father and three big brothers were killed by her boyfriend, Peter Nawkins.

'Wow,' Wren said. 'Remind me not to get old.'

But it was far more than that. There was something of Christine Keeler about Carolyn Burns, she had exactly that kind of exhausted beauty. But it was not the passing of time that had ruined her.

It was something closer to destiny, or fate, or whatever you want to call the ending that we reach without choosing. The sixteen-year-old girl who smiled under her family's Christmas tree with her parents and her brothers had never grown old. She had been annihilated along with her father and brothers.

Some crimes are not over just because someone does time, and the bodies are buried and they fade from the headlines.

I saw the burn on Whitestone's neck. The stress on Wren's pale face. And the empty workstation of DI Curtis Gane.

Some crimes last a lifetime, I thought.

When I came out of work Charlotte Gatling was standing under the big blue lamp just outside 27 Savile Row with a dozen photographers coming towards her, all with their cameras and their questions in her face. Her right hand was furiously twisting over her left wrist as she looked for a way out.

'Charlotte! Eyes this way, Charlotte!'

'Charlotte, Charlotte, Charlotte!'

'Is Bradley still alive?'

'Why did he do it, Charlotte? Why did Peter Nawkins kill them?'

There should have been some beefy young uniforms around her, and some nice, efficient Media Liaison Officer or Family Liaison Officer. But there was nobody and she was backing up the steps against the wall, her hands in front of her face as if to protect herself.

'Please,' she said.

I forced my way to the centre of the little pack, raising my hand to slap away any camera that got in my face, and I took her arm. She looked at me without recognition.

The X5 was double-parked on the kerb and I got her into the passenger seat. Cameras pressed against the glass as she covered her face with her hands. That's the shot they'll use, I thought. She was giving them what they wanted without even trying.

'It's OK now,' I said, and I put on the blues and twos, the combined siren and flashing lights which ask the question: What the hell are you doing getting in my way? I turned them off as soon as we were on Regent Street.

'Thank you,' she said.

'No problem. But—'

'I know,' she said, raising a hand to stop me. 'I shouldn't have been standing out there alone, only your people had new pictures of children – fresh sightings – and they wanted me to see them.'

I waited.

'They're not Bradley,' she said. 'They're never Bradley.'

I nodded.

'People want to help, but they just get in the way,' I said. 'The public. Even the press. Mostly decent people. They have children, too. It's even worse when they don't care. And that happens too.'

'But they talk as if Bradley is dead. And he's *not*. I can feel it.'

I said nothing, even though I was weary of all these cast-iron certainties. She was certain that her nephew was still alive. Just as Sean Nawkins had been certain that his brother was being stitched up. Just as Echo was certain that her uncle was an innocent man. Everybody was totally certain, right up to the moment that they were proved totally wrong. Not that I blamed Charlotte Gatling for clinging to the hope that her nephew was out there being treated with love and affection. I knew I would have clung to that hope myself.

'You don't know what it's like,' she said, reading my mind. 'If I didn't believe he was alive – if I didn't believe that someone, somewhere, is treating him with kindness – I would go insane.' She stared at the West End without seeing it. 'Are you going to catch . . . this man?' she said.

'I guarantee it,' I said. 'Where we heading?'

'Fitzrovia,' she said. 'But I can walk.'

'I'll feel better if I take you to the door.'

'Thank you. Do you know Fitzroy Square?'

'Sure.' I had always liked Fitzrovia. I liked the area's history – George Orwell and Karl Marx dreaming their big dreams, and bands like the Rolling Stones, Bob Dylan and the Sex Pistols playing their small clubs. And I liked all the beautiful houses that I would never live in.

'I thought you lived out of town,' I said.

'My family live in Lower Slaughter, Gloucestershire. It's where I grew up. But I never go there.' She hesitated. 'My father and I – we're not close.' That sounded like classic English understatement. 'I prefer to live in our town house in Fitzroy Square.' She laughed bitterly. 'I think my father prefers it too. We've had the house for – I don't know – fifty years.'

'I bet you're named after Charlotte Street.'

She almost smiled. For the first time.

'How did you know that?'

'Just guessing,' I grinned.

We were silent for a bit, the traffic crawling north, clogging up around Oxford Circus, and I thought about the options that rich people have, and I pictured Fitzrovia, perhaps the least-known area of central London, quietly sitting between Bloomsbury to the east and Marylebone to the west, and Fitzroy Square, a big leafy square full of discreet old money.

'How's – your injury?' she said.

My stab wound twitched at the name check. 'Healing,' I said. 'And how are you coping?'

She shook her head. 'Not sleeping. Not eating. Not working. I keep thinking about my sister. And her children.'

She didn't mention her brother-in-law. Maybe that was natural, I thought. And maybe not.

'What work do you do?'

'I write,' she said. 'For children.'

I was impressed.

'Stories for kids? My daughter – Scout – she's five – she loves stories.'

'No, not stories. I write apps.'

'For the phone, you mean?'

'Phones. Tablets. You can run them on anything. You heard of an app called Human Nature? That's one of mine. That's the most famous one. Have you heard of Shazam?'

'It tells you what song you're listening to,' I said, happy to prove that I wasn't a complete idiot.

'Human Nature is the same principle, but it tells you what you're looking at in the natural world. Trees, flowers, plants . . .'

'You thought that up?'

She nodded. 'I wrote it. This is me.'

I had pulled up by Fitzroy Square. It is a huge square but you can't drive in.

'Scout is always asking me the names of trees when we're out walking our dog,' I said. 'And I can never tell her. How would I know the name of a tree?'

'Download the Human Nature app.'

I looked at her face. I would never get tired of

237

looking at her face. Because her beauty was more than some lucky roll of the genetic dice. Charlotte Gatling was decent and brave and smart and it showed in her face.

'Your wife has probably heard of it,' she said.

I nodded. 'Maybe.'

She pushed her hair from her forehead.

'Thanks for the lift, Detective Wolfe.'

I watched her walk away.

And when she had disappeared into a house on the far side of Fitzroy Square, I took out my phone and downloaded Human Nature. It was such a simple, clever idea that I drove across to Regent's Park and took a walk in the moonlight, learning the names of all the trees, thinking how happy Scout would be to have a daddy like me when we walked Stan on Hampstead Heath, as I looked through my phone at the cypress, the beech, the elms, the birch and the ash, my head filled with wonder at the Japanese cherry tree and the Indian bean tree and the way that Charlotte Gatling pushed her hair from her forehead.

CHAPTER 23

Sergeant Ross Sallis of Tottenham Police Station had fourteen stone of muscle on him and fifteen years of experience. He was one of those big, hard old onions – onion bhaji, sargie, sergeant – that are the unbreakable backbone of the Metropolitan Police Force.

'You really think we're going to have the Slaughter Man in the neighbourhood?' he said.

He was driving me down Tottenham High Road in the misty morning sunlight, the bright yellow-and-blue Battenberg livery of his motor – a car pool Ford Fiesta, far too small for a man as big as Sergeant Sallis – making us as conspicuous on that long, bleak street as an ice-cream van in the Sahara.

'I don't know,' I said honestly. 'But it's enough of a possibility that I have to see Carolyn Burns. She could be in real danger.'

'It's all a long time ago.'

'True. But under certain circumstances, men get fixated about old girlfriends.'

He chuckled. Sergeant Sallis laughed easily and often, and that was probably not a bad policy for a copper who had spent his entire career working Tottenham.

'And what circumstances might those be?' he grinned.

'When they're desperate.'

Sergeant Sallis was accompanying me because the family were – as we say – known to him.

'Her boy more than her,' he explained. 'Eddie Burns. We had some dealings when Eddie was in his teens. Ten years ago. More. He was hanging around with the wrong sort. Bit of truancy, bit of weed. No major drama. Boys will be boys and all that. But Eddie stuck out around here.'

'Why's that, Sergeant Sallis?'

'Because he's white.'

Carolyn Burns and her son lived above a green-grocer's shop on Tottenham High Road, almost in the shadow of White Hart Lane. Sleek new Mercs and Beemers with blacked-out windows purred into the car park of the football ground.

Carolyn Burns lived in a different sort of Tottenham.

There was a metal grille in front of the staircase that led to the flats, and Carolyn Burns had to come down to unlock it for us. She was an unusually small woman, as though she had suddenly stopped growing on the night that Peter Nawkins came for her father and her brothers.

'Carolyn, this is DC Wolfe of West End Central,' said Sergeant Sallis.

I showed her my warrant card. She glanced at

it for a fraction of a second, chewing her lower lip thoughtfully.

'DC Wolfe wanted a quiet word, if that's all right,' said Sergeant Sallis. 'Just a courtesy call.'

Everything about the big sergeant was reassuring.

'You'd better come up,' she said, and I tried to see the girl she had been all those years ago, the girl that had smiled under the Christmas tree. But that felt as if it was somebody else.

It was a small flat that stank of cat food and cannabis. I couldn't see a joint and I couldn't see a cat. The TV was blaring some football match being played in front of what looked like a totally empty stadium. A foreign match, then. Sergeant Sallis smiled at nothing in particular as he walked across the tiny room and turned it off.

He nodded at me to begin.

'This is a little bit more than a courtesy call,' I said. 'Ma'am, I have to inform you that you're going to be issued with an Osman warning. We believe that there is a real and present danger to you from a man we are seeking to help with our enquiries. The paperwork is being processed right now. If we – the Metropolitan Police – believe that someone is at risk of being killed or seriously injured then we give them an Osman warning. It's both a warning and an offer of police protection.'

'I know what an Osman warning is,' she said. 'I had one once before from you people. When I was

241

a girl. When it all happened. It was called something else in them days.'

Them days.

I gave her my card. 'All my contact details are on there,' I said. 'If you have any worries—'

'Peter would never hurt me,' she said, cutting me off. 'He didn't hurt me then, and he'll not hurt me now.'

A boy appeared in a doorway. No, not a boy – a man in his late twenties but dressed like a boy. One of those new men that seem stuck in time because they never get a job, and they never leave home, and the years drift by as they stare out at the world from under a baseball cap.

'Hello, Eddie, lad,' Sergeant Sallis said, apparently delighted to see him. 'How are you doing? Did you stick with the college course?'

A brief shake of the head.

Eddie Burns probably wasn't a bad kid. But he had the social skills of a lettuce.

'Peter would never hurt *us*,' Carolyn Burns said. 'So why don't you go back to—' She looked at my card and smirked. '—*Savile Row* and stop wasting my time?'

'Peter Nawkins is a convicted killer, ma'am. He served twenty years. He is being sought in connection with four recent murders.'

She laughed. 'I don't care. He wouldn't hurt me. Never. You don't know him. You don't know anything about him. What do you think – that I'm going to be grateful to you for coming to my home uninvited? I want to be left alone by you people. You've done nothing for me. And you never will.'

'Has Nawkins attempted to contact you?'

'No.'

'When was the last time you saw him?'

'At his trial. The day he went down.'

'Nothing since then? You didn't visit him in prison? You didn't see him when he got out? You've never been to Oak Hill Farm?'

'What did I just say?'

I looked at Sergeant Sallis. He smiled sympathetically.

But his eyes said that it was time to go.

When we were down on the street Sergeant Sallis said, 'It's difficult to help people when they don't want your help.'

'That's true,' I said, angry at myself for feeling humiliated.

'She's a bitter woman,' Sergeant Sallis said. 'Life has not been kind to her. And – when you stop and think about it – she's never actually done anything wrong.'

I nodded. It was all true.

I glanced up at the flat. Eddie Burns was watching us, a fat moggy in his arms.

Sergeant Sallis and I walked back to his car pool Ford. I thought I heard him sigh, as if dreading folding his huge body back into the driver's seat of that tiny car. He paused with his hand on the door and looked across the roof at me.

'You really think Peter Nawkins is going to come to see her?' Sergeant Sallis said. 'She hasn't seen him for half a lifetime.'

'Maybe not,' I said. 'But he might come to see his son.'

CHAPTER 24

Sometimes she wept.

Mostly Mrs Gane sat at her son's bedside and talked – she talked of the kind nurses, and the bad tea in the hospital canteen, and she talked of Curtis's operation and, after the doctors said there would be no operation because the injuries to his spine were far too severe, her conversation drifted to home, to her church and her cat Molly and the changes she saw every day in the Lewisham neighbourhood where she had spent her adult life.

But sometimes she wept.

She was talking about a dispute with her Romanian neighbours that revolved around Molly's toilet habits when the tears came without warning and stunned us to awkward silence. Wren and I looked helplessly at each other while Whitestone awkwardly put an arm around the old lady's shoulder.

'Don't cry, Ma,' Curtis pleaded with a cracked grin.

'Come on,' Whitestone said gently. 'Let's go and see if that tea has improved, shall we?'

Wren went with them. When we were alone, Curtis Gane looked at me and smiled.

'You got to get me out of here, Max.'

I nodded, smiling along with him. 'Once you're well enough for physio—'

He feebly held up a hand that contained some sort of tube feeding into a vein on his wrist. The tape that held it was coming loose.

'I mean it – you've got to get me out of here.'

He wasn't smiling now. I had been standing in the corner of the little private room and now I sat on his bed. I still did not understand exactly what he was asking.

'Anything I can do,' I said.

'What do you think is going to happen to me?' he said. 'I'm not going back to work, am I? I'm never going to walk again, am I? It's all dead down there. It's all gone. I am never going to make love to a woman or bring a child into the world or walk down Savile Row.'

I saw him as I had first seen him. The cocky young DI with the sharp suits and the shaven head, his childhood in Lewisham giving him a strange kind of superiority complex. That shaven head was covered with rough stubble now, and I saw the receding hairline that he had contrived to hide.

And my heart fell away as all at once I understood exactly what he was asking.

I stood up and backed away from him.

The neck brace stopped him moving his head. But his dark eyes followed me.

'I told you,' he said. 'This is not me.'

'Some people live good lives,' I said, and the

words sounded easy and empty to me, although I knew they were true. 'They come from wars – they survive terrible accidents – they live without arms and legs . . .'

He was quite calm now.

'Heroes,' he said. 'All of them. And I salute them. The soldiers that carry on with missing limbs. The men and women who adjust to life in a wheelchair.' He could not move his body enough to shrug. But I saw it on his face. 'What can I tell you? *I don't want my mum taking me to the toilet.* That's it, really. That's all you need to know. I'm not strong enough for that. I'm a grown man and I can't go back to being a baby, Max. I can't do that to her. And I can't do that to myself.'

I glanced towards the closed door. I could feel the stab wound in my stomach pulsing.

'It's impossible,' I said quietly.

'It's actually very easy,' he said. 'I'm not asking for a one-way first-class plane ticket to some Swiss clinic. Just a pillow and a few minutes of your time when nobody's about. You're a strong man, Max. You put a pillow over my face hard enough to stop me breathing for a few minutes and it's soon done. You'll know when it's done. You would be doing me a real favour. And you would be doing my mother a great kindness.' Finally there were tears in his eyes. 'Please,' he said. 'There's nobody else I can ask.'

The door opened and Mrs Gane came in with Whitestone and Wren. They were laughing now.

'What are you boys talking about?' asked Mrs Gane, smiling at both of us.

'Old times, Ma,' said her son.

I went to pick up Scout. Her friend Mia lived in a townhouse in a quiet street in Pimlico, so close to the river that I thought I could hear it. I stood on the doorstep, my heart still beating wildly from the hospital, and through their window I could see what I could only think of as a normal home.

The father home from a job where nobody suffered injuries they would carry to the grave. The mother calling out to the children. The parents still together. An elderly Golden Retriever lazily climbing on to the sofa and settling down for a nap. It was all so normal that I felt like weeping with envy and admiration.

I could see paintings on the walls, and books, and I could hear voices. There was a tall thin man, mid-thirties, taking off his tie as he turned on the news, and then a woman came up beside him and slipped her arm around his waist. They saw me and smiled and waved.

'Scout's dad!' the woman mouthed.

I nodded and grinned, thinking, Perhaps Scout and I are normal, too. Just a different kind of normal.

As they let me inside, Scout came bombing down the staircase with Mia, while a kid sister, maybe a couple of years younger, hung back at the top of the stairs.

'Do we have to go right away?' Scout said, breathless, by way of a greeting.

'The girls made some cookies,' Lissy said. 'They're good with coffee.'

I agreed to coffee and home-made cookies and my daughter happily raced back upstairs with her friend. Lissy and Roger took me through to the kitchen. They knew I was a cop. The dad – Roger – did something with money in the City that I didn't really understand and Lissy was training to be a psychotherapist.

'Mia loves your dog,' Roger said. 'Stan?' He smiled at his wife. 'She's bugging us to get a Cavalier.'

'Our old mutt doesn't do much any more,' Lissy said, passing me a plate of crumpled brown ruins that were possibly meant to be cookies. I took a seat at their kitchen table.

And then their faces fell.

They were looking at my stomach, their eyes wide with horror, and the growing stain on my T-shirt. They had never seen anything like this in their happy, normal home.

'You're bleeding,' Lissy said.

I got up quickly, calling for Scout with my mouth full of cookie, my stab wound pulsing like some living thing and my face burning with shame.

CHAPTER 25

In the morning I was sipping a triple espresso from Bar Italia and wading through the overnight sightings of Bradley Wood when Wren came and sat on my desk.

'I was looking at the statement you took from the farmer's daughter,' she said.

'Maybe we should stop calling her the farmer's daughter,' I said. 'She hasn't lived on a farm for thirty years.'

'Carolyn Burns,' she said. 'Formerly the farmer's daughter. She lied to you.'

She placed a thin green file on my desk.

HMP Belmarsh
Adult Male – Category A

'Her Majesty's prisons have been required to keep records of visitors to maximum-security prisons since 1984,' Wren said. 'The year the IRA almost blew up the British Government in the Brighton bombing. Don't ask me why they changed the rules after that – just a general tightening of security in the wake of a major terrorist attack.'

'It's always the way,' I said. 'Some little bearded loser fails to blow up a plane and suddenly we all have to take our shoes off at airport security.'

'The Slaughter Man was four years into his stretch in 1984,' Wren said. 'So we don't know about the first four years – but for the rest of his time in HMP Belmarsh, he received only two visitors.'

I picked up the file and looked inside it. The letters were faded with time but mocked me loud and clear.

'Carolyn Burns looked me in the eye and told me she had not seen him since she was sixteen years old,' I said. 'According to prison visiting records, she saw him once a month. For years.' I shook my head. 'Peter Nawkins killed her father and her three brothers with a cattle gun. And then she's going to see him once a month?'

'Maybe she loved him. Maybe she hated them. Look at the name of his other visitor.'

Another faded name. *S. Nawkins,* it said, the letters blurred by the years, although these entries were less frequent than for Carolyn Burns and then stopped completely a few years before he was released. I flipped through the yellowed pages.

'The brother,' I said.

'Look again, Detective.'

S. Nawkins (Mrs)

'Not the brother – the brother's wife,' Wren said. 'Didn't she die?'

I nodded.

'Somebody burned her alive,' I said.

Carolyn Burns stared at us through the metal grille, her face twisted with contempt. Her gaze drifted from Whitestone to Wren to me but she addressed Sergeant Sallis.

'Not again,' she told him. 'I don't have to talk to them if I don't want to.'

'It's easier if you do, Carolyn,' the big sergeant said mildly. 'There are a few points they need to clear up.'

She stared at him, still thinking about it.

Whitestone stepped forward.

'Miss Burns? DCI Whitestone. We know you were a regular visitor when Peter Nawkins was in Belmarsh.'

'I know my rights.'

Less certain now.

'As Senior Investigating Officer, I can designate you a significant witness in our investigation,' Whitestone said. 'If I do that, you'll be compelled to provide a visually recorded interview. And if you lie to one of my officers during a visually recorded interview, you will find that all your rights will not save you from more trouble than you can handle. So why don't you open this gate and we can talk to each other like civilised human beings?'

Burns opened the gate and went back upstairs without waiting for us. Sergeant Sallis stood back, smiling pleasantly, as we filed inside.

The front door to the flat was open.

Carolyn Burns and her son were sitting on the sofa, waiting for us, the young man glancing uncertainly at his mother as she kept her eyes fixed on Whitestone. The flat still stank of cannabis and cat.

'It must be tough for a country girl like you,' Whitestone said, smiling for the first time. 'Living in the city, I mean, after spending your childhood on a farm.'

Carolyn Burns laughed.

'Is this the bit where you pretend you're my best friend? You never met my father. You never met my brothers. Vicious bastards, the lot of them. It was growing up on the farm with them that was tough for me. Are we done bonding? Shall we get on with it?'

'Fine,' Whitestone said, taking an armchair opposite Burns and her son. 'The bonding's all done now. Why did you lie to DC Wolfe about visiting Nawkins in prison?'

Burns shrugged, no longer thrown by her lie.

'No reason I should do your job for you,' she said. 'It's all there in the records, right?'

'So you didn't hate Peter Nawkins?' Wren said.

Burns looked at her. She snorted with contempt. 'Why should I hate him?'

'For what he did. For killing your family.'

'Who says he ever killed anyone?'

'The court. The jury. The judge. Are you suggesting he was wrongly convicted?'

253

'I'm suggesting they don't know him. They never knew him. Not like I do.' She ran a shaking hand across her thin mouth. 'Like I did,' she said.

I drifted to the window and stared down at the street. The traffic was crawling down Tottenham High Road. A traffic warden was moving along the pavement as if in slow motion. I watched him write a ticket and slip it under the windscreen wipers of a Nissan Micra.

And I saw that the car had a wing mirror missing.

And as I kept staring down at the car while the traffic warden moved slowly away, I felt my next breath stick in my throat.

I remembered black-and-white CCTV footage of a man having his face repeatedly bounced off the side of a car on a garage forecourt, his head banging against the car so hard that in the end the man was unconscious and a wing mirror had been smashed to pieces, the broken glass glinting in the lights of the garage forecourt.

And I saw the Nissan Micra with the wing mirror missing.

And I knew we had to get out of this place.

Now.

I turned to look at the room.

Carolyn Burns and Eddie on the sofa and Whitestone opposite them, so close in the tiny flat their knees were almost touching, with Wren perched on the edge of the armchair.

Sergeant Sallis stood to one side, smiling benignly,

as if goodwill on all sides would get us through any unpleasantness.

He looked at me and smiled, nodding briefly, and I looked desperately at the closed doors behind him.

All three were closed. Two bedrooms and a bathroom.

Carolyn Burns and her son were looking at me.

'Boss,' I said. 'We should do this at West End Central. *Now.*'

Carolyn Burns stood up, her arms stiff with tension by her side. She seemed to be having trouble breathing too. There was suddenly less air in the little flat.

'Mum?' her son said.

I heard a sound in one of the rooms and then the door opened and Peter Nawkins came out with a twelve-bore shotgun in his hands.

Somebody screamed and Wren was on her feet but Whitestone did not have time to get out of the chair and if I moved I wasn't aware of it as Nawkins pulled the stock tight against his shoulder and pointed the shotgun at the head of Sergeant Sallis and pulled the trigger.

It was like a bomb exploded in the tiny room, the sound so loud that when it was over I heard nothing at all, just the aftershock of that single shot ringing somewhere behind my eardrums.

Sergeant Sallis was on the floor.

I looked down at him, fully expecting to see half of his head a smashed and bloody pulp, brains and hair and bone sprayed all over the cheap wallpaper behind him.

But Sergeant Sallis was staring at me with his mouth open. Blinking with confusion. Alive.

Behind him there was a hole in the wall the size of a fist.

Nawkins had missed. But how had he missed?

Sound came back. But not my hearing. Not fully. The deafening shot in that confined space made everything sound as though it was coming from underwater.

Mouths were moving. People were screaming. I staggered forward, my balance gone with my hearing. With a stricken look on his face, Peter Nawkins was staring at the uniformed policeman sitting on the floor.

The shotgun was still pressed hard against his shoulder.

Only seconds had passed.

I looked at Sergeant Sallis again, struggling to understand how he was alive, then I took a step towards Nawkins on legs made of water.

He turned towards me, as if noticing me for the first time, and I watched him as he aimed the double-barrelled shotgun at my chest, a good place to aim because there was less chance of missing the target.

Everything froze.

I stopped, staring at the business end of the shotgun, aware of a boy cursing, the noise somehow penetrating the deafness. Wren and Whitestone were on their feet, staring at Sergeant Sallis sitting on the floor, dumbfounded that he had survived being shot at point-blank range. Nothing made any sense.

My legs moved. My fists clenched. A short left hook, I thought. Break his jaw. One chance. Don't miss.

But I stopped as Nawkins took half a step back, the barrel of the shotgun levelled at my eyes now, as if he couldn't decide the best place to shoot me.

We stared at each other. Nothing was moving. Everybody was screaming. My ears hurt. Then he jerked the shotgun away with his right hand and swung it at my face, the old wooden stock connecting high on my left cheekbone.

It was like being hit with a hammer.

I went down and stayed down, dizzy and sick, waiting for the sound of the second shot.

I lay there waiting and still it never came.

All I heard were screams and tears and cries for help.

All I heard was a front door crash open.

All I heard was the sound of a man running when there was nowhere left to run.

CHAPTER 26

I got up off my knees, slowed down by sickness more than pain, that deep and debilitating nausea that comes from being struck in the face, very hard.

I wanted to sleep, or at least to slip into the blackness, but I leaned against a chair, staring down at Sergeant Sallis.

He was still sitting on the floor, his face paralysed with shock. There was still a black hole the size of a fist in the wall behind him. And he still wasn't dead.

'You're OK,' I told him, as I struggled to stop myself from falling.

He blinked at me. 'I can't hear you,' he said. 'I see your mouth move, but – nothing.'

I got down on my knees and placed my hands on his arms. Everywhere there should have been the stink of blood and ruin. It felt like a miracle that he was suffering from nothing worse than shock. But I knew that there were no miracles.

'What happened?' Sergeant Sallis said.

'He missed,' I said.

'What? Missed? How could he miss?'

'Because he had no reason to kill you.'

I got back up. Getting up was easier this time.

Carolyn Burns and Eddie were standing inches away from me, pointing at the hole in the wall and screaming at each other. My hearing was coming back but I could not register one word of it.

I looked around the small room. There was nobody else here. Then I heard Whitestone and Wren shouting down on the street. I patted Sergeant Sallis on the back of his head, just to let him know he was still breathing, and I stumbled from the flat.

Through the metal grille of the open gate I saw Whitestone and Wren inexplicably getting into the back of a response car, as if it had been waiting for them. But then I saw the two young uniforms in the front, both women, eyes wide with alarm, and I knew they must have flagged it down.

It pulled away with a shriek of burning rubber, the back door still open, Whitestone shouting instructions as the blues and twos came on, the lights and sirens swirling and screaming.

I stood on the pavement, cursing. I could feel my cheekbone swelling to the size of a boiled egg.

Then I saw Peter Nawkins.

He was jogging down the pavement, maybe one hundred yards away, heading south towards Tottenham Hale, nothing but gridlocked traffic between him and the response car, looking back at the sound of the sirens.

I could not see the weapon.

Then suddenly it was in his hands.

There were motorbikes and cyclists edging their way through the stalled traffic and Nawkins stepped into the middle of them and pointed the shotgun at a motorbike messenger.

The biker bumped on to the pavement and tore away, his bike flying up on to the back wheel. Nawkins tried again.

Still standing among the traffic, terrified faces at the windows, pointing his shotgun at the next biker. And this time the biker raised his hands and fell backwards from his bike. Nawkins got on the bike, glanced back once and took off, turning into the one-way system that feeds in and out of Tottenham. I heard the horns and curses and I knew that he was going the opposite way to everyone else.

The stagnant traffic on the High Road was getting out of the way of the response vehicle, pulling on to the pavement, crashing into each other with the soft crunch of metal, and I saw Edie Wren leaning out the window, trying to get a fix on Nawkins.

She ducked back inside and they picked up speed as they went after him, following the bike into the one-way system, against the tide of the traffic.

And I began to run.

They soon lost me.

And the traffic that parted for the blues and twos had continued on its journey by the time I ran into the Tottenham Hale Gyratory. I ran between the oncoming cars, the curses and horns and faces twisted with rage, the traffic always faster here, the drivers swerving to get out of my way, the palm of my hand touching the cold metal as I ran on, my body tensed, waiting for the crunch of steel and glass and rubber into flesh and blood and bone.

It didn't happen. Not to me.

Instead I stopped when I came upon the crashed response vehicle, its front crumpled against the metal pole of a speed camera, the pole bent at a sickening angle and resting across the smashed glass of the windscreen.

Whitestone was still in the back seat, holding her forehead. Wren was standing by the wrecked car, apparently unharmed but dazed, her phone in her hands. And beyond the inflated air bags in the front of the vehicle I could see the bruised and scuffed faces of the two young uniforms.

'Max!' Wren shouted. 'He's heading for the reservoir!'

I went off after him.

Nawkins had had his own crash. The stolen motorbike was bent and mangled under the front wheels of a large lorry. Nawkins had not done a lot of damage to the lorry but the driver was standing on the road, bent double as he vomited.

The traffic had ground to a halt here, other vehicles concertinaed into each other, drivers getting out, voices shouting, fingers pointing, and

I saw the great expanse of the Walthamstow reservoir system off to my left, ten interlinked reservoirs that go on for miles.

I climbed the fence and dropped inside. The reservoirs looked like a sea, dead calm, and the city seemed to slip away. It was curiously still and silent in here, the roar of Tottenham's chaos coming from another world.

Then I saw two men running towards me, awkward in their wellington boots. Two fishermen, their rods abandoned by a pair of green tents.

'Over there!' they said, pointing towards a rough clump of bushes fifty yards away. 'He's got a fucking shotgun!'

They didn't stop running.

I heard sirens. More sirens. And when I looked back there were response vehicles everywhere. I wondered if CO19 were here yet, Scotland Yard's specialist firearms unit, and then I saw them – the big BMW X5s, the Armed Response Vehicles of CO19, and the black gleam of the weapons, the HK G3Ks of the snipers and the MP5 sub-machine guns. There are around 550 Specialist Firearms Officers in CO19 and it looked like every last one of them was here.

I hesitated, looking back at them as they took up their positions, wondering how far these reservoirs stretched and if CO19 had all the exits covered, and most of all wondering if I should keep after Nawkins or bail out now. And then there was no choice to make because Peter

Nawkins came out of the bushes, still holding his shotgun.

I stood perfectly still.

Nowhere to run, nowhere to hide and all that lifeless water making this place look like another planet.

He began walking towards me.

'Put down your weapon,' I said.

He didn't stop. Forty yards.

'I'm arresting you for the murder of the Wood family,' I said. 'Mary. Brad. Marlon. Piper.'

He shook his head, and looked over my shoulder at the blue lights splitting the grey gloom of winter.

Twenty yards.

'You do not have to say anything,' I said.

Ten yards.

'But it may harm your defence—'

He raised the shotgun.

'*Put the thing down and step away from it now!*' I told him, my heart pounding, my stab wound throbbing, the blood in my veins pumping as fast as it could. 'There's no way out.'

'Wrong again,' he said, and turned the shotgun in his hands to fit the barrel in his mouth, his eyes blinking as he eased his right thumb into the trigger and pulled.

There was no separation between the shot and the back of his head exploding. It happened in the same instant. And the sound of the second shot was very different here. It seemed to echo across those ten reservoirs, that vast expanse of water, that sea in the city, and I looked up at the sky as the black flock of birds took flight in alarm.

Nawkins had fallen backwards into the water.

What remained of the back of his head leaked into the still waters.

I looked down at my hands. They were covered in blood.

And my heart began pumping, wild with joy, and I felt the tears of gratitude sting my eyes and choke my throat.

Because it wasn't my blood.

The woman attacked me from behind.

I was standing by the side of the road, a carton of bad coffee in my hands, boiling hot, far too hot to drink although I drank it anyway, letting it scald my throat, enjoying the way it reminded me that I was still alive, watching the paramedics stitch the gash in Whitestone's forehead, armed officers and uniforms and blue lights everywhere, when the woman came up behind me, screaming a torrent of filth as her fingernails raked across my face.

She wanted my eyes. She wanted to take them out. She was trying to blind me.

And as I felt the boiling hot coffee splash across my shoes, I thought that she was doing quite a good job.

Her nails raked down my forehead and across my eyebrows and into my eye sockets, trying to stay there, attempting to sink into the eyeballs, and then trying again, all the while screaming, screaming, screaming.

I thought it was Carolyn Burns come to punish me.

But as they finally pulled her off, I glimpsed the dog tattoo on the inside of her wrist, the Akita that looked more like a German Shepherd, the image streaked with blood from my clawed face.

It was Echo Nawkins.

Sleeveless shirt. Pink miniskirt. Dressed for the start of summer in the middle of winter. She turned to scream at me over her shoulder as a couple of uniformed officers led her away.

'*Blood on your hands!*' she screamed. '*Blood on your hands! Blood on your hands!*'

'Shall we do her, sir?' a sergeant asked me, and I wondered if he was local and if he knew Sergeant Sallis. 'Book her for assaulting a police officer?'

I shook my head. I didn't have the heart for it. And I could live without the paperwork. And the truth is that she had shocked me. It was as if Echo knew that Peter Nawkins had not murdered the Wood family. Not *believed* – with the usual sentimental blinkers of the ones who dote on the wicked – but as if she *knew* for a stone-cold fact.

I thought of Sergeant Sallis sitting on the floor of the flat that stank of cannabis and cat, his face frozen with disbelief that he was still breathing, and the hole in the wall where the shotgun had been very deliberately fired.

It was as if she knew.

Peter Nawkins had not killed anyone for half a lifetime.

MARCH

MORTAL REMAINS

CHAPTER 27

It is not easy to hide a dead body.
Two reasons.
Killers are stupid.
And bodies decay.

Twenty-four hours after Peter Nawkins had emptied a twelve-bore shotgun into the roof of his mouth, I stood before the map of London that covered an entire wall in MIR-1 and, as I stepped back to take a better look, I thought – no, it's not easy to hide a body, not even here.

Not even in this city of ten million souls.

Not even in a metropolis that sprawls for thirty miles either side of a river that is more than two hundred miles long. Not even in London, a special city with countless acres of green and blue, all those parks, woods, commons, gardens and heathland, all those ponds, canals, lakes, rivers and reservoirs.

London, with its sixty thousand streets and all those garages, skips, recycling bins, brand-new patios and old dank basements. And below the floorboards, under the manholes, far beneath the concrete and the earth, deep down in the subterranean network of drains, pipes and sewers that carry away the city's waste – it still wasn't easy to get rid of a body. Because killers are stupid and bodies decay.

I stood alone in MIR-1, staring at the map of my city. Behind me, at my workstation, Bradley Wood smiled out from the computer screen, forever four years old and happy, with his Han Solo figurine in his small fist.

I took another step back. It helped me to see better.

Killing someone is the easy bit, I thought. Disposing of a body is the hard part.

Killers are blind with adrenaline, terrified of being caught, sweating with panic. They have no time. Their hands and clothes are covered in enough evidence to put them away for a lifetime. Every fibre of their being is telling them to flee.

The ones who attempt to hide their victims are never thinking clearly. They are unlikely to be reflecting deeply on the immutable facts of death and decay.

Putrefaction, the pathologists call it.

It is the reason you can put me down for cremation.

The process is slowed by cold and quickened by heat, and it is affected by the weight of the corpse, and by the kind of clothes they were wearing at the time of death, and if there is undigested food in the stomach, and wounds, and if the body is in water, and whether the water is warm or cold.

But if a body is not stored in sub-zero temperatures, then nothing stops the process of putrefaction.

I glanced towards the window. It was still bitterly cold but the worst of the winter was over. The snows were melting. The seasons were changing. But even among all that awakening life, the cruel facts of death remained. They are never pretty.

At the moment of death, everything shuts down. The heart doesn't beat. The blood doesn't flow. The last breath has gone. There's a myth that hair and nails continue to grow after death, but it's not true – skin tissue shrivels at the time of death, so it can appear as if hair and nails have kept growing. But they haven't. The only thing that hair and nails are going to do from now on is fall out.

After death, the body's tissues are destroyed by bacteria escaping from the intestinal tract, melting the body down. The internal organs break down in strict order: intestine, liver, kidneys, lungs, brain and finally the prostate or uterus.

After thirty-six hours the head, shoulders and abdomen turn green. Then the gases accumulating in the cavities cause bloating, beginning in the face. The eyes bulge. The tongue protrudes. The head swells. The bloating reaches the stomach and finally the skin, which fills with blisters.

The nose and mouth look as if they are leaking blood, but this is purge fluid, a result of the total destruction of body tissues by bacteria. The body's blood vessels collapse and this results in an intricate road map known as marbling. By now the body has turned a shade of green so dark that it is almost black.

Then the body splits open like fruit that has been left to rot in the sun and releases its gases.

So the murdered dead always sleep uneasy.

They are discovered by dog walkers and drain cleaners and DIY enthusiasts tearing up the floorboards, digging up the garden or knocking through a wall. They are discovered by neighbours who find they are living next door to the unmistakable stench of rotting flesh.

And they are discovered by someone like me who goes into a house of horrors and kicks down the front door.

Although not always. I thought of Winnie Johnson, the mother of Moors Murder victim Keith Bennett. Winnie died after almost fifty years of trying to find out where her murdered twelve-year-old son was buried on Saddleworth Moor, outside Manchester. I thought of Winnie now, and the long years of leaving her flowers and toys and tokens of love on random parts of the moors.

Yes, it happens. Yes, it is easier to hide the body of a child than the body of an adult.

But killers are stupid.

And bodies decay.

And if Bradley Wood was dead, I believed with all my heart that we would have found him by now.

My fingertips touched the map of London.

'He's still alive,' I said quietly.

'Detective Wolfe?'

I jumped back from the map, a breath caught in my throat.

Charlotte Gatling was standing in the doorway. She bit her lower lip. 'Why did he do it?' she said.

I did not know what to say to her. I grasped for some truth that she could understand.

'I can't explain madness to you,' I said as gently as I could. 'Nawkins was criminally insane. He had some kind of obsession with your sister. If it had not been Mary – and her family – it would have been someone else. He should never have been walking about. After the first murders, all those years ago, he should have been in a high-security psychiatric hospital. He should have done his time in Broadmoor instead of Belmarsh, and they should have let him die there.' I hesitated. She saw it.

'Please go on,' she said.

I was thinking of Wren.

'A colleague of mine said that Nawkins was a deeply unhappy man who was enraged by the happiness of others. Nawkins saw a happy family and he had to destroy it. My colleague – she's not a psychologist; she's not a shrink – she's just a cop, the same as me. But her theory makes as much sense to me as anything.'

I did not know what else to tell her.

'I'm sorry,' I said.

'What will happen to those children? The ones you found in the house on The Bishops Avenue?'

I shook my head.

'Social services will try to send them home, even though some of them will have been running away from their homes. Most will go into care. I can't pretend they will have happy endings. I wish I could.'

She thought about it, and nodded.

'This world is a sewer made by what men want,' she said.

We stared at each other. She remained in the doorway of MIR-1.

'What are you doing here?' I said.

'I had an interview with the Family Liaison Officer. Looking at CCTV footage. Some pictures taken with an iPhone. Reading reports. I come in once a week. I used to think it was a sign we were making progress. I don't believe that any more. Pointless, really.' I could see that a lot of the hope had gone out of her and I hated it. She shook her head. 'All these ridiculous sightings that lead to nothing,' she said.

Her face reddened. Perhaps because we both knew the FLO offices were all on the first floor. There was no obvious reason for her to be up here. But she wasn't lost.

'I just wanted to thank you,' she said. 'And your colleagues, of course. I know you put yourselves in harm's way to bring Nawkins to justice. But everyone's gone home.'

It was true. In every sense. It was the end of the working day. And our murder investigation was winding down.

DCI Whitestone and DC Wren were at home with their wounds and their loved ones. Our only suspect was dead by his own hand and, although we would never have publicly admitted it, the Met was reluctant to throw endless resources into the search for a four-year-old boy who by now had been missing for two months.

'I know that my nephew has had a lot of attention,' Charlotte Gatling said. 'And I know all the statistics. A child missing every three minutes. One hundred thousand children missing every year. Some new ones have disappeared in the time I have been standing here talking to you. And I know not every missing child has the attention you've given to Bradley.' She recovered her poise. 'That's why I wanted to thank you.'

'It's my job.'

'But you're doing far more than just your job, aren't you?'

She indicated the image of her nephew smiling on my computer screen. I had thought she had not noticed it. I had been wondering how to get across and press quit before she saw it. But she had seen it the moment she came to the door.

'Your job is done,' she said. 'You're a Murder Investigation Team. And now the murders have been solved. And we both know that every day that goes by reduces the chances of Bradley coming home. *But you're still looking.* Everybody has gone home but you're still up here, thinking about him, not giving up, still trying. It's true, isn't it?'

'Yes.'

She took a single step closer to me.

'Why are you doing it?'

'Daddy?'

Scout lifted her head at an empty workstation. She rubbed the sleep from her eyes and swung back and forth on the swivel chair, her feet not touching the ground. Below her Stan stirred himself at the sound of her voice, yawning and settling into his stretching exercises. Downward-facing dog, upward-facing dog.

Scout slipped off the chair.

'Toilet,' she said, heading for the door.

'You OK with that lock?' I said.

'It's an easy lock,' Scout said, padding from the room, her dog at her heels.

I looked at Charlotte Gatling.

'I do it for her,' I said.

CHAPTER 28

What I didn't tell Charlotte Gatling was that the information from the public about Bradley had almost dried up. The cranks and the time-wasters and the well-meaning citizens had moved on.

Twin girls, five years old, had disappeared from a park in Notting Hill while under the supervision of an Italian nanny who had an obsessive need to Tweet. While the young Italian was attending to her Twitter timeline, the girls vanished. The twins' parents both worked in the City and the disappearance prompted countless think pieces in broadsheet and tabloid about parents who work, the balance between parenting and the office, and how we put our children in the care of strangers.

Bradley Wood was yesterday's news.

With Whitestone and Wren still on leave, PC Billy Greene and I spent the next day wading through what remained of the alleged sightings of Bradley. Dispatching uniforms to Trace, Interview and Eliminate. Logging it on HOLMES. But it was all thin stuff and I did not feel guilty about leaving Billy Greene to it when the darkness fell on Savile Row.

I had an appointment at the Black Museum.

Sergeant John Caine and I stood in the quiet corner of the Black Museum that was devoted to the Slaughter Man.

Nothing had changed. After all that effort, all that hard work and routine, all that fear and blood, everything here was still the same. I wasn't sure what I had been expecting, but the display was exactly as it had been when I first saw it, and that shocked me.

The cattle gun that looked like a hand drill was still sitting on a small card table. The ancient newspaper article was still in its dusty glass case, the yellowing paper disintegrating with time.

RITUAL SLAUGHTER ON
ESSEX FARM
Slaughter Man executes father and sons
in midnight killing spree

A killer was jailed for life yesterday for murdering a father and his three grown-up sons with a bolt gun used to slaughter livestock . . .

And the two photographs that accompanied the article were the same as they ever were. The large, good-looking boy with the totally blank expression being led away in handcuffs by a uniformed officer.

And a family dominated by men grinning under their Christmas tree.

'Will you update it?' I asked the keeper of the Black Museum. 'Now that Nawkins is dead?'

John Caine shook his head. 'Now that the Slaughter Man's story has a happy ending? Don't think I'll bother. This place is not really about the likes of him.' He nodded towards a much larger, much cleaner glass case nearby. 'It's about the likes of them.'

The faces stared back at me from inside a glass case that was labelled OUR MURDERED COLLEAGUES. Official photographs, just standard Met mugshots, and yet all those eyes of murdered policemen and -women twinkled with mischief and smiles played around lips pressed tightly together for the photographer.

Sergeant John Caine said, 'And how was Peter Nawkins at the end?'

I thought about it.

'He was in bits,' I said. 'He looked at me as though he had never killed anyone in his life.'

Sergeant Caine laughed bitterly. 'Yes, the jails are full of totally innocent men, aren't they?'

We walked through the deserted Black Museum, John Caine switching the lights off. It is probably the biggest collection of murder weapons in the world but I paused in front of the display of a woman who never held a weapon in her life. Maisy Dawes, the Victorian maid from Belgravia who was set up for a burglary and then destroyed for a crime she did not commit.

'Maisy Dawes,' I said. 'Whatever happened to the men who set her up?'

'As far as I know, they all died in their beds,' said Sergeant John Caine. 'It was a very good blind. What's on your mind, Max?'

'Sergeant Sallis,' I said. 'The local support who came with our mob to the flat where we found Nawkins.' I shook my head. 'Nawkins didn't kill him, John. He wasn't armed with a handgun, some puny little weapon that can only spray and pray beyond eleven feet. Nawkins had a twelve-bore. And at that range it was easier for him to hit Sergeant Sallis than the wall. Yet he missed. Why?'

John Caine shrugged. 'I don't know, son. Maybe he bottled it. Murderers are not brave. Murderers are cowards. You want to get a drink and talk about it? You can have a triple espresso and I can have a tea and we can live the life of sin.'

'Some other time, John.'

'Got a date, have you?'

'Yes,' I said. 'It's a sort of date.'

I looked for Ginger Gonzalez in the American Bar at the Savoy, but she was not there.

I looked for her in the Coburg Bar at the Connaught and the Rivoli Bar at the Ritz and The Fumoir at Claridges and the Promenade Bar at the Dorchester. But she was not there either.

I was driving home past Broadcasting House on Portland Place when I saw the lights in the grand façade of the Langham Hotel. It wasn't on the list, but then I wasn't sure she had given me her entire list.

The Artesian Bar in the Langham smelled of money. Discreet, unflashy money. Huge windows looked out on the street and made you glad to be inside this place of soft lights and laughter and plush purple leather chairs designed to make you stay.

Ginger Gonzalez was sitting at one of the window tables, smiling over a glass of champagne at the man sitting opposite her. When he leaned forward to make a point I saw his face clearly in the candlelight.

The man was Nils Gatling.

I took a seat at the bar, my back to the room, watching them in the mirror behind the bar. The bartender approached me.

'What can I get you, sir?'

'Triple espresso.'

I saw his surprise and glanced at my watch. It was knocking on for midnight.

'Better make it a double,' I said.

'Yes, sir.'

It was a good bar.

Nils Gatling and Ginger Gonzalez had the easy intimacy of old friends. But that was her way. For all I knew, they had met five minutes ago.

The waiter brought my coffee. I knocked it back as Nils Gatling walked behind me, heading for the door. Ginger was still sitting at the table. When she saw me walking towards her table, her eyes blazed with anger. Then she recovered.

'Detective Wolfe,' she said.

'Has your companion gone?' I said.

'He's retired for the night. He has a suite upstairs.'

'Nils Gatling has a suite at the Langham? The family have a house in Fitzroy Square! It's less than a mile away. Why does he keep a suite at the Langham?'

There was something like pity in her eyes. Did I know nothing of the rich?

'*Because he can*,' she said.

I sat down in a chair that was still warm.

'I need a girl,' I said.

She laughed shortly, as if all men were the same in the end.

'What sort of girl?'

'Kind,' I said. 'She has to be kind. That's very important. And smart. Really smart. University educated. Oh, and she has to be very beautiful.'

Ginger Gonzalez finished her champagne and sighed.

'No wonder you're unlucky in love,' she said.

Ginger dashed off a text message and then we waited. I had another espresso and Ginger had another glass of champagne. For the first time since I'd met her, she seemed slightly drunk.

'How long have you known Nils Gatling?' I said.

'A while.'

I could see that she did not want to talk about it. Client confidentiality, I guessed. Maybe being somebody's pimp is like being their doctor.

'Surprised, Detective?' she said.

I nodded. 'He has a wife, doesn't he?' I said.

She smiled with genuine amusement.

'And what do you imagine *that* means? Brad Wood had a wife, didn't he?'

'Is that how you know Nils Gatling? Through his brother-in-law?'

She quickly shook her head.

'God, no. I knew the old man first. Victor Gatling. The daddy of them all.' She hesitated. 'Victor Gatling was just about the first proper man I met after I got off the banana boat.'

'You mean the first rich man,' I said.

'I mean the first man who knew how to act in this world. The first man who knew how to treat a woman. I was very young. He liked me. And his wife had just died.'

'And it didn't work out.'

'I wasn't what he needed.'

'What did he need?'

'To spend time with his family. But we stayed in touch. I've known Nils for years. And I've done work for the company, OK? Gatling Homes.'

'I never knew you were in the property business. I can see you as an estate agent.'

'They have a lot of clients they need taking care of.'

'I bet they do.'

'Here she is.'

Zina was tall and pretty and tired looking. I stood up to shake her hand. She did not sit down. I dropped some cash on the table and we left.

She was Romanian, I found out as we were walking to the X5, although she said it had been ten years since she had left Bucharest. She was twenty-six. In another world she would have been a businesswoman or a mother.

I didn't ask to see her university degree.

The three of us drove east.

Ginger and Zina in the back of the X5. I glanced at them in the rear-view mirror but mostly I listened to their typical London conversation – *Where are we to live?* What areas were up and coming, where would be next, where the cafés and restaurants were good, where was safe, where was too dangerous, where was too expensive, what was still affordable, where you could still get a bargain.

'I'm thinking of Shoreditch,' said the woman.

I cleared my throat. 'What about money?' I said. I wasn't thinking about Shoreditch.

Zina looked out at the street. We were passing Liverpool Street. The last of the half-cut commuters were staggering to the train out to Essex.

Ginger lightly touched my shoulder.

'You can pay me later,' she said. 'Cash, credit or banker's draft. You don't have to worry about payment now. I know you're good for it.'

I nodded and we drove in silence for another few miles.

'This is it,' I said.

There were patients enjoying their cigarettes outside the doors of the Homerton Hospital, huddled up inside their dressing gowns, shaking with cold. One of them had some kind of oxygen tank. Another had the bloated hands that I recognised as a side effect of chemotherapy.

Nobody even looked at us as we went inside.

A policeman, a pimp and a prostitute.

We blended right in.

Curtis Gane had been moved to a private room. We stood outside the door and for the first time I wondered if I was doing the right thing.

'He's still in a lot of pain,' I said to Zina. 'And he's angry. And he's depressed. And he knows he is never going to walk again. So he's not going to—'

Zina lightly kissed my cheek.

'I understand,' she said. 'Don't worry. You've done a good thing.'

She slipped into the room and closed the door. Ginger and I bowed our heads, listening to the sound of Gane waking.

'. . . *who are you?*'

I reached for the door when I heard the alarm in his voice. Ginger placed a hand on my arm. She shook her head.

'We've done this before,' she said quietly.

'*But I can't do anything,*' Gane said, and the shame in his voice tore at my heart.

285

'It's all right,' Zina told him. 'I'm just here to hold you.'

Ginger and I didn't speak until we reached the cancer patients sucking on their cigarettes outside the main doors.

'*Salamat po*,' I said. 'I mean it, Ginger. Thank you very much.'

'You speak Tagalog.'

'I'm a policeman in London,' I said. 'I know a few words in fifty different languages.'

She ran a fingertip down the side of my face.

'You know the word *gwapo*?' she said. 'Tagalog word for *handsome*.'

'I know *bola-bola*,' I said. 'Tagalog word for *bullshit*.'

She laughed.

'What about you, Detective? You want me to make a few calls? Or do you have someone waiting for you?'

It was getting late.

Time to relieve Mrs Murphy.

'Someone's waiting for me,' I said.

CHAPTER 29

I watched Scout sleeping.

Stan appeared in the doorway, sniffing the air and eyeing the bed, wondering if he could get away with sneaking in and curling up next to her for a few hours. I shook my head at him and he followed me out as, very quietly, I closed her bedroom door.

Mrs Murphy was putting her coat on.

'Scout wants a dress,' she said.

Stan climbed on the sofa, listening with interest. Mrs Murphy scratched the back of his neck and he closed his eyes in bliss.

'A dress?' I said dumbly. Beyond the great windows of our loft, Smithfield's lights were blazing. The dome of St Paul's Cathedral rose under a full white moon.

'A Belle dress,' Mrs Murphy said. 'You know – *Beauty and the Beast?*'

I shook my head, a bit desperate. I didn't know.

'Her friend – Mia – the little Australian girl – is having a princess party,' Mrs Murphy said.

This was all strange new territory to me. I felt

as if I had stumbled on to a stage where I was the only person who didn't know his lines.

'What do I have to do?' I said.

'You have to go online,' Mrs Murphy said.

And so I did.

Stan slept at my feet as I sat in the kitchen with my laptop, frowning at little girls around Scout's age smiling as they posed in ballgowns of silky golden ruffles. It was made apparent to me that I was also going to have to fork out for Belle gloves, Belle shoes and a Belle tiara.

I found myself grinning.

Scout was really going to wear this stuff?

And then I felt a stab of something and I knew it was the loneliness of the single parent. It came out of nowhere and I was shocked by the force of it, like a punch to the heart that you don't see coming.

It's not just the bad times that you have to go through alone, I thought.

It's the good times, too.

'Rocky's got the spite,' said Fred. 'Speed. Timing. Power. That's all good stuff – but you don't go anywhere without the spite.'

We were ringside at Smithfield ABC watching Rocky dismantle his sparring partner. He was in with a light heavyweight who had on a threadbare Wild Card vest and one of those Cleto Reyes headguards with the bar across the front. Those headguards are designed to protect the mouth but Rocky had hit it so hard and fast and often that it was coming loose.

I could see Rocky's mean streak now, and I saw it was hidden well, buried deep, behind the big easy grin and the default charm, and I thought of how he had looked me in the eye and told me he knew nothing of the men from Oak Hill Farm going to The Garden. I would have been happy to see the man in the ring with him give him a good hiding.

But the sparring partner was struggling. Breath coming harder, the feet more flat-footed, a look of dazed confusion in the eyes. Rocky had dragged his opponent into the trenches and it seemed to put a joyous spring in his step. That mean streak was obvious to me now.

Rocky hit his man with a seven-punch combination. Jab, right cross, left hook to the body, left hook to the head, right cross, left upper cut, jab and away, pivoting to an angle of safety, out of harm's way as his man lurched desperately towards him, flailing now, and walked on to Rocky's big right.

There was something sickening about the damage it did. The big right rocked the man's brain as much as his body, and although he did not go down, the strong legs not deserting him, it was one of those moments when those of us who love boxing are forced to ask: What is it exactly that you love? The bell went and the two men embraced as a ripple of applause went around the ringside.

Fred shot me a rueful grin. There was no clapping in Smithfield ABC. It was not about applause in here.

But as he approached his first professional bout, Rocky's sparring sessions were drawing a sizeable crowd. There was an excitement around him. A journalist was taking notes. Two photographers were taking pictures – with cameras, not phones. There were men we had never seen at the gym before – white men in suits and ties, who had the hard-eyed, smooth-skinned look of boxing promoters.

They loved his story, and they loved his style, and they loved his spite. Although you would never have known it outside the ring, when he was fighting there was a viciousness in him, a cruelty, and that would be his best friend in his chosen career.

'He's going to make somebody a lot of money,' Fred said. 'I hope he makes a little for himself and his family.'

Echo Nawkins sat by Rocky's side on the steps to the ring as a journalist talked to him. She sat close by her man, and every now and then the palm of her hand would run over the curve of her belly, as if stroking the baby that was growing inside her.

Oak Hill Farm, I thought. They marry young.

Neither of them gave any indication that they were aware of my presence. Then, the interview over, they walked across to me.

'I know you're angry with me,' Rocky said. 'Because I didn't tell you we'd done work at The Garden.'

'You make it sound as though you forgot my birthday,' I said. 'It's a lot more serious than that.'

Rocky began taking off his hand wraps, unspooling the black, sweaty, threadbare cotton.

'The trouble is,' Rocky said, 'you looked at Peter Nawkins and saw a killer. I looked at him and saw a decent man who had paid for his sins and was trying to build a good life.'

'The trouble is,' I said, 'you withheld information during a murder investigation. The trouble is, that's against the law. Obstruction of justice. Impeding a police investigation. It's not too late to do you for being an accessory to the crime.'

'I *tried* to tell you the truth,' Echo said, coming towards me. 'And you weren't interested in the truth!' Tears came as her mouth twisted with anger. 'And now he's gone.'

She began to sob helplessly.

'I'm sorry,' Rocky told me, holding her close. 'About everything. I truly am.' He led Echo away as my phone began to vibrate.

MIR-1 CALLING, it said, although Wren and Whitestone were still on sick leave. I did not even know there was anyone still up there.

'An old lady wandered in,' PC Billy Greene told me. 'Says she saw Bradley Wood with a UM in a UV.'

I almost laughed. Another sighting of another

child with an unknown male in an unidentified vehicle.

'Why don't you just take a statement from her?'

'Because I think she's telling the truth,' he said.

'I've got three grown-up children and seven grand-children,' said Mrs Margaret Duffy of Stow-on-the-Wold.

'That's lovely,' I said.

She looked at me as if she might tear out my throat.

'I'm not making small talk, young man,' she said. 'I'm telling you that I know how children act. I raised three of them myself, and spent a lot of time with one of my grandchildren when my daughter was between husbands. I know all their moods. I know when they are sulking, and when they are tired, and when they are frightened. And I never saw a little boy like this one before. That's why I caught the train to London. That why I've come to see you rather than wasting time with the yokels in my area.'

She considered her surroundings.

'So is this the Major Incident Room?' she said.

'No, this is the room where we conduct inter-views,' I said. I indicated PC Greene standing by the door.

'Mrs Duffy, why don't you tell me exactly what you told PC Greene here?'

The old lady gave Billy an affectionate look.

'He's been very courteous,' she said approvingly.

'Young William. Told me that I should speak to a more senior officer.' She looked at me, still in my sweaty boxing kit, profoundly unimpressed. 'That would be you.'

I waited.

'Since my local newsagents closed down, I walk to the service station for my morning paper. I like my morning paper. There was a man with a child. And you never saw a little boy quite so lost. As though he thought life had become a dream. Or a nightmare.'

I pushed the photograph of Bradley Wood across the desk. The classic shot of Bradley smiling in his mother's arms as he waves his favourite toy at the camera.

'Is that the child you saw, Mrs Duffy?'

'The child I saw was older,' she said. 'When was that photograph taken? You should have a more up-to date photograph. Children can change a lot in just a few months, you know, Constable.'

'Detective,' I said, trying not to sigh.

Another crank. Another fruitcake. I got up to go.

'Oh, pardon me all over the place, *Detective*,' she said, rummaging in her handbag. 'The answer is – I can't say for certain if the child I saw is the child in that photograph because your photograph is so old. But he dropped this before the man dragged him out to the car.'

She placed an eight-inch Han Solo figurine on the desk.

Classic Han Solo – white shirt, black waistcoat, leather boots. The cocky captain of the *Millennium Falcon.* I picked it up, aware that I had stopped breathing.

'And that's the same toy, isn't it?' said Mrs Margaret Duffy.

I pressed the doorbell of the big house on Fitzroy Square.

'He's alive,' I said, and I held out my hand.

Charlotte Gatling stared at the battered little Han Solo figure in my palm. Then she took it. And then she kissed me.

Awkward, desperate kissing, mouths that were out of practice, our lips missing then finding each other. Warm breath, no words.

The heat of her in my arms. A moment that had been delayed so long it felt like it would never come.

And yet here it undeniably was – her face next to mine, her skin under my fingertips, her hands in my hair, the beautiful fact of her, suddenly full of hope, wild with hope, giddy with it, still gripping the eight inches of intergalactic space cowboy and pressing them into the back of my head.

She took me inside and closed the door.

CHAPTER 30

We stood in the hall as I told her everything I knew.

A torrent of words, the taste of her still on my mouth.

The phone call from PC Billy Greene. Mrs Margaret Duffy of Stow-on-the-Wold in the interview room at West End Central. The child she saw and recognised at the service station. The dropped toy. How she had travelled to London to place it in my hand. And Mrs Duffy's certainty – total certainty – that here was the boy on the news, although he was older now, and Mrs Duffy a woman, mother and grandmother who knew from personal experience how a child can seem older overnight.

Then I found myself lapsing into cop speak, telling Charlotte about the HP action that I had raised on HOLMES2, the highest-priority directive that would have eight forces cancelling leave, and the fast-track action authorised by my SIO, DCI Whitestone, that would have every officer in the land understanding that this was a positive sighting, before I abruptly stopped, and told her again what really mattered.

'Bradley's alive,' I said.

Charlotte stared at the Han Solo figurine in her fist, nodded and took a step towards me.

Then there were no more words for a while.

There were no words in the hallway where she took my hand, and no words on the staircase as she led me to the top floor of that grand house on Fitzroy Square, and no words in the bedroom, where we undressed quickly in a state of shy wonder, and there was absolutely no space for words with our mouths so busy seeking each other, and finding each other, there were no sounds at all beyond our gasps and cries as we made love with fierce, tender urgency and the night fell outside and the room was lit by nothing but the street lights of Fitzrovia.

There were no words as we lay with our limbs entwined, stunned and breathless, so close in that moment that I could not tell where she ended and I began.

I gently pulled her towards me and I kissed her mouth, and I could have kissed it forever, feeling the blood flowing, the heat rising and a wild joy inside me.

'Max,' she said. 'This is difficult for me.'

'I understand,' I said, not wanting any words, feeling they were unnecessary.

I kissed her face again, her shoulder, her arms, her hands, loving her taste and her touch, and it was only then that I saw the band of white scar tissue around her left wrist, the unmistakable bracelet of self-harm.

'No,' she said softly, pulling her arm away, hiding it under the sheet. 'You don't understand anything. But you're kind, aren't you? You're good.'

She kissed the back of my hand. Tears shone in her eyes. She was starting to scare me.

'It's not you,' she said, and I felt myself flinch.

When someone says, *It's not you,* what they usually mean is, *It's definitely you.*

But not this time.

'Tell me,' I said. There were more kisses. 'Trust me.'

I didn't know what was happening.

I didn't understand what had gone wrong.

'What is it?' I said. 'Tell me why it's difficult for you. Because it doesn't feel difficult to me. It feels like the most natural and right thing in the world.'

She did not look at me. She could tell me or she could look at me. But she could not do both.

'There are things that happened years ago,' she said. 'When I was very young. After my mother died.' She took a deep breath and slowly, slowly released it. 'Everything fell apart. My father was drinking – oh, God, he was drinking so much.' Now she looked at me. 'He didn't know what was happening.'

The dread was building inside me.

Something dark had entered this house, this bedroom, this bed.

'What happened to you?' I said, feeling my heart fall away, dizzy and sick, suddenly knowing what had happened to her.

And I saw her make that old gesture, her right hand over her left wrist, wringing the skin, and I saw now it was to cover the scars she had cut into her flesh all those years ago.

'You were abused,' I said, numb with shock and grief.

She said nothing.

'Who was it?'

She still said nothing.

Because she knew I wanted to kill the man who had done it.

Kill him tonight.

'At home?' I said.

A small downward nod of her head. Not looking at me.

'Home. Yes.'

'What about Mary?' I said.

'It was worse for her.'

'Because she was older?'

She laughed.

And I had never heard such bitterness in a laugh.

'Because she was *prettier*.'

The silence built between us. Now I wanted to know everything. I wanted to hear how bad it really was.

'Is that why your mother killed herself?'

She was suddenly furious.

'*My mother did not kill herself.* She fell – she fell in front of the train . . . my mother . . .'

The words trailing away, the fury subsiding.

'Who?' I said.

'Let's stop talking about it.' She kissed me. 'Can we? Let's be like we were.'

She put her arms around me.

'Do you know who abuses children?' I said. 'It's almost always their family members. Nearly all the time, the statistics are overwhelming. Strangers? That happens. But not as often as people believe. It is usually someone trusted. Someone with access.' I shook my head. 'You're talking about your father.'

She buried her face in a pillow.

'No,' she said, her voice small and muffled.

'Your mother killed herself, didn't she?'

'Yes.'

'Why did she kill herself?'

'Why does anyone kill themselves? Because life was unbearable.'

I got out of bed.

'I'm sorry, Charlotte.'

It was true. I was sorry about everything. The mother. Her pain. And I was sorry about what I had to do now.

I wasn't sure what was happening. I did not know what it meant. But I was certain that there was someone I needed to see immediately.

I began to retrieve my clothes from where they had been discarded. I started to put them on.

She sat up in bed.

'Please listen to me,' she said. 'My father was a good man.'

I kept getting dressed.

She got out of bed, grabbed my arm and threw me around.

'*Listen to me!*'

It was the voice of one who was used to being obeyed, the voice of someone who had grown up surrounded by hired help.

'You can't go,' she said. 'You're *not* going. I don't want you to go!'

'And I don't want to go. I want to stay with you. I wish I could stay with you forever. But I have to go.'

'This is *private*.'

I nodded. But I didn't stop getting dressed. Her eyes were wild with misery.

'I didn't tell you because I want you to *do* something! I told you because I want you to *understand*.'

That was the moment to stay.

'I have to work now,' I said.

She cursed me. 'You can't *tell* anyone! You can't *use* this!'

I tried to kiss her one last time.

She turned her face away.

'*No*.'

'I have to go.'

'If you go now, then I don't want you to come back.'

I heard her crying as I went down the stairs.

Han Solo was on the floor of the hallway. I picked him up and slipped him into the pocket of my leather jacket.

Then I stepped out into Fitzroy Square, turning up my collar against the black and bitter cold.

CHAPTER 31

'I know why Mary Wood was seeing you,' I told Dr Joe. 'And I know what happened in that family. I don't mean the Wood family. I mean the Gatlings.'

We were in a bookshop in Notting Hill. It was after closing time but the place was full of happy, bright-faced people drinking wine and waiting to hear Dr Joe talk about a book he had written. We had stepped away from the crowds and into a quiet corridor of books. Intelligent chatter drifted down to us. People were happy that he was there.

'Max,' he said quietly. 'Mary was there for the same reason as all my other clients. She was trying to learn how to be alive in this world.'

'I know she was abused,' I said. 'When she was a girl.' I thought of the white band of scar tissue around Charlotte's left wrist. 'And I know that's why it was hard for her to be alive in this world.'

I saw by his face that it was true.

'Ah, Dr Joe!' I said. 'You should have told us.'

'I would have told you if it was relevant to your investigation,' he said. 'It wasn't. The man who did it died years ago.' He hesitated. 'Mary's coach. Her skiing instructor.'

I shook my head. 'That's not true,' I said. 'She lied to you. About that, at least. It's a lot closer to home. The same old story, Dr Joe. The abuse came from within her family.'

I saw the doubt on his face.

'Why did she stop seeing you?' I said.

'I don't know.'

'I do,' I said. 'Because there was something else she needed to do. To make it bearable. I think Mary had decided it was time to stop talking to you and start talking to the law. She was going to tell the police that she had been abused. I think she was ready. She was ready to tell the world. But sometimes it takes years, doesn't it? To find the words. To find the words to say that you've been abused. Sometimes it takes forever.'

'Yes,' said Dr Joe. 'And sometimes it takes even longer. How do you know about this?'

'Because it wasn't just Mary who was abused. It was both girls. Charlotte, too. After their mother killed herself, they were both abused by the old man. By their father. Victor Gatling.'

'No,' he said. 'You're wrong, Max. Mary loved her father.'

I banged on the door of Nils Gatling's suite at the Langham, looking at his DO NOT DISTURB sign.

A woman's voice came from inside.

'Leave it outside!'

302

I kept knocking.

Zina opened the door. The girl who had held Curtis Gane in his hospital bed.

We stared at each other, both of us surprised to see the other. What was I expecting? That she was going to hold Curtis Gane forever? Perhaps that is exactly the lie that you buy.

I followed her into a hotel suite that felt more like a house.

Zina was drunk. Sloppy drunk. And something else. Her words slurring into one another when she told me he was in the other room, her robe falling open.

She had some kind of downer in her veins. And then I saw the bubble-wrap package of pills on the dresser. Little white pills with a cross cut into the top.

Rohypnol.

Nils Gatling came into the room in a dressing gown.

'Let's talk about your sister,' I said.

He paused, sizing me up. He wasn't frightened. It should have been a warning but I ignored it.

'I have two sisters,' he said. 'Which one would you like to talk about, Detective?'

'Let's talk about the one who was murdered. I know why Mary was in therapy. She was abused as a child. And she was going to tell the world.'

He looked at me for a moment.

And then he laughed.

'No,' he said. 'You only *think* you've discovered

the reason she was in therapy. You see, the reason my sister needed help is because she was disturbed and delusional. There were suicide attempts. A history of self-harming.'

He saw the doubt on my face and smiled.

'God knows my brother-in-law was a useless little maggot – but I didn't envy him his married life. Mary was deeply troubled. If Peter Nawkins had not killed her then she would probably have done it herself. Three things run in my family – blond hair, blue eyes and paranoid-schizophrenia.' He sighed. 'It's the cross we bear.'

I shook my head.

'I think that if she hadn't been killed by Nawkins, she wouldn't have killed herself. What she would have done is *talked*. She would have gone to the police. Therapy did what it could. Dr Joe did what he could. But she needed closure.'

'Dreadful word,' he said.

'And maybe it's the wrong word,' I said. 'But I've seen too many victims. And they need the truth to come out, because if it doesn't it chews them up like cancer. Your sister needed the truth to come out because what had happened to her was eating her alive. She needed justice.'

'She *did*. She *did* talk. Talked for hours when she should have been training. I imagine it will all be on the record. All the dreary lies. All of her sick fantasies. My mother, too. All the women in my family suffered from the same sick fantasies.'

The women in his family.

His mother. His sisters.

Yes, I bet they all suffered from something.

'Nobody listened,' I said. 'I've seen that too. She tried to talk and nobody listened. And at last – all those years later – she was ready to try again.'

There was a knock on the door.

'Leave it outside!'

The knocking continued.

A flash of pure fury on Nils Gatling's face.

'Get that door, you stupid whore!' he said.

Zina swayed into the room. She looked at him with doped eyes.

'Get it yourself,' she said.

He took one step towards her and his hand cracked hard across her face. He was about to do it again when I took his wrist.

'OK,' he laughed. 'OK.'

'He likes to hurt me,' Zina said, the red palm print on her blotchy white skin, making her uncertain way to the door. 'He likes it too much. It's the only way he can get hard.'

She smiled at her small triumph. But Gatling just laughed.

'Touch her again,' I said, 'and I'll break your arm in three places.'

He smiled at me.

'Look at you,' he said. 'Defender of the weak.'

I let go of his wrist. This was running out of control. I had to get him to West End Central. We had to get an interview on tape. If we stayed here, I would want to hurt him.

Zina got the door. We didn't see the room service boy. It was a large suite. She came pushing a trolley.

Champagne. A bucket of ice. Two glasses. Dinner for one.

'I need you to come into West End Central,' I said. 'I need a statement. You are going to be interviewed under caution.'

'Do you mind?'

The champagne bottle was in his hand.

I ignored him and took out my phone. I wanted everything ready for us when we arrived.

He hit me in the centre of my head with the full champagne bottle. I went down on my knees. The bottle came down on the back of my skull. Something broke and it wasn't the bottle.

Zina was screaming. My ribs were wet and freezing cold. I had grabbed the linen tablecloth on the room service trolley and dragged down the ice bucket with me. Ice cubes everywhere. Something exploded in my ear. I realised he must have kicked me.

And then as blood slid into my eyes, the pain suddenly came all at once – in my forehead, in the back of my skull, in my ear.

Gatling was on the phone.

'Get here now,' he said.

And then, very carefully, the toe of his shoe aiming at the fragile bone just above the ear, Nils Gatling kicked me in the head until the sweet blackness came and took me away.

★   ★   ★

I awoke and stared at Zina.

I had not moved. I had no idea if I had been out for a minute or an hour. I felt the rush of nausea that comes with dislocated time. I had been knocked about quite badly. But not as bad as the girl who had left Romania ten years ago.

She was in a chair, her head slumped forward.

The front of her chemise was drenched in blood where her neck had been opened up.

'*Oh God . . . oh Jesus,*' I said.

I tried to get up.

Sean Nawkins was there.

He looked at me.

'Do him here,' he said, not taking his eyes off me.

'No,' said Gatling. 'We've already got to get rid of the whore. Unless you want to leave them both for the maid.'

There was a bottle of water in his hands. One of those small bottles of mineral water that they leave in hotels. They helped me to my knees. It was such an unexpected act of kindness that the tears stung my eyes in pathetic gratitude. Then Nawkins sank his fingers into my chin and pulled my mouth open.

'Drink it,' Gatling said.

I shook my head.

'*Drink it.*'

I mumbled something.

He put his head close.

'Fuck you,' I managed.

'Get his mouth open and keep it open.'

Nawkins gripped my chin with one huge hand

and my nose with the other. My jaw creaked open. The water was poured in. My throat convulsed in spasms, the vomit rising, bitter in my mouth.

But Nawkins had my mouth closed, and the vomit went down my throat with the water.

'Wait twenty minutes,' Gatling said.

The room began to slip away.

Time had chunks cut out of it.

I wanted to lie down and sleep forever, but I was being dressed, put into a hoodie that was too small for me, and then I was going down the hall, dizzy and sick, my legs not working, one of my friends holding me up on either side, into the service lift, larger and shabbier than the lift I had come up in.

We were going out the back way. A young hotel worker was outside sneaking a cigarette.

'One too many,' Gatling said, and the kid laughed, quickly hiding his cigarette.

'We've all done it, sir!' he said.

I felt myself falling into the deepest sleep. The sleep that is next door to death. It felt like all I had drunk was water, for when mixed with any liquid, Rohypnol has no taste and no smell.

It dissolves completely. And then so do you.

The effect that it has on psychomotor performance of mind and muscles can be compared to tranquillisers only if you understand that it is ten times more powerful.

Rapists love it.

Because it means they can do what they like with you.

CHAPTER 32

I woke up with a hammer being tapped against my front teeth.

'First I knock all his teeth out,' Sean Nawkins was saying. 'Then I can saw off his fingertips in twenty minutes.' He thought about it. 'Half an hour at the outside.'

The hammer's claw traced a rough sphere around my face. It dragged across my forehead, my cheek and my jaw and then up the other side.

'Then remove his face,' he said. 'Make a nice deep cut and then I can peel the skin right off.' He turned away. 'Then we burn him. And they don't find a man. Just burned, chopped-up meat.'

I was aware that I was unable to move. At first I thought it was the betrayal of my mind and muscles that prevented me from moving. But then I realised they had taped me to a chair with what must have been a good few rolls of brown duct tape.

At some point I had been sick because there was a streak of yellow bile hanging from my mouth and sticking to my bare chest.

Scout, I thought, or said it, and maybe even screamed it.

The Rohypnol was a thick fog in my brain and I could no longer tell what was real and what I had only dreamed.

There were lights in this new room and they were far too bright for me to see. I briefly wondered if I was dead already and cast in some over-lit corner of hell.

'*Oh, please, God,*' I said. '*Oh, please, Jesus . . .*'

'What's he saying?'

'Just babbling. It's the rophies. He's out of his skull.'

I heard bells. Temple bells, Japanese bells.

I opened my eyes.

I was in the big house in Highgate. I was in The Garden.

I was in the two-storey atrium that I had walked into a lifetime ago, the great white open space with a wall of glass at the back. The blackened stain of the failed fire still covered one high wall and half the floor of the kitchen and dining area. The long dinner table with places for twelve people was still there. Beyond the glass wall there was still only blackness.

And the gentle chime of the bells from the Japanese garden.

Nils Gatling was standing at the window, looking at his phone.

Nawkins was putting my clothes into a black bin bag. It was only then I realised I was naked.

There was a coffee table between us. There was a metal jerrycan on it, a hammer and a hacksaw and a tall glass vase of fresh-cut lilies.

My mind was not working properly. It was very likely that it would never work again. Rohypnol stays in the bloodstream for eight hours and I would be dead by then.

I could not think. I could not see. I could not breathe without being overwhelmed by a sudden tide of sickness.

But I saw one thing.

The man at the window.

And I saw him clear at last.

'Not your father,' I told Nils Gatling. 'You.'

And I did not know if the words were in my mouth or in my head but I saw the little rich boy running wild when his father was out of his mind with grief, when his father was waking up drunk, when his father wished he was dead too.

And I saw Gatling sneaking into the rooms of his sisters, and doing what he wanted, with nobody to stop him.

And I saw Mary slaughtered because she was finally going to talk to the police, all the secrets were about to pour out, because in the end they always come out, even if it takes a lifetime . . .

And I only knew that the words were not in my head when Nawkins tied up the black bin bag and came to me to tap the hammer against my front teeth again.

'You certainly talk a lot for a dead man.'

He picked up the jerrycan and emptied its reeking contents over my head, my arms and my legs. I retched on the stink of petrol.

'Drink up, Detective,' Nawkins told me. 'Because I am going to light a match on your next breath.'

Already I thought I could smell my roasting flesh.

'Burn it,' Gatling said contemptuously, not looking up from the phone. 'That's your answer to everything, isn't it? No more fires, Nawkins.'

It was not a request. It was a command and I saw the look of disappointment on Nawkins' face. He was a man who liked his fire. And I remembered the farm where the Slaughter Man left no prints because someone had torched it.

'You want him gone, don't you?' Nawkins said. 'He can't be found, can he? The fire will stop him being found.'

Gatling indicated the blackened stain in the kitchen and dining area.

'Tried that already, didn't you? How did that work out, you moron?'

'Your wife wasn't burned by townies,' I told Nawkins. 'She wasn't burned in a riot. That's all bullshit. She was burned alive by you, wasn't she? What did she do to deserve that?'

I saw his body tense but he didn't look at me.

'You want him gone, don't you?' Nawkins said.

'There's a better way,' Gatling said.

Suddenly it all fit.

I looked at Sean Nawkins and I saw a burning

caravan with a screaming woman inside and I remembered the visitors' records at a maximum-security prison that recorded Sean's wife visiting his brother Peter week after week, year after year.

And I saw the total certainty of Sean Nawkins' daughter dragging her nails down my face, not believing but *knowing* that her Uncle Peter was innocent of the crimes he was accused of.

'What you looking at, pig?' Nawkins shouted.

I smiled at him.

'I'm looking at a man whose wife and daughter both went to bed with his brother.'

He raised the hammer, murder in his face.

'And that's why you set him up,' I said.

He hit me with the hammer.

A hard crack across the cheekbone that tore off an inch of flesh just under my eye.

I hung my head, trying to control my breathing, attempting to master the pain. It was a few minutes before I could speak.

'Gatling?' I said.

'What?'

Not looking at me. Still fiddling with his phone.

'This is what happened,' I said. 'Sean Nawkins here was meant to shut your sister up. Stop Mary blabbing to the law. Very popular these days. Historical sex crimes that come back from the dead. You can do a lot of time for old sex crimes. Doesn't matter how long ago it was. No statute of limitations on raping children. Victims are finding their voice. And justice. Justice at last. What was the idea? Kill the whole family to make it look like a spree kill?'

Gatling almost smiled.

'It worked, didn't it?'

'Did you know Nawkins raped Mary? I bet that wasn't in the plan, was it? That's why you loathed Mary's husband. Nobody's meant to touch Mary apart from you. But he did, Gatling. Nawkins here. Ask him. That information was never released. But it's true. Ask him.'

Silence in the white room. Gatling was staring at Nawkins.

'Is this true?'

'No! He's trying to save his worthless skin . . .'

'Gatling?' I said.

'What?'

'Where's Bradley?' I said.

I began to call the boy's name.

'BRADLEY! BRADLEY! BRADLEY!'

'Shut him up, will you?' Gatling said, and Nawkins furiously covered my mouth with duct tape. Then he covered my nose, my eyes, my ears. He kept going until all the duct tape was gone.

And suddenly I could not breathe. My mouth. My nose. He had covered too much. He had left no airways. He wanted me dead now.

I tried to calm my heart.

I realised I could no longer breathe through my mouth and most of my nose was blocked by the tape. But I could suck in air through one tiny corner of one sinus. It was enough. And the top of one eye could see a slither of the room above the tape that nearly blinded me.

And that is how I saw the security guard.

A young Nepalese, probably ex-British Army Gurkha, maybe the same one who had been here on the first day. He was standing at the end of the driveway, looking towards the house uncertainly. Gatling and Nawkins were talking at the garden window. They had not seen him. The guard continued to look at the house.

My legs were taped above the knees. But I could still move my lower legs. I lashed out at the tall glass vase on the coffee table. I missed and cracked the top of my bare foot against the side of the table. The pain shot up my legs and wrung my testicles. I swallowed the sickness because I knew that if I was sick now then I would choke to death.

I aimed another kick at the glass vase and this time connected. The vase went flying, shattering against the far side of the coffee table, broken glass and water and fresh lilies everywhere.

And through my tiny window on the world, I saw the security guard coming up the drive.

He rang the doorbell.

Nawkins leaned close to me.

'I was going to do you quick,' he whispered. 'But now you're going to be done as slow as I can make it.'

I lashed out with my foot and connected with something hard and human. His fingers dug into my neck like claws, forcing my head down, and I could feel the cold air from the open door and the murmur of civilised conversation.

'Thank you so much,' Gatling was saying. 'Yes, the police released the house . . . I'll be staying here tonight, but thank you for your concern.'

'Sir,' said the Gurkha, and he went away.

The front door closed.

Footsteps on the driveway.

The door of the guard's car door, opening and closing. The car driving away.

I could have wept.

And then we were all alone in the big house at the top of the highest hill in the city, and there was a silence that sounded like the end of the world.

The blind, I thought.

Peter Nawkins was the blind.

Peter Nawkins was Maisy Dawes.

And he was perfect for the role.

'Wait until the guard knocks off,' Gatling said. 'Then we can take this one out the back.' He patted me on the head. My heart pounded in my chest. The air wasn't enough. It wasn't nearly enough.

I was suffocating.

'I know just the right place to bury him,' Gatling said.

The wall at the back of The Garden was covered with ivy.

At a certain spot it could be pulled back to reveal

a sally port – a secret double doorway whose original purpose could only be remembered by men who had been dust for a hundred years.

But when the ivy was pulled aside the hidden sally port provided entry to The Garden, just as it had on the night that Nawkins came to annihilate a family, just as it gave them passage into Highgate Cemetery on the night they carried me to the place of the dead.

They carried me deep into the Victorian jungle. I tried to keep a map in my head. Through the wall. Down the steps to Egyptian Avenue. A right to – where? – Dickens' Path. And then left and downhill to Comforts Corner.

But my mind was still weak and dizzy with the Rohypnol, I was in the middle of the drugged fog now, and by the time they dropped me hard on the ground, I was lost.

I could see nothing. There was only the blackness.

But I could hear the sound of earth being dug up, and then the sound of ancient wood, rotten with the ages, creaking and cracking as it was prised open.

There was the smell of the grave and strong arms were lifting me.

'You want to sleep with a whore?' Nils Gatling said, close to my ear. 'Here's one you can sleep with forever.'

Then I felt the rustle and crack of human bones beneath me as they lowered me into the coffin.

CHAPTER 33

*E*nough.
    Sleep now.
    Close your eyes.
Think of nothing.
Slip into the darkness that is total and unbroken and all you will ever know.
Let your breath do the work.
Let it be over.
Embrace the blackness and end all of your suffering.
End it. End it. End it.

The pain revived me.

I had no idea how long they had waited for the security guard to end his shift but I guessed it was hours rather than minutes because the pain sliced right through the Rohypnol fog inside my head.

They had knocked me about quite a bit, but the pain that woke me was from the single cut high on my cheekbone where Nawkins had caught me with the claw of the hammer.

The pain – the fierce sting of a fresh, deep cut on top of a bruise – was enough to lift the mist just enough to make me realise that they had buried me alive.

I screamed.

I thrashed like a dog with a dying rat in its mouth, the ancient bones cracking and snapping and breaking beneath me, sticking into my flesh, the tape that held my arms loosening, as if it had no dominion in this terrible place. I tore at it with my fingers, my teeth, pulling it away from me, wanting it gone.

There was so much of it but I knew that I was reaching the end of it when it began to tear away hair and skin. Then I lay there panting, and the roof of the universe was damp, rotten wood just a few inches above my face.

I lay there breathing, the blackness around me unbroken and absolute.

Then I began to punch.

'*Scout!*'

I thought of her and I drew another breath. I thought of her and she gave me strength. I thought of her and I said her name aloud and the sound of my daughter's name was full of the rage to live.

And I punched the way I had been taught to punch for month after month, and year after year, wasting nothing, no room to waste anything, lifting my fists the few inches to the wooden ceiling, slamming them home – left – right – left – right – banging away, a small animal gasp escaping my lips with every blow, left – right – left – right – *ah!* – *ah!* – *ah!* – *ah!* – my elbows tucked into my ribs, as if protecting myself from the body shots that robbed your breath and were worse than anything that anyone could do to your face – left – right – left – right – *ah!* – *ah!* – *ah!* – *ah!* – until my knuckles were torn raw and bleeding and I had to stop to master the pain and to find my breath again.

While I was resting I wrapped thick scraps of discarded duct tape around my hands, makeshift gloves to let me hit harder. Later – it felt like an hour but it could have been seconds – I began again.

And the wood cracked. A tearing sound, like sudden thunder, and it made me lash more wildly, which did no good at all, because the wood cracked no more and yet my energy seemed to be seeping from me, and I lay in the grave with the sweat pouring and the tears streaming and the salty sting in my eyes.

And I noticed the air.

There was not so much air.

The air was being used up.

I turned on my side, feeling the panic surge, trying to fight it down with slower breathing. But I found I could not lie on my side. There was no room when I was sideways. The coffin would not counter such movement. It wanted me to rest on my back and to rest like that until the end of time.

I cursed out loud, lashing out with one foot, and felt it smash through rotten wood and into the cold earth. It took a while to pull my foot back. I knew then that the wood was ready to fall apart. I just had to hit it the right way. And I had to do it before the air was gone.

But I was so tired.

I closed my eyes, although nothing changed when my eyes were open or when my eyes were closed. I rested for as long as I could. Then when I felt the darkness pulling me down, telling me to sleep, telling me that I had done my best and now it was time to rest, I steeled myself for one final effort.

I could no longer punch because my knuckles were a bloody mush. So I used the weapons of the dirty fighter.

Elbows. Knees. Forehead. Hit them with anything. Hit them with everything. Getting into a mad rhythm.

'*Scout! Scout! Scout!*'

Grunting with each impact. Left elbow into wood – right elbow into wood – lashing up with right knee – then the left knee – and finally raising myself off the ground, in a stunted little sit-up, the bones beneath me pressing into my back, then breaking as I smashed my forehead hard against the wooden sky.

And it did no good. The wood creaked and cracked and even split. But I remained in the tomb that I would rest in forever, exhausted now, and finally giving in to the hot, bitter tears.

I said one word out loud.

'*Scout.*'

And I would have wept.

But then I felt the rat.

It came into my little wooden world through the

hole that I had kicked with my foot. It slid between my legs and – responding to my cry of pure horror – slid across one thigh, its long tail like a diseased snake sliding over my bare flesh, and I heard its teeth chatter close to my head as it paused to smell and savour the bloody meat of my face.

I kicked and screamed and thrashed, lashing out like a dying animal that finally understood he was fighting for his life.

The coffin lid split, and cracked, and fell apart.

And the sky caved in. Cold, hard dirt pouring down, hitting my chest and then my face, and then everywhere, a sky full of dirt chilled by winter, all at once in my mouth and in my eyes and clogging my nostrils.

I tore at the earth with broken fingernails. I scratched and I clawed and I dug. It tried to bury me. I refused to let it. But the weight of the world pressed down on me, a world of dirt that was suffocating me. And I fought against it, knowing that when I stopped fighting it would be time to die, trying to lift myself up and yet held down hard, truly fighting more than digging now, the way a desperate man fights, with a kind of helpless and terrified ferocity, the earth so cold and so hard with the winter, and I realised that I was no longer breathing, I was drowning, a man drowning in dirt, gagging on a mouthful of the stuff, my throat closing down as my lungs and heart made ready to burst.

Then I was half-sitting up, the weight of the dirt

world still pressing down on me but unable to hold me, and I felt one hand break through the ground, the air sweet and cold, and then I was pulling, crushing bones to dust beneath my feet.

Fingers in the night air, then one hand, then one arm flailing above ground, pulling myself up, the top of my head and then my face, retching dirt and sucking air, vomiting dirt, sucking it back in, feeling it clinging to tongue and teeth and throat, gasping like a drowning man breaking the surface with the last of his strength, and suddenly I was lying there, panting and gagging, half-buried and half-free, the pain everywhere, still with the dirt of the grave in my throat and eyes and nose.

Alive.

A pair of fierce yellow eyes bored into me. The scarred old fox and I stared at each other in disbelief. Then the fox ran. And I slept. Or I fainted. Or there was still enough of the Rohypnol in my bloodstream to make me cling to the darkness as if it was my lover.

I did not move until I shuddered with cold and suddenly knew that I would freeze to death if I did not move.

Watched by all the angels with no faces, I pulled myself from the grave and found that I could not even begin to stand. Nowhere near it. Forget standing. So I crawled.

Dragging myself slowly, feeling the rough ground beneath my knees and elbows and forearms and shins and feet, the pain without respite, glad for the remains of the duct tape that still clung to my limbs and gave me some protection.

I crawled hoping that the night would end and that help would come. But the night was without end and no help came. When I could crawl no more I lay down and trembled with the cold, whimpering like a wounded animal.

The last thing I remember was looking up at the monument where I had stopped. Rising out of the undergrowth was a statue of a sleeping dog. It was a massive thing, more the size of a car than a dog, and I wondered if it was really there or just inside my dreams. It didn't matter now.

Beyond the dog there was a stone plinth with words that shone in the last full moon of winter.

TOM SAYERS
PUGILIST
CHAMPION OF ENGLAND
BORN 1826
PIMLICO, BRIGHTON, SUSSEX.
'IT'S A MAN'S GAME.
IT TAKES A GAME MAN
TO PLAY IT.'

I closed my eyes and passed out with one hand on Tom Sayers' dog.

CHAPTER 34

'Oh, God Almighty,' Rocky said. 'What have they done to you?'

It was freezing cold in Highgate Cemetery. The hour before dawn. He came jogging out of the mist, for it was the time that boxers do their lonely running, the insurance against the catastrophe of total physical exhaustion when there is still fighting to be done.

I was lifted by hands that felt both strong and gentle, and I stared at faceless angels in the undergrowth as the remains of the duct tape were pulled from my body and he began to dress me in his tracksuit, zipping up the top to my chin, easing me to the ground and struggling to pull up the bottoms. He helped me to my feet and I held on to him for support as we slowly walked downhill to the gates where his elderly white van was waiting.

'Twenty-seven Savile Row,' I said, repeating it when he did not react. '*Twenty-seven Savile Row. West End Central.*'

'No,' he said.

Then we were heading south, the traffic already

building around Archway, and I may have slept because we were around the Angel when I glanced at his face and saw it set in hard lines as we turned east for the City and the East End and Essex. And I knew that the last place in the world Rocky would ever take me was a police station.

I cursed him once. For not taking me where I wanted to go. For all the things he had not told me. He smiled grimly at me and shook his head, and I closed my eyes knowing that he had saved my life.

Then I slept.

I awoke to the sound of skipping.

The leather rope whipping through the air, faster and faster as thin-soled boxing boots lightly touched the ground. I flexed my body, feeling where it hurt, and tried to stretch my arms and legs. My hands touched the wall. The bed was tiny, and so was the room. I was in a small caravan. There was a baseball bat in one corner. My hand reached out for it.

'You're safe here,' Echo said.

She was standing in the doorway. As always she was dressed for summer and courting. White shorts. A T-shirt that didn't quite reach the jewel in her navel. High, clunky heels. But she seemed older now, and her pregnancy was unmistakable.

'You don't need a baseball bat,' she said, unsmiling. 'Rocky's not going to let them hurt you any more.'

I lay back on the bed, reflecting that baseball bats are a vastly overrated form of personal protection.

'What happened to you?' Echo said.

I took a breath. From the fading light outside, it looked like I had slept for most of the day. The remains of the Rohypnol felt like the worst hangover in the world. But I could remember everything. And I could think clearly.

'Your father and Nils Gatling,' I said. 'They happened to me. They know each other, don't they?'

She shrugged. 'My dad's done work for him for years. Gatling's got property all over London. It's been a steady earner for my old man.'

I almost laughed.

'And you didn't tell me?' I said. 'And Rocky didn't tell me?'

Her gaze never wavered.

'You're the law,' she said. 'We try not to tell you anything.' Then a flicker of the old anger. 'But I *did* try to tell you about my uncle, didn't I? I *told* you my uncle was innocent. But you wouldn't listen.'

'You don't want to talk to us but you want us to listen,' I said. 'You can see how that might cause problems, right?'

She took a breath and let it go.

'My father and Nils Gatling,' she said. 'What have they done?'

'They did each other a favour. That's what they did. Gatling wanted to silence his sister. And your father wanted to punish his brother.'

I saw the shock on her face. Her hand protectively rubbed her belly and the baby that was growing inside her.

I sat up and looked out of the window. Rocky was skipping, stripped to the waist, He radiated supreme fitness, and I wondered when his first professional fight was happening. It had to be soon.

'Why would Nils Gatling want to kill his sister?' Echo said.

'He wanted to stop her from going to the police about historic sex abuse. Horrible things, revealed at last. Her family – they were collateral damage.'

She did not ask me why her father had wanted to punish his brother. She didn't need to.

'You knew Peter Nawkins didn't kill them because on New Year's Eve he was with you,' I said. 'I should have believed you. And I think I would have – if you had told me.' I thought of Sergeant Ross Sallis of Tottenham Hale, and the way he had looked after having a shotgun fired near his face at close range. And I thought of the Burns family, the father and his three grown-up sons, and what Peter Nawkins had done to them after they tried to castrate him.

'Your uncle didn't kill Mary Wood and her family,' I said. 'But it's a bit of a stretch to call him innocent.'

She laughed bitterly.

'So it's never over then?' she said. 'My uncle did his time but it's never forgotten by you people?'

'Not if it makes enough headlines,' I said. 'Fame comes and goes. Infamy lasts forever.'

I noticed she had a fresh black eye and I knew her father must be close by. I looked again at the baseball bat. Vastly overrated, but better than nothing.

'When's your baby due?' I said.

'The end of the summer,' she said.

'Who's the father?' I asked.

She shook her head quickly as the caravan door opened and Rocky appeared in the doorway. He slipped an arm around Echo's waist and placed a kiss on her lips.

'They're back,' he said. 'Outside the wire. One of them chucked a bottle at me so I've come inside. It's been bad since your Uncle Peter died.'

I looked out of the window and I saw a large group of locals gathering on the far side of the wire. A solitary female police officer was among them, her hands raised, pleading for calm.

'What do they want?' I said.

He grinned. 'Same as always,' he said. 'They want us out. Are you all right?'

I nodded. 'Thanks,' I said. Then I shook my head. 'You should have talked to me, Rocky. You should have told me that you worked at The Garden. You should have told me everything. You ever see Nils Gatling around Sean Nawkins?'

He shrugged and looked away, even now reluctant to give up what he knew.

'You really should have told me that,' I said. 'You

329

should have told me what you knew about Echo's father.'

'I don't know anything about her old man,' he said. 'Apart from the fact that he's a fucking psycho.'

'He's more than that,' I said. 'Sean Nawkins is a murderer. And now he's going down.'

Rocky nodded, attempting a grin that failed miserably, and I found myself hoping that it was his child she was carrying. Suddenly an awkward silence came between us. He didn't feel he could ask me who had given me a beating, and I couldn't talk to him about Echo's baby.

'I can't believe you two are still here,' I said. Echo's black eye looked fresh. 'So close to your father,' I said.

'That's ending,' Rocky said. 'Got my first pro fight on Friday. York Hall. A six-rounder against a Serbian who's 6 and O.'

Rocky had the kind of fitness that glows. Fighting fit, they call it. I had no doubt that he was ready for his life to begin.

'Good luck with that,' I said, and indicated the pair of them. 'Good luck with everything.'

Rocky looked at Echo proudly.

'Get a few wins under my belt and then we're moving out of here,' he said. 'It's no life for a fighter. Not knowing when you're getting moved on. You need stability. You need routine. Get a little flat in Billericay. Somewhere with a bit of green for the kid but that's handy for the London trains.'

I nodded. It seemed like a good plan.

Then I stood up, shrugging my shoulders, feeling where it hurt. I did not have any injuries that would stop me doing what I needed to do. Better get on with it, I thought.

'I need you to do one more thing,' I told him. 'I'm going to give you a direct number for DCI Patricia Whitestone at West End Central. I want you to call her right now and tell her that I have arrested Sean Nawkins for the murders of Mary Wood, Brad Wood, Marlon Wood and Piper Wood. Can you remember that?'

They were silent.

Rocky looked at Echo.

'I can remember it,' she said.

I gave her the number.

Then I nodded at the pair of them and stepped outside their little caravan. I was still wearing the hoodie he had put me in. It said KRONK GYM – DETROIT on the front. I zipped it up as far as it would go.

I was close to the front gate of Oak Hill Farm, a part of the camp where there were smaller caravans. The crowds beyond the wire seemed to have increased. I looked for the reassuring sight of blue uniforms but all I saw was the young woman I had watched from the caravan and her colleague, a young man who was at the main gate, talking into the radio on his shoulder. He looked scared.

They had parked their car inside the gates. That was a mistake. You park where you inform the

331

public that they are going no further. Parking inside the gates was lousy tactics.

From somewhere close by I heard the sound of breaking glass, followed by ironic cheers. Then more breaking glass.

I walked faster. I wanted this done.

I saw the smoke before I saw Sean Nawkins. Thick black smoke rising from the skip behind his bungalow.

Screams. I turned to look at the wire. The young copper was in the middle of the crowd. Now the woman was talking urgently into her radio, calling for backup. I listened for sirens. Nothing. I stared at them for a moment, knowing they needed my help.

But I kept walking.

More breaking glass. And a much louder cheer this time, as a small burst of fire exploded on the scrappy patch of grass where I had seen the horses on that first day. I stopped again, waiting to see if they were going to throw more petrol bombs. But when a couple of beer bottles came over, shattering harmlessly against the roof of a caravan, I kept going.

The front door to Sean Nawkins' bungalow was open. I walked round the side of the building to where the skip was burning. Nawkins was emptying petrol from a plastic jerrycan on to perhaps a dozen black bin bags that he had tossed into the skip. I wondered what was in the bin bags apart from the clothes he had worn last night.

I wondered if Zina was in them.

'I'm arresting you for murder,' I said, and he looked up at me as if he was staring at a dead man, taking a terrified half-step backwards, his jaw suddenly slack with terror.

'No,' he said, denying my existence more than his crimes. 'Not you.'

'You do not have to say anything,' I said, moving towards him as a bottle smashed against the side of the skip, and then another bounced off the roof of his bungalow without breaking.

He clutched the jerrycan to his chest, as if defending himself from a ghost, and all at once a burning bottle hit his shoulder and there was a soft pop of air – *whap!* – and Sean Nawkins erupted into a ball of flames.

He staggered towards me, his head a corona of flame and his flesh already melting, his hair on fire, his eyebrows and hair the first to burn, his mouth twisted and screaming, one hand holding the side of the skip, his body stooped by the all-consuming agony, his face blackening as his features burned away.

Then a bottle must have struck me because I was momentarily stunned, dizzy and sick, a searing pain in the back of my skull and broken glass glistening on the front of Rocky's tracksuit top.

Sean Nawkins was lying at my feet.

Flat on his face, the flames subsiding, most of his clothes gone, revealing that every inch of his flesh was the colour and the texture and the stink of badly burned meat.

I backed away, one hand on the back of my head, another over my mouth, and I stumbled round the side of the bungalow and into a full-scale riot.

The locals had entered the camp.

The residents of Oak Hill Farm were pouring out of their caravans and bungalows to meet them. There were men with lead pipes, women with baseball bats, dogs barking and children screaming. Just inside the main gates the two sides clashed like medieval armies, coming together in a sickening collision of metal and flesh, broken glass and blood.

The two uniformed officers were nowhere to be seen but their car had been commandeered by the locals. Two large men in polo shirts, all clinical obesity and bad tattoos, not young, bellowing from the windows, were driving the squad car across the neat little flower beds, weaving across the lawns.

I saw Rocky and Echo in the doorway of their tiny caravan. She was calling a name.

'*Smoky! Smoky! Smoky!*'

Her dog.

I saw the Akita, maddened with terror, standing on a lawn next to a child's swing, barking wildly. Then Rocky was running towards the Akita, and the men in the stolen squad car had seen him too, and began driving towards him.

Rocky got to the dog first. Clapping his hands, shouting instructions. For a moment the great Akita was oblivious but then he responded, and

Rocky was turning back, the Akita at his heels, the squad car with the two screaming men getting closer to them with every second.

The car not swerving now.

The car aimed at man and dog like a heat-seeking missile.

Echo was in the doorway.

Her dog was much faster than Rocky and it bounded ahead of him, disappearing inside the caravan, its tail already wagging with happiness, and Rocky was almost there, almost there when he stumbled and fell and lay unmoving and spread-eagled on the scrappy grass of Oak Hill Farm.

The squad car ran over his arms just above the elbows.

I saw his face contort with agony as he screamed at the heavens.

The car swerved away, the two men laughing wildly.

Then I heard the sirens and I turned towards the gates of Oak Hill Farm, and began running towards them.

CHAPTER 35

I put on the blues and twos and we drove west as night came closing in, the heavy traffic on the motorway to Heathrow melting away before us, the tail lights pulling over to the hard shoulder at the approach of the BMW X5.

'Mary talked,' DCI Whitestone said beside me. She was leafing through a thin green file that looked as if it was twenty years old but had never been touched. 'When Mary was sixteen years old, she went to the local police and made a formal statement about her brother's abuse.' She closed the file. 'Nobody believed her. Nobody was listening.'

'They would have believed her this time,' I said. 'The world has changed.'

'They didn't even bother to lose the file,' Wren said. 'Did the father lean on the law back in the day?'

'The sad thing is that he probably didn't even have to,' Whitestone said. 'The big man's name would have been enough.'

'But why take out the family?' Wren said. 'Nils Gatling wanted to shut his sister up. Why kill the husband and the children? Why abduct the little boy?'

'Making it look like a spree kill was part of the blind,' I said. 'And so was the cattle gun. What kind of nutter uses a cattle gun for mass murder? Somebody who's done it before.' I thought of what John Caine had told me in the Black Museum. 'You kill with what you know. And it was a good blind – the Slaughter Man looked perfect for this – especially after Mary Wood gave him a glass of lemonade and a smile and he started collecting her pictures.'

'So Nils Gatling and Sean Nawkins had known each other for years?' Whitestone said.

I nodded. 'Gatling owned property all over London, and Nawkins had a limitless supply of cheap labour. And once Nils realised that Mary had decided there were things she intended to tell the police, she was as good as dead. All he needed was someone to spill the blood. And Sean Nawkins had his own reasons for setting up his brother, the Slaughter Man.'

'But why was Mary so determined to talk now?' Wren said. 'After all these years? Because she wanted justice? Because she wanted to save her marriage? Because she wanted to stay sane? Because men should not get away with this stuff – no matter how long ago it was?'

'All of the above,' I said.

I thought of Charlotte in my arms. I remembered how she had looked when she told me not to get too carried away. *This is difficult for me,* she had said, and I knew that was why Mary had decided

337

to finally go to the police. Because her life could never be what it should be while the cruel and bitter past dragged her down, and held her heart, and stopped her from loving, trusting and holding someone the way she should. *This is difficult for me*, Charlotte had said, and I knew she spoke of the victim's terrible burden, and it was exactly why Mary was ready to tell the world what her brother had done to her.

'Nils Gatling wanted to silence his sister and Sean Nawkins wanted to punish his brother,' Whitestone said. 'But are we really certain that Peter Nawkins had an affair with Sean's wife and daughter?'

I shrugged. 'I know that Echo spent New Year's Eve with her Uncle Peter and I know that her mother visited him in Belmarsh for years. That's it. I don't know for certain what either of them did with him. Nights of passion? A cup of tea and a cuddle? No idea, in all honesty. There's no question that Peter Nawkins was an extremely violent man – when Burns and his sons tried to castrate him he came back to their farmhouse and fired a cattle gun into their brains. But if the world left Peter Nawkins alone, he was happy to leave the world alone. He didn't shoot Sergeant Sallis when he had the chance. If you caught Peter Nawkins on a good day, or even if you just treated him like a human being, I suspect he could be gentle and kind. But Sean Nawkins was a psychopath.'

'Sean's wife and daughter couldn't stand to be

around him,' Whitestone said. 'He was a vicious, woman-beating bastard. A woman like that – and a girl like that – they're going to look for a way out.'

'And sometimes they don't look very far,' Wren said. 'In this case, the caravan next door.'

I looked in my rear-view mirror. The cars that pulled on to the hard shoulder stayed there to let the rest of our convoy through. There were two CO19 ARVs, response cars, patrol cars, and a few motorbike outriders who couldn't keep up with me. Somewhere in there was a Child Abuse Investigation Team.

'We've got to lose the circus before we go in,' I said. 'They have to wait for our call. I don't want to frighten that little boy.'

I felt rather than saw Whitestone and Wren exchange a glance. But they said nothing, as the city and the suburbs made way for green rolling hills and houses made of honey-coloured stone.

And I drove to Lower Slaughter.

In the walled garden of a manor house, a small boy was playing by himself.

Bradley Wood looked older and darker than any photograph I had ever seen of him, but then that is true of almost all missing children. At a garden table, an elderly Filipina housekeeper was dozing with her head on her arms, an iPad on the table in front of her. We didn't disturb her.

'Bradley?' I said, crouching down so that our eyes were level. 'I think this belongs to you.'

I held out a plastic eight-inch figurine of a space cowboy.

'Han Solo,' he said, taking it from me. 'I've been looking for him.' He looked beyond me at Wren and Whitestone, as if expecting to see his mother, and I felt a wave of raw grief surge through me. The things men do, I thought. The things men do for those few spasms of pleasure, and the things they do to hide it away.

'Bradley?'

'Yes?'

'Did anyone hurt you, son?'

He thought about it. Then shook his head.

'Would you tell me if someone hurt you?' I said.

A short nod.

I believed him.

'Can I go home now?' Bradley said. 'Uncle Nils keeps telling me, *Soon, soon.*'

'You can go home right now,' I said. 'And you don't even need to say goodbye, OK? You go with these ladies. They've got the *Millennium Falcon* parked outside.'

He gave me a slow, shy smile, and in his face I saw his mother, his brother, his sister, the entire star-crossed family.

Most of all I saw his aunt.

Wren was holding out her hand. 'I'm Edie,' she said. 'And the Metropolitan Police Force is always with me.'

Bradley laughed uncertainly, but he took her hand.

I looked back at the house. A man with a shaven

340

head was standing in the doorway. He had arms built up on weights that bulged from his short-sleeve white shirt and a gut built up on lager that hung over his black trousers. The kind of body-guard that had been turning up all over London. Apparently they were even out in the countryside. He disappeared back into the house, talking on his mobile.

Whitestone and I watched Wren leading the boy round the side of the house.

'Max?'

'What?'

'I have to ask you – did Charlotte Gatling know the boy was here?'

'No,' I said with total certainty. 'She never came to this place. It wasn't home to her. It was more like a torture chamber. And it tore her heart out that Bradley was missing.'

'You know that the CAIT people – the child protection unit – are going to have to turn him over to social services?'

'That can't happen. Not to him. Hasn't he lost enough already?'

'Max, they're not going to release him to someone from this messed-up family.'

'Then just take him to her in London,' I said. 'You and Edie. Get the kid to someone who loves him. Charlotte can argue about it later. She's smart. She's rich. She *wants* him. He *needs* her. They need each other. She can hire the best lawyers in London. Please. Bradley can't go into care.'

Whitestone thought about it. But not for long.
'What's the address?'
I gave her the address in Fitzroy Square.
And then we went into the house.

There were screams coming from the first floor.
'What have I told you?' a woman with a West
Country accent was shouting. 'What have I told
you about doing your bloody business in the bed?'
Screams. Slaps. The sound of tears.
We entered an enormous room.
An old man lay on a four-poster bed.
He was wearing nothing but a gigantic nappy.
It was Victor Gatling.
And Victor Gatling was crying.
Bitter, heartbroken tears. He looked into my eyes
and, although I was no expert, I estimated that
his dementia was at least ten years old. There was
a red mark on his cheek.
A man and a woman were either side of the bed.
They were both grotesquely overweight, and the
tattoos that covered the flopping blubber of their
bare meaty arms looked out of place amid all this
rural splendour.
The fat man lifted his hand to strike Victor
Gatling again, but he saw the muscles tighten
around my mouth and that was enough to stop
him. The fat woman was less wary. She took a
fistful of the old man's thinning white hair and
shook it hard.
Then she stared at Whitestone defiantly.

'What the fuck do you want, you four-eyed bitch?' the woman said, a fleck of spit flying from her mouth.

Whitestone took out an Airwave radio and said that she wanted social services and some uniformed officers in here immediately. Then she started towards the bed.

'Madam,' she told the fat woman. 'That's DCI Bitch to you.'

There were a lot of bathrooms.

I found Nils Gatling in the master bedroom's en-suite bathroom at the very top of the house. He was wearing a cashmere sweater and his underpants. His legs were thin and hairy and the sight of him half-dressed made my flesh crawl. I was hoping that the sight of me risen from that shallow grave in Highgate Cemetery might kill him. But he looked at me with that old familiar contempt.

'Step back, pig,' he said. Between the thumb and index finger of his right hand he held an old-fashioned razor blade. He pressed the razor blade against his wrist. He did not break the skin.

I laughed at him.

'Go ahead,' I said. 'Don't stop on my account.'

I glanced over my shoulder. Nobody else was coming. They were all happy to leave him to me.

'But slashing your wrists is a slow way to die,' I said. I nodded at the bathtub. 'You need to speed up the blood flow or it's going to be more pain than you can handle, pal. Trust me. Hot water is

343

good. A bath is great. But you need to cut something serious – an artery or a vein – so push down really hard, OK? And don't slash *across* – that's just in the movies, and a common mistake – you have to slash *down*, towards your wrist from about two-thirds of the way to your elbow. Otherwise you're going to cut a tendon and you will not be able to do both sides. What would be good is if you were really hydrated – you need to drink as much water as you can to enlarge your veins and make the blood flow good and fast. Get a few litres of water inside you. Sparkling or still – it doesn't matter. Whatever you fancy. But make it a *long* cut. How sharp is that razor? It doesn't look that sharp to me. You should use a brand-new blade. And – this is important, so pay attention – you have to do it quick or you'll back out. And what's really perfect is if you can do both wrists. So you cut one wrist and then immediately put the razor in the other hand and do the same again. But you should do the weaker side first. You're right-handed? So cut your left wrist with your right hand and then change sides. There's just one problem . . .'

He licked his lips.

'I never met a bully yet who wasn't a coward,' I said, and I took my time crossing the bathroom, turning him around and putting on the handcuffs. Hinged ASP handcuffs in steel and black that let me have a good look at his lily-white wrists.

There was not a mark on them.

'One thing I don't understand,' I said. 'You let the boy live. Sean Nawkins was let loose to kill your sister, her husband, those two teenage kids. But Bradley was spared and brought here. Why didn't you tell your man to do the entire family?'

I felt him tremble with rage.

'What kind of animal do you think I am?' he said. 'I would never hurt that child. Do you think—'

There was more but I didn't have the patience to hear it. There is not one evil bastard in the world who can't find a good reason for their mindless cruelty. I don't need to hear it.

The steel handcuffs snapped shut behind Nils Gatling's back and I yanked them towards me, so that he stumbled one step backwards and our faces were very close. He hung his head. His breath came in ragged gasps. His eyes were shining with self-pity.

'You done?' I asked him. 'Because you look done to me.'

His courage came back by the time we reached the motorway.

He was in the X5's passenger seat, leaning forward, half-sitting on the hands that were cuffed behind him. A warning signal went *ping-ping-ping* because he was not wearing the seat belt, but I was not taking him out of the cuffs. I saw the cocky, knowing grin on his face and I waited. I looked in the mirror and I could not see the rest of our convoy. Somehow I had lost them.

Nils Gatling chuckled to himself.

It was dark now and the traffic towards London was thin. I watched the accelerator increasing with a kind of detached interest, as though it didn't really have much to do with me. I saw the sign that said LONDON and I longed to be home.

Nils Gatling moved in the passenger seat, as if he was both deeply amused and mildly uncomfortable.

'You don't *seriously* think that my sister could possibly be interested in a man like you, do you?' he said.

I said nothing.

'You see, when you get them started that young – as I did with both Mary and Charlotte – then they are never really the same again,' he said. 'There's some damage that can never be repaired. And I have that over you. And I will *always* have that over you. Every time you kiss her, you are tasting my—'

There was black ice on the motorway.

You can't see black ice very well because it is not black at all – it is transparent, ice that is devoid of air bubbles, clear ice, a thin layer of ice so clear that you can see the black stuff beneath it. But it is not invisible.

You can see it if you are trained to see it.

And I saw it. I was trained to see it.

And I knew that if the BMW X5 hit the black ice and lost traction and went into a skid I could not pull out of then Nils Gatling would likely put his face through the windscreen and bounce one hundred yards down the motorway, almost certainly breaking his neck while my face was buried deep in a big comfy BMW air bag.

Shut his mouth forever.

I deliberately steered on to the black ice, and the X5 went into a sickening skid, the back of the big car swinging around like an executioner's axe.

There was a moment when I could have put the bastard through the windscreen. But I let the moment pass.

And I found myself going through the drill on muscle memory alone.

Don't panic.

Don't brake.

Don't oversteer.

Turn into the skid.

And I gained control of the X5 and then the black ice was suddenly behind us and we were on smooth motorway with the lights of London ahead of us.

I felt calm and crisp and strong.

Nils Gatling was panting with terror in the passenger seat, wondering what had just happened. He kept his cakehole shut for the rest of the journey.

I handed custody over to the duty sergeant at West End Central and they took him down to the holding cell. And then I did something that the black ice on the motorway almost stopped me from doing.

I went home to Scout.

★   ★   ★

I got a call from Edie Wren when I was fixing our breakfast. They had found Nils Gatling at first light. At some point in the night he had ripped his cashmere sweater to shreds, tied it to the bars of the custody cell and hung himself by the neck until dead.

I think I was expecting the call.

Because sometimes bullies and cowards don't have the nerve to kill themselves and at other times they lack the nerve you need just to stay alive.

CHAPTER 36

The days were getting warmer.

On the last Sunday of the month I stood at the window of our loft, the great market still and silent on its day of rest, and I could see the seasons changing before my eyes.

Above the dome of St Paul's, the fierce winds of late March made it seem as if the whole of the sky was moving. But the days were lighter now and it felt like the long winter was finally gone. Something cold and dark had been lifted from our city, and it was suddenly beautiful again.

As the cathedral bells rang for morning prayers, so close they sounded as though they were coming from our kitchen, I got down on the floor to do one hundred press-ups. When I had to pause at fifty for a triple espresso, Stan raised his head from his basket and looked at me with mild surprise.

It was true. Somewhere between long hours and a stab wound, I had let my fitness slide.

I had missed too many of my regular sessions with Fred. But they would always be waiting for me. The heavy bag, the speedball, the pads and the sparring. The endless sweat and the occasional splatter of blood, with The Jam and The Clash and James Brown always on the sound system. I looked forward to getting fit with Fred.

He had called me with bad news. Rocky's injuries in the Oak Hill Farm riot had ended his career as a pro before it had even begun. The last Fred had heard, Rocky and Echo had moved out to Essex, the way generations of Londoners had moved out in search of a patch of grass to call their own.

I was sad to hear that Rocky had stopped training. But he had the woman he loved. They had a child on the way. They had a new home. Life was not over for him. It was just beginning.

The training may have been over for Rocky, but for an ordinary man like me, it never ended. My kit bag was already packed to go, because Fred had taught me that the first thing you do when you get back from the gym is to pack your kit bag for the next time.

My body ached with the bone-deep weariness of someone who is still recovering from being given a beating by experts. But there were no reasons worth giving. There were only excuses.

With the bitter tang of the espresso in my mouth, I forced out the remaining fifty press-ups, noting the build-up of lactic acid in my arms and the way my heart and lungs were being made to work hard, knowing that the final handful of press-ups – the ones you didn't feel like doing, the ones that would be easy to skip because you had already done enough – were where you claimed real and lasting strength.

And I had to be strong. I had to be fit. I had to be healthy. My heart and my muscles and my lungs – they could never let me down.

Because Scout still had a lot of growing to do.

And I was going to stand by her side every step of the way.

It was late afternoon, the days noticeably getting longer and brighter and milder, and Stan and I were alone in West Smithfield where he sniffed the bins, getting his pee-mail before leaving his own mark – *I, Stan, passed this place* – while I read the inscription from *Oliver Twist* that covers the stone chairs, Charles Dickens' hymn to the ghosts of the meat market.

'*Countrymen, butchers, drovers, hawkers, boys, thieves, idlers and vagabonds of every low grade were mingled together in a dense mass . . . the cries of hawkers, the shouts, oaths, and quarrelling on all sides, the ringing of bells and roar of voices that issued from every public house . . .*'

But Smithfield was silent and empty now.

The meat porters were at home in the suburbs. The clubbers were tucked up in bed. And the tourists were all gathering around the bells of St Paul's.

It was a good and a quiet time and we lingered there until the soft spring light was fading and it was time to pick up Scout from her friend's party.

It was three miles from Smithfield to Mia's home in Pimlico but the route passes through some of my favourite parts of the city, and Stan and I elected to walk.

It was a glorious day. We went down to the river and then along the Embankment as far as Big Ben, then around Parliament Square and took a right into Birdcage Walk before taking the long way round for an excuse to stroll through St James's Park.

The park was where I saw her.

On the far side of the lake.

Charlotte and Bradley, looking exactly like mother and son, both of them shaking with laughter as they tried and failed to float some kind of mechanical boat on a lake that was as still as glass.

A blonde woman in a red coat, dressed too warm for this time of year, and a small boy who looked at her as if she was his everything.

She glanced up and saw me.

I said her name once, and started around the lake towards her.

Then a woman's voice behind me stopped me.

'Excuse me? *Excuse* me!'

It was a voice so posh you could have used it to stir Pimm's. Its owner was one of those Chelsea widows who bought their house early and clung on after the wealthy foreigners from Russia and China and the Eurozone moved in and all the people who fly first class were bought out by all the people who fly in private planes.

Somewhere in her late seventies, the Chelsea widow wore a Hermès scarf, Hunter boots and was carrying a dog lead that had an orange plastic bone containing poo bags. She glared at me with well-mannered ferocity and I felt an enormous affection for her. She had probably lived through the Blitz, knew all the waiters at Wilton's and was as much a part of the old London that I loved as the porters of Smithfield.

'Do you have a Cavalier King Charles spaniel?'

'Stan,' I said. 'Yes, ma'am.'

'Have you seen what your Stan's doing to my Lulu?'

'Lulu?'

'My Labradoodle!'

Stan was struggling to mount a pissed-off looking Labradoodle with a look of abject misery in his eyes. He could not help himself and I remembered something a wise man said about the male sex drive, how it was like being chained to a maniac.

'Sorry,' I said. 'He gets excited. He's just being friendly.'

'*Friendly*? *Friendly* you call it? If you can't control your dog, you shouldn't let him off-lead.'

She was right. I put Stan on his lead. And when I turned back to the lake the blonde woman in the red coat and the little boy with the boat were gone.

And I missed her.

Stan and I continued on our walk. The Union Jack that flew above Buckingham Palace was visible above the oak and plane and mulberry trees that were coming back to life, and I knew this meant two things.

The Queen was at home.

And Charlotte Gatling had taught me the names of the trees.

They were handing out the party bags when I got there.

It was a room full of little girls dressed as princesses. Snow Whites, Little Mermaids, Belles and a few I couldn't place, most of them struggling with a sugar rush. There were a handful of boys dressed as pirates, cowboys and Vikings.

'Scout's been a little bit upset,' Mia's mum said.

I found her in a quiet corner, chin trembling and wet-eyed. A smear of birthday cake down the front of her gold-coloured dress.

I gathered her in my arms, and she felt too warm under her elaborate ball gown. Mia stood protectively by Scout's side, her hands on her hips, looking outraged.

'I *told* Hector,' she said. 'I *told* Hector to stop being mean to Scout.'

I looked around the room. A seven-year-old pirate was grinning as he bothered a six-year-old Pocahontas with his plastic cutlass.

Hector, I guessed.

Mia's family gathered around Scout, trying to comfort her. They were good people but we just wanted to go home.

We jumped into a black cab and were back in Smithfield within fifteen minutes.

I watched her for every second. Scout sighed, dried her eyes and calmed down. When we got home she changed into jeans and a T-shirt and handed me her gold ball gown. I wasn't sure what I was meant to do with it. It was only much later, when I was putting her to bed, that I could no longer resist asking her the question that had been tormenting me since I had picked her up.

'What did that kid Hector say to you, Scout?'

'Nothing.'

'OK, angel. Sleep well.'

I went to turn off the light and her voice held me.

'Foul marriage,' she said.

'What?'

'Hector said that my mummy and daddy had a foul marriage and that's why I'm the only one in my class who doesn't have a mummy.'

I came and sat down on the bed.

'He doesn't know what he's saying,' I said. 'He's repeating something he heard his dumb parents say. He's just a stupid little boy with a plastic cutlass. Did you see his cutlass?'

'Yes.'

'What kind of a pirate has a plastic cutlass? Only a rubbish one. Don't worry about him, Scout. People will always try to hurt you in this world. Don't let them. Never let them hurt you.'

I hugged her and told her that I loved her. Then I turned off the light and left the room. Across the street the market was already stirring. Monday morning was waiting at the end of the night. I stared at the market for a while and then I went back into Scout's bedroom. I didn't turn on her light.

'Scout? You awake?'

'Yes.'

'He didn't say foul marriage. That stupid little kid. He said *failed marriage.*'

'OK.'

'He said failed marriage because your parents are divorced. They call it a failed marriage. That's what they call it. Failed marriage.'

'All right.'

Her voice was very small in the darkness.

'Can I tell you something, Scout?'

'Sure.'

'It wasn't a failed marriage. Your parents split up, but it wasn't a failed marriage, Scout.'

I controlled my breathing. I wanted to get this right. It was very important to me.

And I saw that it was really very simple.

'It ended but it didn't fail. There's a difference. *And that's because of you.* It wasn't a failed marriage because you came along. You were born, Scout. And you are the best of me. You are the one true good thing in my life, Scout. You make this planet a better place and no marriage that produces a little girl like you *failed*, Scout. It didn't work. It ended. And that's very sad. But it didn't fail. And that's because of you,' I said, stroking her hair. 'Because of you, Scout.'

But by then of course she was sleeping.

AUTHOR'S NOTE

When I was a lad, and still wearing a black leather jacket in all seasons, every morning on my way to work I would walk past one of the Great Train Robbers.

Ronald Christopher 'Buster' Edwards had been part of the gang that intercepted the Glasgow to London mail train in the early hours of 8 August 1963. By the time I was passing him on my way to the *NME* office on Stamford Street in the late Seventies, Buster was a florist at Waterloo Station.

But to a no-nothing kid in a cheap leather jacket, Buster Edwards would always be one of the Great Train Robbers.

Buster reportedly bagged £150,000 from the Great Train Robbery and, after the money ran out and he came home from Mexico, he was sentenced to fifteen years, serving nine of them before starting his flower stall outside Waterloo.

I often thought of Buster when I was writing the story of Peter Nawkins, the Slaughter Man, because Buster's life and death – like the fictional Slaughter Man, Buster took his own life – suggest that even crimes that are paid for are never forgotten, not if they are spectacular enough. That's what I learned from Buster Edwards, Great Train Robber and florist.

As Max Wolfe tells Echo Nawkins, 'Fame comes and goes. Infamy lasts forever.'

Tony Parsons,
London, October 2014